DRAKE'S BAY

Other titles by T. A. Roberts

DRAKE'S BAY

T.A. ROBERTS

THE PERMANENT PRESS
Sag Harbor, NY 11963

For information, address:
The Permanent Press
4170 Noyac Road
Sag Harbor, NY 11963
www.thepermanentpress.com

Library of Congress Cataloging-in-Publication Data

Roberts, T. A.—
    Drake's Bay / T.A. Roberts.
        p. cm.
    ISBN 978-1-57962-197-1 (alk. paper)
        1. College teachers—Fiction. 2. Treasure troves—Fiction.
    3. Rare books—Fiction. 4. San Francisco (Calif.)—Fiction.
    I. Title.

PS3568.O2475D73 2010
813'.54—dc22   2009047954

Printed in the United States of America.

To my father

George Whiting Roberts

Lt. Col. Military Intelligence Service WDGS G-2, 1942–1945

And many other roles in my life

CHAPTER ONE

My father walked with me up from the shore at Drake's Bay. It was early spring, still a bit blustery along the coast, but we'd made it mostly under sail until the wind abruptly failed and the sea, never exactly quiet, became indecisive. We anchored and rowed in, where the grass was deep and lush and the elk barely glanced up from their dinner. From the ridge top the schooner looked a masterpiece of the traditional boat builder's craft, a model on a scratched glass tabletop, a museum specimen. We sat, and Dr. Thomas Storey took out his pipe and his oilskin tobacco pouch, and I smelled Prince Albert and the north Pacific Ocean. There was nothing else beyond the bay and its landscape, no other boats, people, cars, or structures, apart from the idle fish pier and shed. I was young, maybe sixteen or seventeen; we'd made this trip many times, and I never knew why, at least not until recently, this was the one I'd remember years later. "So, what are you going to be?" he asked.

I wanted to annoy or test him and I said "rock musician," though I didn't play an instrument and hung out with a totally different crowd at school. He nodded but I thought he hadn't really listened; he was the most distant man I'd ever know. "If you choose to study history, Ethan, remember this. No matter how far away or how far back you go, it's always with us, every minute, and every evil and every blessed thing anyone has ever done."

On that autumn Sunday, Kay and I walked once again past the Williams Institute. It was a cumbersome stone structure just visible to passers-by on Arlington Street. You had the sense it had once been imbedded in its hillside with pretensions of permanence; then, as with other human foibles in California earthquake country, soil creep was expelling it like something the Berkeley Hills had eaten by mistake. We couldn't see much more than the bulging retaining walls, concrete green and scaled, cracked deeply and wet to the touch, but the building's upper floors gave it all away: swaybacked or hogged up depending on where you looked, furred by windthrow from the deodar cedars and capping a few asymmetric and undersized windows. We always noticed the place because the steps leading up from the street often had strange, found-art objects like old sporting trophies or castoff clothing, neatly folded. And because it felt unsafe somehow, and scary in a B-cinema sort of way. But we were curious nonetheless.

We were on a regular routine of aerobic walking in those days. The truly aerobic part was long gone by then, but we stuck with it for the companionship; two people in love who seem to show it best when sharing views of architectural detail, or French lupines and bougainvillea or the mossy, morose oaks along the way, making up stories about where the roaming housecats were headed or discussing what we might have for breakfast. That day we stopped for coffee and a shared newspaper in Kensington. It was early and the town center just starting its mellow, upper-middle-class rhythms of brioche and strollers and L.L. Bean, the first week of October, California in suspended summer that can last till Christmas in some years. When we'd found a table outside with the right combination of sun and shade we disassembled the *Chronicle* in our usual fashion, real-estate section for her and me sorting through everything else, for something of interest to a historian.

"Ethan," she said after a moment and without preamble, "it's for sale." Kay's dark hair fell forward slightly when she read the paper in her usual pose, newsprint spread out on the table and pinned down by her elbows, fingers netted beneath her chin. There was something about *real estate* that made her young and sexy again, not terribly odd for a woman who'd spent years living aboard a sailboat in San Francisco Bay with no special affection

8

for the nautical life. The walks often ended with wistful visits to open houses. It made me feel guilty, but only to the point of wanting to indulge her. She'd never asked to move ashore, not directly. However, neither of us was still young. "The Williams Institute. They're open today. We should go." I paused long enough for her to say: "You're thinking of something else you have to do." She made a little noise like an alarm going off. "Too late."

"No, no. I'd like to go, really." She smiled, knowing I'd like a lot of things better.

The open house wasn't until one, and it was quite warm when we'd retrieved the distant car and found a place to park. The hills on the east side of San Francisco Bay seem to rumple upwards about as fast as they slump downwards towards the sea. Between tectonics, or whatever it is, and the long Indian summer, the clear air and our mood, it seemed in the moment that we would live forever, that we had ample time to dawdle over a 1920s folly of a manor house no one would ever think of buying. We knew it was called the Williams Institute only because beside the precipitous driveway the barely readable name had been etched into the concrete, in a shallow cove in the wall that also contained a splintered redwood bench. We had no idea, nor had ever tried to find out what it might have been, though it seemed fitting that such a large, odd place had a label. We walked up the drive under a canopy of softly chattering eucalyptus leaves overhead and finally saw it in full frontal exposure. Georgian, I suppose, if Georgians could be in ivy-ravaged stone instead of brick and have a gambrel roof. The front was that plain expanse with identical nine-over-six pane windows, a high, relatively narrow box with a cupola on top and a chimney at each end. In short, a house both noble and decrepit, and boring. I'd been expecting something more cinematic.

I said, "I don't see any signs." Normally open houses go to great lengths to advertise themselves and their smiling agents. Bay Area real estate has much in common with the Chicago Mercantile Exchange, even in down times, and can be entertaining for its frantic display and competitive commotion. This was exhausting or sort of fun, depending on your energy level and provided that you yourself have someplace to go home to.

"Door's open, though," said Kay, always the braver one in these situations, and strode through. Inside, the temperature dropped ten degrees. It was surprisingly well kept given the outside, 1940s ponderous furnishings and oriental carpets in a large foyer that ended in a staircase. There was something of Julia Morgan here, William Randolph Hearst's architect, noble arches defining the rooms beneath barrel-vaulted ceilings, and smooth, tea-brown tiles under the carpets. The wainscoting was a dark mahogany and what light there was came from a stained-glass window on the staircase. It was hard to tell the function of the room, unless its function was reception, like the entry of a small hotel without a front desk. A young woman with sharp, severe Berkeley-intellectual features and cropped sandy hair was sitting in a wingback chair and somehow in the poor light reading *Architectural Digest* magazine.

"Can I help you?" she asked without rising. Kay introduced us, said that we lived in Kensington, had always been curious about the property and, oddly, that we were retired, none of which was especially true, some of it patently false, all suggesting that we were serious people. There was a general atmosphere of play-acting on both sides when visiting open houses, or so Kay had informed me the previous time she made up a good story.

"I'm Karen Molina, the resident curator." A trace of accent; southern European, but there was little darkness about her open and friendly face. She looked a little like Meg Ryan. Kay asked if that meant people lived here, the surprise evident in her voice. "No. I should have said 'property manager,' except that I stay here occasionally. The house is owned by a European family who never come to the states. I am a post-graduate at UC and keep things tidy and academically organized for the times when they consider selling." No hurry to leave the security of the University of California, I noted, but spending a decade there after getting a

Ph.D. at Berkeley was not unknown. It had taken me about that long to get started on life.

"The Williams family?"

She rose to shake our hands. "How do you do? The Willems, actually." She spelled it carefully. It was odd we'd looked at the stone sign all this time and never read it correctly. "Yes, but two generations away from the one that started the institute." She looked from Kay to me with an expression of amiable calculation, then asked if we'd like to see it. We paused at the turn of the staircase, under a stained glass in the shape of a rose, as if she thought we'd need a rest. "The institute part was never fully realized, but you'll see how it was set up for resident scholars. History, as you'll guess from the collections." Kay tugged my sleeve. *History, honey. Your thing.* We reached a long, balconied landing that faced the back of the building and was the recipient of most of the rose's pinkish light. Also darkly wainscotted, it connected two very large rooms the size of elementary school gymnasia and two capacious suites of rooms at each end. The rooms at the end were identical opposites, four-poster beds facing the fireplaces, sitting rooms and baths adjacent. One was obviously Karen's, with a computer on a Duncan Phyfe satinwood sewing table and an MP3 player on the bedside table. No TV, however. Karen apologized for a mess that didn't exist and walked us to the southernmost door of the two center rooms. "Get ready to sneeze from the book dust."

The sun—we were now facing west through one of the dormers at the bay and the late afternoon—cut a swath through the dust, which wasn't bad at all, just enough to get my allergy started. But the room had the deep spicy smell of old books: a little like balsamic vinegar, I'd always thought. Besides two leather chairs and long tables covered with sheets, there was little but books in the room. In the angular light they were furnishing enough, not just shelves along the walls, laddered to the high arch of the ceiling, but freestanding as shelves human-proportioned and other smaller shelves like end tables near the chairs.

11

I was already thinking about football on the small TV over our chart table. I'd had a life of too many books, and the boat had shelf space for about six of them. It did not seem like Kay's kind of place either and I expected her to say something polite and resigned, already thinking of another house to visit before the universal closing time of four o'clock. But instead she was all cornices and floor tiles with Karen, and they chatted in the way women strangers do, polite and bright, the kind of conversation men savor as long as they can stay out of it.

The other room had no dormer window but a relatively recent skylight addition. It was large but dwarfed by the size of the space it tried to illuminate. Absent the dormer, the shelves went all the way around. There was more of the beauty of books here, embraced by them. There was a comfortable oriental rug on the floor, facing couches with a library table with low bankers' lamps. By the bindings, I saw that these books were much older. I glanced around for the appropriate equipment and found it: humidity and temperature controls. If Kay expected me to be drawn in, I was determined to disappoint and stayed mute; so she asked Karen what was the nature of the collection.

"Fifteenth- to seventeenth-century first editions, mainly. Never very well organized, I'm afraid. But they are valuable I know, and are not for sale along with the house, of course. They'll go to the university or to private collectors at auction."

We returned downstairs and viewed a kitchen straight out of Dickens, great soapstone sinks for the plucking of chickens and washing dirty dishes for ten dinner guests, and a stove just barely electrified. No place to sit and chat. A room off each end of the foyer, walls painted a burgundy that had stood the test of time well, except for a single dagger-shaped water stain from one of the upstairs baths. The space in front of the kitchen was a formal dining room, where the discussion turned to mahogany tables and the wood's susceptibility to fade in natural light, bow-fronted china cabinets and collections of ceramics. The other was book-less, but had a clubby feel nonetheless. The fireplace had a mar-bled mantle carved in animal figures, brass rail in need of polish, wingback chairs so softly commodious I started considering a nap instead of the game.

When we were outside, Kay said: "Well, you were the usual bored and tolerant hubby. We've been looking up at that house for two years. Did you notice anything at all?"

"They cut the dormer off and replaced it with a skylight to protect the books," I said.

She sighed. "We couldn't even afford the delftware." Seated in the car she paused and said, "Maybe we could."

"Could what?"

"Afford the china."

"OK, let's make them an offer."

"I'm serious, Ethan. You're a professor of history and the oldest thing you own is a wooden schooner." She wasn't really serious, because at some level she knew I'd buy the china and store it in a vault somewhere if I thought that would please her. It had been that way from the day we met.

"You," she'd said when we first spoke, ten years before, "look like a history professor should look." I was packing my briefcase after a dazed bout with the students in Hist 344, 19th Century Europe. It was a night class; no time to get back to the boat, dinner a taco and a coke at the union. The time had just relapsed to Standard, the November campus cold and musky smelling. The corridor outside the room would be empty, an existentially long, despairing tunnel of beige walls with regular, identical overhead lights. I was evenly poised between wanting to flee and wanting to hear what she had to say. She gave me no choice; Kay never really gave me a choice from the very beginning. As if answering the response I had not given, she plunged in again, counting the points on her fingers. "Three-piece suit of respectable cut but old beyond imagining; prematurely grey beard trimmed with garden shears, rimless spectacles. You're underfed, underappreciated and easily bored by anything that happened after the Treaty of Ghent." She'd been up to the front a couple of times with questions that suggested a skepticism about history, both its facts and its relevance. Not a bad attitude for a student, really. But I was going to have to glance down at the class list before I remembered her name. She took note of my silence while I did so. "Including me, I'm afraid."

"Treaty of Ghent was way later than I usually teach," I said, deciding to meet her intensely focused yet guileless stare. "Ms. O'Toole, isn't it?"

"Kay."

Flirting with graduate students was not much better than flirting with undergraduate students, but the old bachelor in me had few defenses beyond a slavish adherence to routine and a poorly trimmed beard. She was short with raven hair in a long black braid tight as rope, and wearing a jean skirt with a floral sleeveless top in spite of the rummy weather. She had the kind of strong womanly face that would grow more beautiful as she aged, but which now made her look like a failed fashion model going back to school to learn a trade. Her coloring was more the Welsh brand of Celtic, and she had a habit of touching the side of her neck with the tips of her fingers as she spoke. "I'd always thought the standard was tweeds with leather patches," I said.

"Do you have tweeds with leather patches?"

"As a matter of fact I do."

"There you go then." She was running out of steam. A little older than she'd first looked, perhaps an extension student. Still easily ten years younger than I was.

"I'm glad I meet your preconceptions."

Strangely, she looked crushed, as if this really was a gambit of some sort and she'd completely failed. I was entranced. No one reacted strongly to anything I said, normally, and I rarely spoke just to be provocative. "I'm tired and I need a cup of coffee before I start home. Will you join me?" She said yes, with a smile that said *finally*.

We were both genuinely fatigued, and it was just coffee. She was pre-law; from a solid Central Valley farm family; living with two other women in the Sunset. She had a cousin in the History

Department at UC Berkeley. She loved my lectures, so she said. Why else would she be there? I was tenure track, a little late in the race, lived on a boat. Never married. "Wow. Hunh. Are you gay?" Not an impolite question in San Francisco in the 1990s.

"No. Just . . . solitary."

She considered me for a moment. "Could we . . . have coffee again . . . after Thursday's class?" She blushed and sneezed at the same time. I said I supposed that would be all right. Being pursued is wonderfully tonic. When we parted at the parking garage, my only thought was that Thursday was six long days away.

WE WERE back on board, house-hunting done for the day, and had the teakettle singing when the cell phone rang. I sat at the chart table and heard a vaguely familiar voice asking for Dr. Storey. "Your wife left your business card with me," said Karen from the Willems Institute. "You're a history professor at San Francisco State?"

"Just a moment." I punched the mute button. "Did you give my card to the woman this afternoon?" She nodded, handing me a mug of Lipton sweetened with honey from her father's farm. I asked Karen what I could do for her.

"You know," said Karen, "the family has asked me to find someone to organize and evaluate the library collection."

"You probably want an appraiser more than a historian." Evenings in the crumbling manse after a day on the other side of the bay sounded like miserable work—traffic considerations alone made it unsavory.

"Oh, we already have the appraiser; he suggested a professional historian." I gave the hourly rate I charge for private consulting. A surprising number of people want historians in California, a land without much history. It was usually private indulgences of genealogy or finding where the San whatever Rancho was actually located. My fee was usually high enough to discourage the more frivolous enquiries. "I hope you don't mind, but I looked you up on the internet. You wrote an analysis of logbooks from the English explorers; much of the collection dates from that period. I don't believe the owners would have a problem with your fee."

"Excuse me." I muted again. "They want me to box the books, or something. What do you think?"

"Why are you asking me?" This was a wholly unlikely response from Kay. She'd been telling me what to do for a decade, ever since she moved aboard and threw away all my suits and jackets with leather patches. "See if they'll pay you in delftware."

"Karen, we can talk about it, I suppose." She said that the appraiser would be there Monday, coincidentally. In a coequal coincidence, I was meeting a Berkeley colleague for lunch, and I agreed to stop by afterwards. Karen was effusive in her thanks.

We moved to the table in the cockpit with cups of tea. We still needed the shade cloth stretched between the mainmast backstays, though the air was now much cooler. This was the best time of day aboard, when the wind died and the salt smell from the sea muted down and mixed with old boat perfumes of varnish and teak and a salmon casserole cooking in the galley. The other boats lay quiet, their owners back in their houses in the hills. Kay had changed into a long skirt with a paisley print and pulled her hair into a ponytail tied with black ribbon. She'd cut her hair last year. She smiled at me and touched a spoke of steering wheel with a caress I'd assumed, from the very first time she did it, was foreplay. Sunday evening, something in the stove that wouldn't be done for an hour, feeling now the powerful appetite for her that had never flagged in our relationship. Now my turn in the dance. "I'm interested in that house," I lied. "If it was a bit better kept I could see you there, hosting a formal dinner party."

She moved closer on the settee and put her hand on my knee. "How you humor me, Ethan." She kissed me behind the earlobe so as not to interfere with my finishing the tea. When the sun blinked down behind Telegraph Hill we went to the broad double bunk in the forepeak, where through the hatch overhead she could still see the sky when we made love.

"You are the steadiest man I've ever met," she'd said, when after another coffee outing in 1994 I took her sailing. A fifty foot wooden boat can be a major production to get underway, but *Drake* had been home and retreat and transport for twenty years at that point, and thanks to this and a flawless autumn day I did indeed look pretty steady. With all plain sail up, a touch of southerly flow preceding a distant storm, and a reliable autopilot, we heeled just enough to make the lee rail gurgle and she pulled along like an amusement park ride for adults. Kay was dressed in jeans and a pink BERKELEY LAW sweatshirt and had heeded my advice about footwear and layers. She let me do everything, which is a pretty good indication that she had been out on boats before as an amateur. But when I disengaged the pilot and had her steer I could tell that, unlike a succession of beer-besotted colleagues with quarrelsome preteens and, worst of all, racing sailors, she got it. Holding the wheel of a traditional full-keeled wood boat is like being part of the ocean itself, so integral is the hull and its motion to the water, and so completely is all of this felt by the person at the helm. Like leading a horse in a meadow, joyous and frivolous at times, then attentive, always part of its landscape. "I want to go to Hawaii with you," she said. She had started saying things like that from the first night, heedless of potential rejection, ignoring old Ethan's Fear of Commitment as if the notion that we would not be together in some way was just too preposterous to consider for an instant.

Even when I invariably took her literally: "I've only got forty gallons of water and there's a storm coming tomorrow."

"We'll give each other sponge baths." The remark made me giddy with desire. We hadn't even slept together yet.

I guess that was the point, because docked and trimmed, I had my first girlfriend in a couple of years; first in more years who made it to the sanctum of the forward bunk. She was a serious lover, rather unlike her flirtatious other self, without games but possessed of a deep and gracious sexuality. She had a subtly voluptuous body and allowed me to look for a time as she lay back, one knee raised and hands crossed over her stomach. Curves like a boat, I thought much later. I was a goner, though it was many months before she came to live with me. When she passed the California Bar some years later, and our combined incomes—though never affluent—meant we could afford a house even at Bay Area prices, we stayed right where we were. Even when things turned dark for us.

I woke very early on Monday morning, before five. I shut the hatch quietly, slipped off the edge of the bunk and into my slippers and robe and shuffled aft, closing the bulkhead door behind me. I lit the brass lamp opposite the starboard guest cabin, for warmth as well as light, checked to see if there was hot water in the head and started a pot of coffee. This was ceremony for me, an old one that survived cohabitation. The black water outside, the morning silence made more profound by the tiny tugs and creaks of a tethered boat, then by the chuffing of the percolator. And a luminous darkness beyond the pools of light thrown by the oil lamp and the spotlight over the chart table, formed by equal parts reflected harbor light through the ports, all the tiny pin lights on the control panel and the digital display on the radio, and the deeply comforting glow of the mahogany walls of our little world.

You are the steadiest man I've ever met.

I pulled my notebook from the drawer and examined my week. A relatively light course load this semester, two senior seminars, though, with students who needed to be discouraged from pursuing careers as historians. More immediately a journal article to finish, coauthored by Brian Haggerty, the Berkeley historian I was meeting for lunch. The coffee was ready and I heated some of the casserole from last night. Never one for conventional breakfasts, though that was one of the few things about me—beyond the schooner I suppose—that would be considered unconventional.

When I'd eaten I brought out my laptop, and using the marina's wi-fi connection, I searched on Williams and Willems Institute and the same name with Collection and Library. Nothing useful, though the Willems family in Luxembourg were well-respected European academics and appeared to be the ones who'd started the institute. I still had a few minutes before the Bay Bridge seized up with traffic, so in the interest of simply being professional and because I hadn't gotten a phone number from Karen, I collected the Sunday paper from the salon table, teased out Real Estate, and steadily, methodically went through the Berkeley/Kensington section to find the listing. Since it hadn't been a realtor but obviously a private listing, the phone number would likely be Karen Molina's.

I realized, of course, that the number Karen had called from yesterday was in the cell phone memory, and this whole exercise was not really necessary. But not until I'd confirmed that the listing was just not there, anywhere. My memory of Kay leaning over the paper at the cafe, even the pattern of advertisements I could read upside down across the table, made me feel certain that she had had this page under her gaze when she'd made the announcement about the open house.

CHAPTER TWO

"How are things at State?" Brian Haggerty asked while we waited for cioppino just outside the Berkeley gates. Through the window behind him I could see a sky begging to rain. A single drop trailed down the window and an undergraduate, dressed as a street urchin, had stopped to watch it. First rain since May.

Brian was a bit of a snob about the difference between UC Berkeley and San Francisco State. He hid it well, behind a veil of interest in the workings of our blue-collar institution, but only for the first few minutes of any meeting. He asked after Kay: a cousin. And although that was perfunctory as well, the connection with Kay was what originally brought us together; and we now were coauthoring an analysis of the Thomas Jefferys' 1761 *A Summary Of The Voyages Made By The Russians On The Frozen Sea, In Search Of A North East Passage.* Captain Cook had blundered around with this volume for a time. We were basically writing a concordance between what Cook found and what he thought he'd found. And since academic journals need a bit more than random curiosity, it was a study of how expectations shaped reality as experienced by Cook, or anyone else.

"We haven't had a student strike all semester," I said.

"That's what I like about State. Everybody knows they're eventually going to have to work for a living."

We talked about the manuscript for a while, professional talk of two old colleagues in an abstruse field, incomprehensible to anybody around us. It would sound very erudite, except for occasional detours into movies, restaurants, car problems and academic gossip. When we'd finished a carafe of wine (neither of us had classes that afternoon), I asked him if he knew about the Williams (or Willems) Institute.

"The building in Kensington?" he replied.

I nodded. "They're selling off their library."

"Who on earth told you that?"

"I was there yesterday."

He seemed about to say something, then stopped. "I'm not surprised you didn't know anything about it," he continued after a moment. "It's one of UC Berkeley's best kept secrets, especially from other university historians. A private collection, opened only twice since 1960. How did you get in?"

"Kay arranged it somehow."

"Get out of town. Half the book perverts in Berkeley have howled under those eaves at one time or another, for a generation, and a copyright attorney gets in? How did that happen?"

"You should ask her." I hadn't, and for some reason didn't want to.

Brian was an academic of the jolly sort, slightly red-faced and overweight, with long thinning blond hair and the kind of infectious fascination for his discipline that made him a favorite on the local PBS station. He was ambitious and shrewd and mildly unscrupulous in some respects, but on the other hand had Kay's grey eyes under an unlined brow, and not an ounce of real malice in him. He looked at me as if I were a tasty dessert. "Well, Ethan, if you're straight with me I'll tell you everything I know."

Fat chance, I thought. "I'm meeting with the . . . caretaker in half an hour. They want to hire me to catalogue the collection."

He removed his glasses and rubbed his eyes and momentarily lost control when his eyes were shut. "They're offering that job to someone from *San Francisco State*?" He opened his eyes and caught himself. "Serves us right, really. All our whining and posturing over the years. Cal professors win all too many Nobel Prizes, that's the problem. All right, here you go . . ." he drew a breath. "The Willems were a family from Luxembourg which had the misfortune to be comfortably installed at the University of Antwerp when the Nazis invaded in 1940. They were already internationalists, of the period anyway, and saw the writing on the wall in the nick of time. In 1939, Professor Manfred Willems

21

of the Antwerp Library watched Belgian authorities ship the $200 million from their treasury for safekeeping . . . to *France*. Didn't seem to him that his collection should travel that road. So he packed up the cream of it—which had been donated to the University but was still legally theirs—and took off for the USA. The collection was for safety's sake divided in half on two ships, one of which was torpedoed and sank. The other reached New York with the professor and his young wife just in time to be impounded by Roosevelt because the State Department thought it was Danish, and all Danish assets were impounded to keep them away from the Germans. This is really all news to you? Think for a minute." I thought. "Here's a hint: *Translated from the High Dutch of S. Muller.*"

"The Jefferys Manuscipt?" This was the main source of the article we had been discussing for the past ninety minutes. "That was part of this collection?"

"One of a few volumes that made their way into general circulation, via a private collector, before the Executive Order. You really should be more of a book person. That's where the real money is in our corner of the academic wilderness." For all Brian's swashbuckling talk, he was basically an easygoing, colorful college man. But a thorough book person; that's why we were such a good team.

"What happened then?"

"Willems went back to Europe after the war with his wife and kids by that time, but in the meanwhile had built that house in the hills. He was never offered anything at the University because of a faint hint of collaboration with the Reich that allowed him to get out in time. Remembering that, maybe your hiring makes more sense. He and his children were very, very bitter about it, so the story goes, and locked down the collection and the house. Other than a handful of visitors and repairs to keep the books safe, the whole thing just moldered away for the rest of the century."

"What's happening now, do you think?"

Brian was a nanosecond from asking to come along with me, but was already, I could tell, thinking about something more strategic. "You should ask them," he said.

I HAD to hustle to get there on time. Karen Molina opened the door to my knock. She was wearing a pale blue cardigan and matching skirt, a faint trace of makeup and a welcoming smile, and she ushered me into the burgundy-painted parlor where a small wood fire was burning. It was not terribly successful in venting its smoke, but the smell was both evocative and soothing. A table had been placed between the wing chairs, with a decanter of something, two glasses, and a plain white three-ring binder. "Sherry?"

"Wine with lunch, I'm afraid. But if I may say so, this is the nicest setting for a rainy-day business discussion I've ever experienced."

"We're trying to butter you up. There's coffee, and fresh scones coming out in an hour. Please sit down." I sat, resisting the temptation to put my feet up on the brass hearth rail and trying not to look curious which, in spite of myself and in direct proportion to Brian's interest, I was. "I'm instructed by the family to tell you a couple of things to start with. All this is in your contract, of course. This is a private collection and beyond the cataloging of the volumes you are not to discuss its contents with anyone; there's a confidentiality agreement for you to sign. You can speak freely with me or the appraiser, but to no one else. I mean to say, don't contact the Willems family and if they contact you, please respond through me." Gone was the Meg Ryanish housekeeper of yesterday and in her place was a woman in her late thirties with profound self-confidence. She was short, just slightly over five feet, sandy hair now pulled boldly back from her face in an attempt at professional severity which failed now because it just made her beauty statuesque: broad forehead and high cheekbones; blackest of black eyes. "I hope I'm not being presumptuous, treating you as if you'd already accepted."

"Well, that's what the sherry and scones were for. I'm yours, I suppose, at least so far."

"Wonderful. Your contract and agreement are in the binder along with a list of everything that I compiled on the collection, just by transcribing what's on the covers or flyleaf or whatever. It's not a very good inventory but it's complete; I've been working on it part-time for years. Think of it as a checklist to make sure you don't miss anything."

"I'm not a librarian."

"We know that. Think of it as an annotated bibliography, entered into a database with standard historical subject fields and a brief commentary on its contents and, to the extent you can, its uniqueness."

"Why wasn't this done before?"

"All of the catalogues were lost at sea, with some of the collection, when it came over from Europe." The ship that was a casualty of war.

"Is there something in particular the owners are looking for?"

"Why do you ask?" To my surprise she seemed troubled by the question.

"Some collections were put together for a purpose, say, family genealogy or the products of a particular printer or a search for who really killed the Princes in the Tower. Maybe you could ask them if there are any database fields that I might otherwise overlook."

"That seems reasonable. But the family lost interest in the collection in the generation after the war, and now Lucius Willems, two generations down, is a historian only as a hobby, really. He'll cherry-pick the collection at some point, but market value is what's important at present. They've only been over once or twice in the last twenty years, to my knowledge. When can you start?"

"No chance I can take the binder home, I'm sure." She shook her head. "Well, let me sign up and work till the scones are ready."

With the paperwork out of the way, we walked up the stairs and into the more serious of the two rooms. It was dry and warm and the lights had been turned on over the library tables, where a computer now sat. Each shelf had a small spotlight that revealed its contents, but there was nothing overhead except the pallid square of the skylight. "I'm curious how you intend to proceed."

"Is there any organization to the shelves?"

"None that I could find." She'd just started in the upper-left-hand corner of the first shelf, up the ladder to the left of the door, and gone left to right, top to bottom of each shelf in its clockwise turn around the room.

"I'll follow your trail, then, and code numerically until it's time to reshelve."

She left me, promising to return with the scones. I pulled a pair of latex gloves from my briefcase and grabbed the first volume. Time enough to learn the software later. The book had a contemporary (more or less) tooled leather cover over wooden boards, but the contents were much older. Karen had merely copied the first printed words *Gronlandia Edur Graenlandz* and nothing else. I hoped the appraiser was a much better book person than I was, but at least I could earn my pay by concluding with some confidence that this was one of the volumes of the Icelandic Sagas. I didn't enter it into the computer because I couldn't find a publication date. I began to lose a little confidence, but that was offset by the delight any historian feels in handling the real thing. Not the book itself, not for me anyway, but the words put down hundreds of years ago, exactly as they had been born in the mind of the writer.

I had better luck with the Russian volumes which came next (I needed literary Russian in my own work), and sat with them for twenty minutes before glancing at the next entry on the list. To my surprise it was entered with an American government publisher—the Superintendent of the U.S. Coast Survey—and the date 1862; it was the Hydrographic Office's *Directory for the Pacific Coast of the United States*. Bit odd for a war refugee from Antwerp. Not rare by any standards. Even San Francisco State had one. However, it's amazing how dramatic, eccentric and cosmopolitan the ordered world of libraries can get. I was once doing some cross referencing of botanical terms from Franklin's Pacific voyages and was intrigued by the stamps on the back cover of a nineteenth-century reference tome. The volume, well-bound and in very good shape, had gone to China, been stamped by the logo of the Manchurian Railway, then a Japanese Government stamp, then the U.S. Occupation Authority in Tokyo, and finally to the library where I was working. So it had gone from England, where it was published for use in India, to China, captured by the occupying Japanese, rescued by the U.S. Army, and sent off to Stanford, which had squeezed its ink onto the bottom of the page, all at the hands of librarians who probably had no good use for it until it came across my path.

I went and pulled the volume, fired up the machine, beat its program into submission, and made up some preliminary fields. When I'd made the entries, I opened it and found out how to get to the port of San Francisco a century and a half ago: *Outside the bar in 15 fathoms, mud and fine sand; or after crossing the bar, 6 to 10 fathoms, fine grey sand with red flecks in some places.* I imagined myself or any other sailor, at night in the fog and a dangerous spot, combing his lead-and-tallow depth line under lantern light for "red flecks" as his only clue to safe harbor or imminent disaster.

Karen appeared, carrying a silver tray with coffee mugs, linen napkins, the plate of promised scones, and a small tub of butter. "Wow," I said.

"No credit to me, Dr. Storey. We're taking on a small domestic staff for the project, which includes a cook for when you and Mr. Burke, the appraiser, are here. He left after lunch; I'm sorry you missed him." Karen had put on lipstick and changed her clothes. I could not for a moment recall what she'd been wearing earlier, but this was less forgettable, showing me a considerable length of black-stockinged leg.

"Call me Ethan."

She poured the coffee. She had fine, pianist's hands, clipped nails and no jewelry. It was fully dark now, with rain pinging against the plexiglass of the skylight, an oddly modern sound in this sweetly curmudgeonly room. "I'll give you one last chance to tear up your contract, Ethan. You seemed to be completely unimpressed when you and your wife were here yesterday."

"When I was a graduate student I developed an allergic reaction to book dust. By the time I had my doctorate I was accustomed to photocopies. Now everything's electronic, mostly. Primary sources have been a sort of forbidden fruit."

"Ph.D. candidates get all sorts of strange ailments and distractions, most of them dragging them away from what they love to do. I speak from experience. My field is anthropology; my doctorate is eight years old and any real field work at least two more years away."

"Well, I appear to be cured." Frankly, I was already thinking of advancing my sabbatical and moving in here. My students never gave me scones, two of which I'd already eaten. This room was as different from my office as a velvet pillow is from a cinderblock.

We talked about a schedule; I proposed two afternoons a week until I could get a sense of the scope of the work. I had several questions, but she asked the first one. "Can I ask you how you came to be here yesterday? You're not someone who's ever expressed an interest in the collection before, obviously."

"Kay brought me for the Open House."

"That's what I thought. We had it scheduled for that day, then cancelled it some time ago, for fear of being overrun by curiosity seekers. Your wife . . . Kay? She must keep careful track of these things. It's funny, but if you'd been more eager about the books, I don't believe I would have recommended you to the Willems as our . . . What shall we call you? Archivist?"

"Sounds appropriately serious." I looked at my watch. "I should be getting home."

"Wednesday, then?"

"How was it?" asked Kay, putting the dishes in the galley sink that evening.

"Karen Molina fed me sherry and scones. They had a copy of the eleventh-century Icelandic Sagas." Whoops, I thought, first confidentiality slip. I wasn't used to holding my tongue, not with Kay.

"She's very attractive, isn't she?"

"Bless my soul, you're jealous."

"Just making an observation." Then she added, turning toward me: "You're still an attractive man, you know, funny old square-jawed sailor's face, beloved uncle beard. Your eyes are as blue as ever."

She didn't sound jealous at all, just satisfied she'd found something for me to do that I liked, and would bring in some extra money. She'd missed dinner the night before, not uncommon among lawyers, even those dealing with intellectual properties like "America's Funniest Videos," and she squeezed in beside me for an after-supper brandy. It had been a long, make-up-for-lost-time dinner that started with crabcakes and ended with cannoli, before she'd be departing on a business trip to New York, the red-eye. I would drive her to the airport and the brandy helped her sleep on the plane, she said. The case, as she had explained it to me, involved depositions on a partnership dispute at a website development company, and she'd be gone the rest of the week and through the weekend.

"How did your lunch with Brian go?"

"We're done with the revisions and off it goes to contribute to the sum total of human knowledge."

"I wish you wouldn't undervalue your work, Ethan. It's not good career planning." She had started using the phrase a year or so before, when rumors began to circulate that she was finally going to leave the stable and become a partner in the firm.

"I'm only honest with you, darlin'."

She finished her brandy in a large swallow and scooted out from the salon table. Her suitcase needed closing and she busied herself with the contents of her briefcase. She carried tons of stuff when she traveled. If either of us allowed paperwork to accumulate on the boat, we'd have been sleeping on deck years ago. When her back was turned she said, "Brian called to ask me how I knew about the institute. I fibbed a little, you know." I watched her shoulders. "There was no ad in the paper."

"You don't say."

"I had some client confidentiality issues."

"Are you involved in the collection somehow?"

"Not directly, but I can't talk about it. Nothing you need to disclose to the institute; no conflict of interest, I mean."

"Well, we're even. I had to sign a nondisclosure agreement, too."

There was a moment of coldness between us, as if we'd had a quarrel. I never knew who led out onto the emotional landscape of our relationship. I suspected most of the time it was Kay, and this time she was acknowledging a lie without my ever asking her about it. It seemed like such a small thing, strange to me but more complex on her side. "Off we go," she said, too brightly. She was inexplicably angry; but by the time we got to the airport, she kissed me deeply and instructed me to behave myself while she was in New York, the way she always did.

I MET the appraiser two days later, a couple of hours after I reported for duty. His name was Adrian Burke, a bookish Briton in his sixties who nonetheless wore khakis and had a ponytail. He was thin to the point of illness, on first examination, a face so drawn he might have had a facelift if the rest of him wasn't similarly stretched and taut. It was an actor's face, large-featured, handsome and angular. His handshake was firm and he immediately projected an energy which dispelled the impression of frailty. I was about ten volumes further along when he walked in without Karen and introduced himself. I put down a record of marriages and property transactions of a French aristocratic family of seventeenth-century France, took off my gloves, and shook hands. "Are you terribly bored, yet?" he asked.

"No, but by my calculations I won't be done for six months. Plenty of time for that later."

"Good heavens. That long?"

"The problem is the confidentiality agreement. Normally, I'd be able to pick up the phone for anything outside my language range or time period. Without that, for half the volumes here each cataloging is a research project in itself. But, for a book-deprived historian, it's going to be fun for quite a while."

He approached the computer. "May I?" I nodded and he scrolled through what I had so far. He smacked his lips and found the volumes on the table, which he examined without touching them. "Fifteen thousand dollars and counting," he said. "This is a very valuable collection."

"How long have you been on staff?"

"I was here several years ago for a time, but never really got started."

We decided that he would track my entries, on days I wasn't working here, and complete a value field we set up in the database. On Saturday mornings we'd meet and discuss progress. He reserved the right to leapfrog ahead of me if he saw something interesting. We chatted amiably for a few minutes. He'd been the book specialist for Sotheby's for twenty years before going out on his own. He lived locally, traveled widely, and had read two of my journal articles, or persuasively pretended he had. "They haven't given you any kind of deadline?" he asked.

"Not so far."

"Any clues to the nature of the collection?"

"What do you mean?"

"What we'd call it at auction. Hopefully something sexier than 'Legacies of Luxembourg.'"

"I asked Karen much the same question. No imprimatur earlier than 1500; the Sagas were a rebinding. Nothing Asian, if you exclude the abundant Russian stuff. Other than that no, the original catalogue was lost and there doesn't see to be any order on the shelves. Very strange; almost like a random selection. I'm not supposed to talk to the family."

Karen entered at that point, with a full tea service that included small sandwiches and daintily cut fresh fruit. "How are you two getting along?"

"Splendidly," Burke said. "Ethan says six months. In two days he found fifteen thousand dollars for the family. At that rate and if the sample is representative, a half million dollars, even without finding a Book of Judges." He was referring to a version of the Gutenberg Bible.

I smiled. "That was fast."

He nodded to Karen. "Occupational necessity, my dear." They exchanged a look. Lovers? Old friends? A joke at my expense? I didn't think I should care. We finished our tea and went back to work. As I left the house two hours later and turned down Arlington, though, I found myself hoping that Adrian was gay. I wanted Karen Molina to like me the best.

There was a call from Brian on my cell and I rang him as I walked. "What can you tell me?" he asked.

"Nothing. They serve tea and apparently I've conquered my allergy to book dust."

"Damn. I figured as much. Well, the word is out on you and there's someone I think you should talk to."

"What do you mean 'the word is out'?"

"I put it on my list server," said Brian who was, after all, a world-class gossip. "When you meet this guy you'll owe me big time."

"Who is it?"

"The last guy that had your job." He waited a beat. "Hah, they didn't tell you, did they?"

"Brian, are you sure you want to be this interested in what I do?"

"Just watching your academic back, old chum. He'll be in town for several days, I think. Can I send him by your boat some morning?"

"As strange as it sounds, I actually have some classes to teach before Thanksgiving. I'll be back at the institute Saturday morning. Sunday's OK. Kay's away for the weekend." It was all so unlike my normal life program: ancient manuscripts, secrets, Nazi submarines, darkly blonde, beautiful women, scones. Although I was uncomfortable with whatever Brian, let alone

Kay, was up to, it was all so damned intriguing. "Why do you think I should see him?"

"Let me call you back when I set it up. Leave your cell phone on for a change. You'll want to see him, I guarantee it."

I was passing through the Berkeley campus when he called back. Many of the students had left after midterms and the place would be like a European park until after the Thanksgiving holiday. Underfoot, the grass was just starting to green after the rains, but it was warming up again and I sat on a bench when the phone rang. Brian said: "He has a partial copy of the catalogue for the collection."

"Brian, I don't know. He should be talking to my employer now."

"OK, OK, but there's some things you need to know. Let me come by instead, that'll keep you clean. He can't make it anyway. He's got some legal thing in New York; certificate of provenance on a manuscript. My kind of guy, really."

It was cold enough for the pellet stove that night, and with Kay gone I could smoke my pipe. But I was restless, too. I was always slightly troubled when Kay was gone, as men with much younger wives tend to be. It was always sexual, of course, but somehow I always feared I'd lose her in some other way first. And in this mood I imagined that her indirect dealing with the institute, and her legal specialty, meant that Brian's man was in New York to see Kay.

CHAPTER THREE

I was in love with Kay by that first Christmas in 1994. She hadn't moved aboard yet, but she came by one day when I was teaching and ran lights up the forestay, across the jackstay and down the main backstay, then along the gunwales so the boat was perfectly outlined in white and amber when I returned in the December darkness. *Hello, Sailor*, read a Christmas card on the chart table, and *Ethan, a woman's heart is a good place to drop anchor. Try it and see.*

Yet it felt like an old man's love, somehow, an old bachelor's anyway. I couldn't seem to be anything but helpless and clumsy in its presence. Not to put too fine a point on it, I hadn't felt like this since I was her age; I was in a foreign country and couldn't speak the language; I was terrified both of screwing it up and of being married and having children. Why on earth had she chosen me? And assuming she'd done so, how could she possibly seem as sure about it as she did? What was the Plan? I knew I didn't have one. How had she known where the halyards were to get the lights up? I suspected her cousin, Brian Haggerty, had helped; he knew the boat well enough after we'd made our second sail in his company. But I had a perfectly bright and utterly adorable vision of her standing on the deck, brow furrowed, tongue protruding slightly, testing each line and shackle until she figured it out.

I thought of her so much over the next few days I slept badly. I was sure I'd make myself ill and of course did so, a wretched hacking cough and low-grade fever that made me call and cancel our New Year's Eve date. It was cold for the bay that week, a Pacific high that brought northeast winds down from northern Nevada. The air was impossibly clear but moonless on New Year's Eve, city lights lost without anything to reflect against. It was

33

a sky my father, whose too-sudden death was still with me four years later, had called a Spanish sky. He thought it evoked California of old, when it was a remote province of Spain, a darkness more purple than black. I never heard anyone else use the term and he was not a poetic man. But I remembered him on winter nights like this, a very quiet scholar who raised his only son by himself. He thought we could both live sustained by boats and history and was nearly correct. *Drake* had been his boat before me, and when he died I sold the house and kept the schooner, which was what he would have wanted.

Inevitably Kay arrived anyway, bearing clam chowder and crackers and fresh-squeezed apple juice and herbal teas. I was in the pilot berth, aft of the chart table. Raised on an elbow, peering through the low porthole that looked inboard, into the cockpit, I could only see her from the waist down as she came aboard, just visible in the backlight of the twinkling Christmas bulbs. She stepped so lightly that I would not have noticed any motion of the boat. Her shoes were high-heeled and an exotic maze of tiny straps. One false move along the deck or cockpit, with its terrain of drains and winches and cleats, and down she'd go, with her carefully packed bags of food. Above the shoes and stockings was the hem of a black party dress. She was now standing in front of the companionway hatch, a long pause as if gathering strength, or uncharacteristically unsure of herself. Gazing through the port gave me the feeling of being in an aquarium, with her a sea creature from a faraway ocean, gently treading water.

Then she set the bags down and knocked. "Permission to come aboard?" And then, "Ethan Storey, if you're with another woman you have *ten seconds* to throw her overboard." She actually counted aloud before sliding back the hatch, stepping through the pilothouse and descending the ladder—backwards because of the high heels and packages. She looked around and didn't see me at first, in my cubbyhole of a bunk. "There you are," she said. And after a moment of inspection: "Thank God, you actually *are* sick." She put down dinner, took off her dress and shoes and slid in beside me.

34

I still hadn't said anything. There was a lump in my throat so big I thought I was choking. She smelled slightly of almonds. I put my head between her breasts for a moment and eventually said: "I'm so afraid of losing you."

She stroked my hair. "I know. Don't be."

She moved in just after spring midterms. She had an amazingly small amount of stuff, for a law student and a woman, but it took place after much measuring of the lockers and inspections of small places to put things, some of which I'd never known about. She made few changes: flowered curtains over the portholes, bright cushion fabrics and a spice rack in the galley. But overnight the boat stopped smelling like mildew and dirty socks and took on a new scent, not feminine but something like flowers and salt. Within a month, colleagues said I was looking younger; students started laughing at my jokes. Within a year I had tenure at San Francisco State, at about the same time as Kay passed the California Bar.

I NEVER doubted that she'd rescued me from something horrible in my life and it never occurred to her to claim credit for it. We simply started living together like it was an arranged marriage, in a culture of perfect wisdom. I would rise early to make her tea and toast. She would get home early and make dinner, almost always something like a soup, stew or casserole; she was a minor genius for that end of the culinary spectrum. The job she was offered, immediately, was in an obscure but successful firm, Jamison and Peters, based in Sausalito and specializing in intellectual properties. Things got a little more hectic for her (things were never that way for me), with late nights and traveling, but we went to each others' conferences and walked in the hills; went to symphonies and plays and football games. Sailed every month of the year, with a three-day cruise every summer. There was enough money and an abundance of the stuff of the life we had together.

35

In 1999, as the tech bubble was bursting in the Bay Area, she was cut back to half time because most of the properties she defended were software-related. We had no mortgage to worry about, so at first it was like a series of three-day weekends. Kay was easily bored, however. In midsummer of that year I first heard about John Peters, senior partner, as a person instead of a name on letterhead. I knew who he was because not only was he her boss, but an avid member of the yachting community, a ferocious sailboat racer. His son was just starting at San Francisco State, hoping to transfer to Cal after his freshman year. For a time we were supposed to do something as couples (sailing probably), but by our fifth Christmas together she no longer mentioned him, about the same time that she started working a fifty-hour week again. Kay was clever, Kay was confident, Kay grew more beautiful each year. Everything about her, even the mysteries, seemed up front and plain for the world to see, puzzle and marvel over.

All of this made for an unpracticed and miserably incompetent liar. This applied even to her silences. If she wanted something, whether it was Ethan Storey or fresh coriander, she did not stop until she got it. She had been gently prompting me to be more ambitious, which in my world meant Department Chair or applying to Berkeley, or at least publishing more aggressively. That stopped in early 2000 along with any mention of John Peters.

We had our New Year's at the millennium as we always did, chowder and cider to commemorate the first one. A glass of champagne before bed. But this year she stood and turned off the music as I was pouring, and sat down opposite me. "Ethan," she asked, "Do you love me?"

"Of course I do."

"You never say so."

I was completely baffled. I knew men were supposed to tell women they loved them and made a point of doing it. "Of course I do," I said again.

"Yes, but it's only because you think you're supposed to and you make a point of doing it." We quarreled so rarely I had no

36

organized approach to the moment. She went on: "We never do anything but sail and go to conferences and have dinner out." Now a counter argument was completely impossible, because, if you'd asked me to name the things that gave me the most pleasure in this life, that would be the list, as long as I did them with Kay.

Maybe, I thought desperately, that was the purpose of this exchange. "You're everything to me."

"Why?"

"Because you're so . . . brave." The word came from the same place as my first desperate cry at our first New Year's. It was honest, beyond my power not to say it.

But it didn't work. "*Brave?* What does that mean?" She saw I was going to fail and she softened. "Oh never mind, Ethan. Happy New Year."

Kay O'Toole with a hidden agenda was such a preposterous notion, and my own view of our life so replete with contentment, that it was two months before I started wondering if she was unhappy, or nursing some hormone imbalance, or, more likely, that I had become someone who didn't interest her anymore. Maybe, in fact, all three things were true.

I was teaching California history that spring, one of my favorites: the story of the Mission padres struggling up the Salinas Valley, battling malaria and grizzly bears, squabbling among themselves, casually dropping names off their religious calendars that became the geographical vocabulary of our everyday lives. On the third of March I marked the day as the anniversary of the first European sighting of the Golden Gate by Bartolomé Ferrelo, Cabrillo's pilot, running down the coast with a strong northern gale. He thought it was a river-mouth, and it wasn't until two hundred years later that Portola stumbled upon the bay by land, having missed Monterey by mistake. Confusion, the whims of nature, religious devotion, greed, duty, and luck: the raw material of history. There were the usual after-class stragglers and I dutifully worked my way through them. March third was also the last day to drop the class, and these students waited to the end, clutching the slips I had to sign, slightly embarrassed. Before any of the three spoke I said: "No harm, no foul, bring on the drop slips." The first two looked relieved and scurried away.

The third looked like he had a point to make. I hadn't had the *why history* question in quite some time, since my lectures were simply more interesting in recent years; and for most students, at least undergraduates, entertainment was justification enough. After all, nobody signs up for a history class in the first place with the idea it would look good on a job application. But an air of confrontation surrounded this one and I knew it was coming. He was a freshman, he said. He had the kind of droop-shouldered look of computer majors, without the childlike good humor of that class of student. He was short, but beyond the size and slouch in pretty good shape, with shorts and a t-shirt and a fresh crew cut. "The course is a waste of my time," he said, handing me the slip. He seemed more angry than argumentative.

I signed it and handed it back. "Why don't you tell me what you really think?"

"How can you make a living with this stuff?"

I had no class to go to; it was a warm morning and the classroom was as pleasant a place to linger as it ever would be. I sat on the edge of the desk. "Well, what does your father do?"

"He's an attorney."

"Attorneys use case law going back to the middle ages. California attorneys sometimes settle real-estate cases by going back to the Spanish land grants." I didn't really believe I could explain history in this way. I was just winging it on a sunny morning.

He seemed to collect himself, but he was trembling slightly. "I think you know my father's girlfriend."

"Oh?"

"Kay O'Toole." He turned and left the room. I ran my hand down the class list. *Clifford Peters.* I crossed it off.

KAY FOUND me later that day, taking on diesel at the fuel dock. Before I'd backed *Drake* out of her slip, I'd unloaded as many of Kay's possessions as I could onto the finger pier. Not a haphazard jumble: I'd taken my time about it, obtaining clean boxes for clothes at the marina market, placing some loose papers in ziplock bags, covering the collection with a tarp, tied down like a mariner would do it. The fuel dock was some distance away, at the far end of the cove. She had no trouble finding me, though. Driving into the parking lot and looking across, *Drake* would give the appearance of a restless bird on a short jess, tied temporarily to the rocky shore.

"How did you find out?" Her voice was barely audible over the chugging of the pump and the rumble of the fuel as it flowed into the nearly empty tanks.

"His son's at State, remember? He announced it to my California History class."

"Can we talk?"

I felt like spraying her with diesel fuel and setting her on fire. "No."

"Where are you going?"

"Port San Luis." A stop before rounding Point Conception, headed south.

"I'll be waiting for you when you come back."

I could not look at her. "I won't be coming back," I said. When I hung up the hose she was gone. My cell phone rang as I was passing under the Golden Gate Bridge and I threw it into the ocean.

The sea was a bit ragged, gusty with eight to ten foot swells, but the weather held sunny. The almanac had a sunset of just after six, and by that time I'd stopped quaking with anger and reduced sail to just the reefed main and jib. Sail changes alone, offshore and in the dark, would be tricky, and I was in no hurry to go anyplace but away. I was in a sense already there. My last view of the shore was Point San Pedro, hundreds of feet high, its white, southern face momentarily tinseled by the setting sun. I steered due south all night, the autopilot blinking its readiness to take over, but what was I going to do? Make dinner and grade term papers? I let it steer only long enough to open all the ports and hatches. The cabin still reeked of her.

The dawn was mostly fog. But without recourse to electronic aids, I could tell I was crossing Monterey Bay by the action of the swells over the depths of the Monterey Trench and the chatter of the Asian fishermen on the marine VHF radio. The wind came up and blew away the fog but it was a wind from the south, a strong low pressure, barometer dropping, which was never a good sign, particularly sailing south in the face of it. The NOAA weather radio took its usual relaxed view of things, but predicted a thirty-knot southerly with showers and this was more bad news. I knew my limits; another ten hours and I'd be exhausted. Port San Luis was a horrible place in a southerly blow. In the last El Niño year, 1998, they'd had seventy-knot winds and fifteen foot seas which pulled boats apart, even when securely moored to buoys. Plus, I needed a very long day to sail there under these conditions. Why had I chosen it? Perhaps because it had been so bleak the last time. They were still ripping out topsoil, and half the nearby town, to cure a blight caused by leaking oil storage tanks. It suited my mood, but when she asked me where I was going I might as well have said Mexico or French Polynesia.

First things first. Course slightly offshore to give me some sea room around Cape San Martin. Another reef in the main. A smaller jib. Breakfast, the first food I'd had in a day. The benison of hot water and coffee. But I was too tired to think my way to a new destination: if Port San Luis didn't work out, I'd just keep going. By midday, on my next tack, I made Point Piedras Blancas and then San Simeon Bay. Even under grey skies and the persistent southerly, it was a seductively beautiful spot: south of the eucalyptus grove which crowned the point like a stylish haircut, it was a wide sandy beach backed by grassland lush at this time of year and rolling gently up a landscape soft as a pile of pillows. It was, if anything, more of a deathtrap than Port San Luis in these conditions. But the coast turned westward here and with wind moderating I could safely raise the foresail and jog along a

40

few miles offshore on a course that would take me all the way to Port San Luis.

I had not thought about Kay during the previous night or much of anything at all. Now, with the boat sailing well, I had settled into a hellish internal video loop of her with another man. I threw up my breakfast and lunched on Tylenol and Dramamine. I could stop this with an effort of the will or something about the boat that needed attention, but it was replaced by thoughts of my own failings as a lover and a man. I wondered, too, if I somehow had gotten it all wrong, if Kay was innocent and I'd taken a spiteful remark from a college freshman as truth. Suppose we'd talked it out? Maybe it was something short of an affair. But that brought me back to the video loop, because her *I'll wait for you* at the fuel dock was as good as a confession, really. We live together for years and I just take the schooner out the Gate and she says she'll wait for me. A confession and an apology and a willingness to . . . make up? Go on?

I raised the old lighthouse and breakwater in the evening. The latter looked like a python which had swallowed a rat, as the breakwater had incorporated a small island about a third of the way along its length. Beyond it were piers belonging to the county and California Polytechnic, and beyond that a startlingly clean, white, newly built town, scrubbed by the rain. There was a brief shower and I was suddenly very cold, even in my foul weather gear. Through binoculars I could see that the transient anchorage was empty except for a largish white skiff tied to one of the buoys and kicking on its line. I tacked out again to get the sails down, but before I did so I called the harbormaster on the VHF. "Well, skipper," he said, "it's been raining off and on all day. The swell's dropped, though, and we're back to something reasonable tomorrow. You'll have a restless night but a safe one. Take the mooring ball just downwind of the buoy that has that dinghy attached." I ran the engine for a long enough time to make hot water, furl the sails, turn on navigation lights and depth sounder, and start the cabin heater. By the time I was ready to make my run in, it was a sultry, pearl-colored dusk. I

41

made a wide turn around the tied boat, found my ball and turned into the swell. I was achingly tired and desperately needed to make the mooring on the first try. The swells were now long and low, more of a help than a hindrance in getting the schooner stopped, and pausing long enough for me to run forward with the boat hook, grab the line and make it fast. As I straightened, I had a good look at the flat backside of the skiff, and raised the glasses which were still around my neck.

Drake, it read. *San Francisco.*

It was my old tender, which I'd left behind at the dock thirty hours ago. A pretty little thing, but basically an unseaworthy nuisance for whatever it was that I'd had in mind. Working largely on instinct I slashed the lines holding the inflatable to the foredeck, dropped it over the side, hooked on the boarding ladder and jumped down. I watched the schooner's navigation lights recede, which were still on and now, in the sudden darkness, the only point of reference. As I pulled alongside the skiff I saw a few inches of water in the bottom, a floating, unopened package of sandwiches and a thermos bottle, a single oar and Kay, in a soaked down parka and curled up in an impossible position on the middle seat. There was a flashlight clipped to the transom of the inflatable, and after tying us together, I shined it on her and called her name. She moved but didn't answer. I stepped over and lifted her bodily out, cast loose and touched her cheek. Stone cold, but with my hand on the side of her face she opened her eyes. "Ethan," she said. "I'm sorry." And then: "I lost one of the oars."

It was a trial getting her back on board, shivering so violently she could barely sit up. I was afraid I'd drop her if I tried to carry her up the ladder. In the end I had to rig a sling and haul her over the side on the main halyard. Once in the cockpit I maneuvered her down into the cabin in small, tentative steps. It was blessedly warm. She stood passively, but unsupported, while I got her clothes off and looked for something dry. Where had all her clothes gone? Oh. I started the shower, which had a little bench to sit on, and pushed her in as the water ran hot. She began to revive almost immediately and looked at me with a strange, sad smile. By the time the tank's two minutes of hot water ran out, I had retrieved my spare long underwear and together we got her toweled dry and into it. She started shivering again and I slid her into the pilot berth, the warmest, driest place on the boat, and joined her. I had plans for hot liquid, but at that moment there seemed to be no idea on earth but to climb in with her. She stopped shivering, wept for a few moments and fell asleep.

I woke at three in the morning, heated two cans of tomato soup and dropped large chunks of cheese into the bowls before I brought hers over. She was slow to wake up and when she did she ate slowly and attentively, asking for crackers and where we were. "On a mooring downwind of where you tied up the skiff."

"I lost an oar."

"I know, you told me."

"But even if I hadn't I'd have stayed there until you came. Because I'm brave. You told me that."

"It's true, Kay." I took the empty bowl.

"I parked your truck by the harbormaster's office. I called your department and told them you were sick. I . . ." her voice trailed off. Then: ". . . resigned from Jamison and Peters."

"Go back to sleep now."

I slept myself, deeply but briefly as sailors do. When we had any light at all I retrieved the old skiff, tied it to the stern, then started the engine and slipped the mooring. The wind was still southerly but the day fair, so that when I made the turn I could set every sail we had. There was a little compass over the pilot berth and Kay had learned a thing or two, so that when she appeared at the hatch with my coffee she knew. "We're headed north."

"Yes, Kay. We're going back."

But it would never be quite the same place.

43

CHAPTER FOUR

In 1933, a local chauffeur named William Hallowell drove a quail hunter to Point Reyes, north of San Francisco and to what was, and still feels like, a wild and untrammeled coastline. Point Reyes ("The Kings") is the most remarkable headland north of Point Conception. The southern face is a vertical, straight slab of durable syenitic granite 600 feet high, but it rises from a wild jumble of hundreds of rocks and crags. The point is an extrusion of an undulating neck of land, which curves to enclose Drake's Bay and its attendant marshes and tidal ponds, multi-hued in shades of green and replete with quail. The name was given to it by the Spanish explorer Viscaino, who was not exploring at the time, but looking for the wreck of the *San Augustine,* a Manila galleon driven ashore in 1595.

Presumably while waiting for his client, Hallowell found a metal plate with the inscription D-R-A-K-E, along with other more obscure words, put it in his trunk and when next cleaning up the car, tossed it into a creek, as people were inclined to do in those days, somewhere along the roads around San Quentin. Three years later a student named Beryl Shinn found a metal plate on the shore of the North Bay, near where Mr. Hallowell had supposedly discarded his. Shinn later took the plate to UC Berkeley: the place to go in those days. My department at State barely existed; in fact the school, then called San Francisco State Teachers College, did not teach history until 1923. It didn't offer history degrees until around 1935, when it had the blessing of the University of California to grant them. So it was the university that got the plate, the institution of the Ballentine family and museum specifically; and two months later it proclaimed that the hand-inscribed brass square had been left behind by Sir

Francis Drake himself during his three-year circumnavigation begun in 1577. It was a controversial and premature announcement. Sir Francis was no help, because after he returned to England in 1580, all of his ship's documents disappeared and no official account of his circumnavigation was ever published.

This is what Brian Haggerty wanted to see me about when he came aboard that Sunday after my first week as Archivist to the Willems collection. Thanksgiving was imminent, but the weather was solidly tranquil, reverting to the day Kay and I first stopped by the institute. No wind to speak of, air layered cool above the water, but progressively warmer as I hauled myself up the mainmast in the bosun's chair for the fall coat of varnish. From my perch and in the perfect air, I saw Brian leave his car, a Lexus, and stretch as if he'd been driving for hours. He was holding a white paper bag delicately and bent down with care to look at something on his car, a scratch maybe, then unlock the trunk and take out a small leather briefcase.

I had a moment of affection for Brian, observing him in this manner without his awareness. He looked like a man aging poorly but gamely, his thin blond locks smoothly coiffed, sporting wraparound shades and dressed for jogging. I'd known him as long as I'd known Kay—she'd introduced us. And though I was occasionally suspicious of his motives, I had the advantage over him that those without ambition have over those with it. In my own mind, I was where I wanted to be and it gave me the luxury of viewing the world as it was, rather than figuring out what it might be coaxed into doing for me.

I was on deck, stowing the chair and its tackle when he arrived alongside. "Kay out of town?" he asked, knowing that watching me varnish fifty feet up gave her the willies. I nodded and offered coffee. He held up the bag. "Chocolate croissants?"

As the coffee perked, he took cups from the rack and the small, lovely, indestructible blue ceramic plates Kay had brought into my life, and set out the pastries. I watched him. He knew the boat well, but setting the table was clearly a displacement activity. "Aren't you going to ask how things are at State?" I asked.

"Do I always start conversations with you that way? Do you ask me the same thing?"

"No, I assume the University of California, as opposed to San Francisco State, will actually survive these troubled times."

"How patronizing. I'll never do it again." While I poured the coffee he collected himself. "You know the story about Hallowell and Beryl Shinn and Drake's Plate?"

"I teach California history, as you may be aware. In some circles I might be considered an expert." I was still somewhat defensive, I suppose, over somehow missing the gossip about the Willems Institute for the past several decades.

"All right, don't be cute. I never realized you were so sensitive." Uncharacteristically, he paused now instead of charging into his next thought. "Did it ever strike you as *odd* that the plate, which we all now know is a fake—a joke at the expense of UC—was discovered *twice*?"

"Well, yes, if you put it that way." He waited for me, chewing his croissant with some pleasure in spite of his obvious distraction. "I always thought that the original plate was forged as a sophisticated prank. Since it was lost and found again, too much time had passed; and by the time Curtis Ballentine announced his discovery to the world, the pranksters were too embarrassed to come forward. Something like that." The plate was in a section of Berkeley's Ballentine Museum devoted to favorite frauds. I hadn't been there in years. "But if you threw it out again tomorrow, down in the brush by Corte Madera Creek, chances are it would wash out in a winter flood and sink. Or if it was found, it would still be in someone's garage."

"OK, that's your first step on the path to wisdom. Rainfall was about average, but six inches fell in January 1935. Enough to flood. The plate the chauffeur found could not have survived in the place where it was discarded. Now take a look at this."

He placed the briefcase on the table, opened it with a flourish and turned it around so I could see the contents. They were two documents side by side, very good, registered (for authenticity) photocopies, but pressed between layers of blotting paper

46

nonetheless. He didn't have to tell me not to touch them. There was enough swing on the chart table's gooseneck light that I could bring it to bear. I took a magnifying glass from the drawer for the first one. The document on the left was an original share in the Dutch East India Company dated 1606. The other was a letter dated 1993 and marked CONFIDENTIAL to the Ballentine Library. It read in part: ". . . to my certain knowledge, very significant portions of the collection have been withheld, and are extant either in Europe or somewhere on the institute grounds. The attached was apparently overlooked because it had been placed, not in the main collection room but in a secondary room in the building, which contains mostly modern works of the period between World Wars I and II. The rest of the collection contains nothing from the period 1580 through 1620, when Drake had his busiest correspondence with northern European cartographers." The letter was signed by Dr. Adrian Burke, the skeletal British book appraiser I'd met the week before. Burke had ended the letter cryptically: "Please advise me if we can pursue matters of mutual interest."

In context, *very significant portions of the collection have been withheld* meant, almost certainly, the lost logbooks of the *Golden Hinde*, Sir Francis Drake's personal logbooks. There had been a dozen or more false leads for Drake's Logs, from Baja to British Columbia in America and as many in northern Europe. Burke struck me as a man who'd delight in such a treasure hunt. "Is Adrian Burke the man on his way to New York, the man you said I should meet?" I asked as innocently as I could. Candor with Brian, about whom I was working with and why, was just an invitation to exposure and the loss of a job I was starting to like.

"I don't know who he is. Google has a Sotheby's auctioneer or something like that with the same name, but I have no way of being sure. My guy is Robert McNally."

Dr. Robert McNally, or "Easy Bob" as a class of grateful students at San Francisco State University had labeled him in praise of his grading practices, was a Midwestern, but mainly itinerant, history professor who'd made a couple of stops on Bay

Area campuses down through the years. He filled in for professors on sabbatical, a sort of "substitute teacher" academic. He had weighed in on the Drake's Plate controversy while here in the 1980s, but I couldn't remember what he actually proposed. "Are you saying Bob McNally worked at the Willems Institute?"

"He did. He'd catalogued about half the collection, when he came across the letter and the East India Company stock certificate, which he copied. He was caught in the act of copying something else—he won't say exactly what that was—and fired, threatened with a lawsuit, and hounded out of town. He's been teaching high school in Des Moines ever since."

"I never heard about any of this."

"Neither had I or anybody else. He was an under-the-radar guy, if there ever was one. I'm surprised you remember him."

"So how—"

"He called me last week, the day after we had lunch. Said he'd read this or that paper, admired my work and gift of making history come alive, blah, blah. Then he asked if, as a professional courtesy, I would check and see whether the Ballentine Library had ever received a letter from an Adrian Burke in 1993. I did so, but wouldn't tell him unless he explained why."

Brian whistled a little tune, squeezed the chocolate out of his croissant and dropped it in his coffee. The cabin was sunny, warm and quiet. There was the sound of a power sander a few slips down and a distant rumble of diesel, which only made his silence more provocative. "What did he say?" I asked.

"He said that he had a strong 'intimation' that somewhere 'close at hand' were Drake's original logbooks that would verify that the first plate, the William Hallowell plate, was genuine, and that the second plate, the one over on campus, *was* a fake, but not as a practical joke. It was a deliberate forgery intended to be discovered, to conceal the real thing until supporting documentary proof could be found, at which point the real Hallowell plate would be . . ." he looked up for an appropriate understatement, ". . . fun to post on eBay."

I thought about it. Francis Drake was the subject of more biographies than any figure of Elizabethan times, and he must be in the top twenty historical personages of all time. Every little indentation in the coast claimed his visit. The Drake's Bay north of San Francisco, though, was simply an exercise in early California real estate promotion, and few serious scholars thought he stopped there. I supposed a very clever man might want absolute proof before challenging the conventional wisdom. A fake plate was just the thing to keep people busy in the meantime. Bit convoluted, though. "Is that his theory or yours?"

"Oh, all Bob's and I was skeptical. When pressed he admitted that the second part was speculation, based on the passionate nature of some of the correspondence he read between the Willems and the Ballentines of the day, and of course the letter from this man Burke. Same kind of snooping that got him fired, I imagine. After I told him a colleague was working with the collection, he said he'd back up his point about what might be in the Willems and send me something, including a copy of the 1993 letter he was asking about. It arrived by FedEx the next day. I think he's looking for a local ally since he can't approach the collection himself, and maybe some university influence in his favor if anything does come up. . . . By the way, do you have any of those cigars I sent you from London?"

I did, and we took our two Havanas out to the sunny cockpit. If there was any discovery of artifacts that would make our world swoon, hardcore academics or self-promoting charlatans or piratical auctioneers, it was Drake's Logs. Elizabethan England was a conspirators' paradise, in which paranoid secrecy made perfect sense. Drake's secret mission was to find the Northwest Passage from the opposite side of the continent, since expeditions up the Saint Lawrence River, the passage from the eastern end, had not turned out well. Also called the Strait of Anian (named before anyone knew whether it existed or not), it would allow the English to turn the Spanish flank in the New World by going after the strait from the west, far north of the Spanish holdings and claiming the strait, and by extension the riches of Asia, for

England. The logbooks, it is supposed, contained Drake's best guess as to how to get into the Strait and was too important to ever reveal. More to the point, they would state whether, where and why he'd left his "plate of brass," establishing English control of the whole area. It's in the nature of many secrets in history to be impregnably protected until such time as proven utterly useless to the world. At which point nobody can remember what they were or where they might be hidden. The document, however, would be priceless even if Drake just wrote out grocery lists.

"Not priceless," Brian said when I'd made that observation. "But a serious collector would consider seven figures a bargain price. May I gather from your bemused expression that you have not found anything remotely connected to these matters?"

"You may. What else did he say?"

"Nothing."

"*Nothing?*"

"Nada. From what he didn't say we can surmise he has no idea where the real plate might be, either. He said he was coming out here and I gave him your name, but then had a message on my machine that he was consulting an attorney before he talked to anybody. He gave me the number of a hotel in New York, but when I called yesterday he wasn't registered."

There was a long smoky pause while we both trimmed our sails a bit. For all Brian's understated cool and my careful detachment, we were both intoxicated by the idea. It wasn't so much the cash value of such a discovery, but a heady combination of the sense of imminent discovery that keeps historians plugging away, and, to be honest, of what Drake's Logbooks might contribute to our stature in the community of academics. To me, this meant my career was not the peaceful coma I'd thought it to be, had in fact contentedly resigned myself to. To Brian, a chance to be on TV. For Easy Bob, a frustrated minor leaguer in search of justification, a chance to start in a World Series game. "But then what happened? If Ballentine had the plate and Willems had Drake's Logbooks, why wasn't the deal consummated when the collection arrived?"

"Well, remember the collection was impounded by the War Department and sequestered from everybody until the war was over, and by that point there was bad blood between the families. Obviously, the government didn't look closely at it either. But why, sixty years later, nothing happened, not even a rumor started, is beyond me."

"Why not ask Sean Ballentine?" Sean Ballentine was the current head of the museum, and everything else the family was into—research and charitable foundations, particle physics, real estate.

"Because," he said, then stopped. "Don't get me wrong; he's a wonderful philanthropist and a great benefactor of the History Department, but he'd squash us like a bug if he thought we had something he wanted." He looked up, over my head. "There's Kay," he said. She appeared, rumbling up the dock with her wheeled suitcase. She looked rested and trim, the in-control traveling attorney. Frozen for a moment in the sunshine, we all could have been an advertisement for boats, cigars, or executive suitcases. I stepped to the dock and kissed her. "Why didn't you call me to pick you up?"

"Rode in with a colleague." She stepped aboard and looked at us. "I forgive you for smoking cigars and varnishing the mast without any help. Hello, cousin. Ah, coffee." Brian was emerging from the cabin with a cup, which he handed to her.

We sat and talked; Kay really wasn't tired, claiming to have finally mastered sleeping on airplanes. This led to beers and sandwiches, and after Brian left, a long discussion of Thanksgiving plans, mainly about whether to invite him this year. Brian could be very charming and clever as a dinner guest, but his wife was an endlessly complaining woman who didn't seem to like him, or us, very much. We had a light supper, and then to bed. Just before sleep it occurred to me that, as I had lifted Kay's bags aboard, he'd put the briefcase away somewhere so she wouldn't see its contents.

I worked at the institute Monday through Wednesday, long days since I had no classes. By midday the second day Burke and I

51

were working smoothly together and had at least one major find, at least from his point of view: Charles Darwin's *Narrative of the Surveying Voyages of His Majesty's Ships Adventure and Beagle.* A first edition from 1839. Worth about $50,000 at auction. We stopped at that point and called in Karen. She seemed more vexed than attentive when I suggested that such volumes might be transferred to a vault. She said she would make arrangements for a private security guard, and one appeared the next day. I made a few other observations. There were more books dealing with navigating the coast of California, among them a catalogue of the publications of the U.S. Coast and Geodetic Survey in the nineteenth century. The publications listed in the catalogue went back much earlier and there were check marks on some of them, books which I later found. These now appeared to me to have a context, of course. If Drake's personal logbooks existed, and if Professor Willems had read them, he would be only half way there, because reported positions in the 1500s routinely had spectacular errors. If he was trying to find out where Drake actually went, he'd be better off with older descriptions of how the coast and sea bottom *looked* to a mariner, proceeding north at four miles an hour. I was starting to believe that McNally was on to something.

We settled down Wednesday afternoon to a celebratory cocktail in the study before the fire, before leaving for Thanksgiving. I had been pondering whether to ask about McNally, but since they had never been forthcoming about him, it seemed to require a level of subterfuge beyond my abilities. I'd had three twelve-hour days, though, to consider and craft a safe and normal-sounding query which would both help verify McNally's claims and get a reaction. We were drinking gin and tonics, mixed by Adrian with an almost balletic flourish, and eating smoked salmon canapés. The security guard, Mike something, a burly and dour Samoan, drank a coke while standing in front of the fire.

"I have a question," I said, when the conversation lagged. They turned politely, Karen in a long paisley skirt and turtleneck, Adrian somewhat festive in tweeds and a burgundy scarf. "What's in the other room?"

Karen smiled tolerantly. "I can't believe you haven't peeked."

Adrian said: "Historians don't browse, they burrow into books like a bird building a nest." To me he said: "It's a collection of mostly fiction from the period between the wars. A lot of mid-century erotica filled with untranslatable terms dealing with female undergarments no longer in use." He took a long drink and winked at me. From his gaunt, waxy face, it was like being winked at by a very well-preserved museum specimen. "Elsewise, hundreds of random volumes in at least six languages. If you're good, we may turn you loose in there as a reward. No real value except as used books, sold by the pound."

This was my opening. "So that was never catalogued, either."

"No, Ethan, everything you're ravishing is a virgin." If Karen had winked I might have forgotten her reply. She leaned forward from her corner of the little table and touched my knee instead. "And there may be other rewards, even better." An odd remark, assuming it wasn't sexual. I was a bit old for that. Could she possibly be hinting about Drake's Logs?

So, I thought, they either don't know about Easy Bob— unlikely in Karen's case and nearly impossible in Burke's, who had signed the 1993 letter McNally found—or were concealing his time on the second floor. "The collection dates from the late thirties, right?"

"Correct."

"Who's been here all that time?"

"Well, there was always a caretaker to keep the place up. There have been visiting scholars occasionally, usually academics who were from Europe and had Lucius Willems' permission to look at the hundred or so volumes he knew were here. The collection has never been opened to any kind of public. If you haven't found out about the feud, I should tell you that there was a longstanding hostility between the Willems and the Ballentines over at Cal."

WE HAD one of Kay's friends from her firm over for Thanksgiving, Molly, a new arrival in California with no place to go. She was effusive and fascinated by our lifestyle; a turkey cooked onboard a schooner being very exotic to someone from Colorado Springs. I showed her everything and explained more in response to her questions, and we were almost to apple pie before I realized how little Kay had said. She'd been perfectly pleasant, except for the culinary panic most women seem to experience before fancy dinners, up until when I opened the wine and she took a cell phone call on deck.

I drove Molly downtown and waited while she found a cab. By the time I got back to the boat it was dark, and I had a peaceful moment contemplating *Drake*, portholes aglow and the sounds of Corelli drifting up the companionway. But below decks all was not well. Kay was sitting with her hands in her lap. "I hope you had fun flirting with Molly." It was the kind of irrelevant, slightly contrary remark that Kay used, sort of like a warning shot, to signal something else was amiss.

"She seems very nice," I said blandly.

"Oh never mind, Ethan, sit down. I have something to talk to you about."

"Brandy?"

"If you must. None for me."

While I poured she said: "Can I ask you some things without your asking me why I'm asking them?" When I'd sorted that out I sat down beside her and said I'd try, but no promises. "Do you know a man from Iowa named Robert McNally?" When I didn't answer right away she said, "He's in your field, I think. History, I mean."

"Bob McNally taught at SFSU for a couple of semesters in the early 1990s, if memory serves."

She lifted my glass off the mahogany and drank a swallow. "I want to tell you a little about my trip last week."

"I'm listening."

"My client is Sean Ballentine, Junior. You know him?"

"I know who he is, of course. And we met him at a party in Berkeley." I couldn't recall the date, but the party was befitting West Coast royalty. The man who, in Brian's terms, would squash us like bugs. He was the scion of the Ballentines of Berkeley, former president of the University of California Regents, donator of the newest wing of the museum, and lord of a manor that sprawled on the crest of the hills above the Willems Institute. There were pink tea roses everywhere, great fences of wrought iron, a Spanish hacienda befitting California elite. The occasion was an award ceremony for Brian, prestigious professor of the year or something. I remembered him as courteous in the manner of the high-functioning super-rich, lots of eye contact and a firm handshake, and a facile warmth that came off him like cologne. "And?"

"That's all I want to say for the moment."

"Wow, that is a little about your trip." She stood and when she faced me she looked very unhappy, eyes on the floor and her arms now placed to hug herself tightly. "Kay, what is it?"

"The call just before dinner was from a police detective in Manhattan. This man, this Robert McNally—who I don't know at all—was found dead in a hotel room. He'd been unidentified for several days because all his possessions were gone and he was registered as someone else. But he'd left a notebook in the hotel safe that identified him and it had your name, Brian's, and Sean Ballentine's in it. It had our address here on the boat, Brian's office number, and the name of the hotel where Ballentine, his business partners, and I were staying. Do you know anything about this?"

"Brian said McNally wanted to talk to me, that he'd worked at the institute ten years ago. He'd been in contact with the Ballentine Museum as well."

"How is Brian involved?" I told her a little of it. I'm sorry to say I wasn't eager to share what I knew with Sean Ballentine's property rights attorney, even if I did sleep with her.

But she seemed a little relieved. "Brian and his wheeling and dealing. That explains it. The police want you to contact them. . . . I said you were away but would call tomorrow. I also said I was your attorney."

"Bit of a stretch, there, but thanks."

55

"This isn't funny."

"Apparently not. Don't worry, Kay. Bob McNally was trying to get in touch with me through Brian, something about the collection."

"The Willems collection?" I nodded. "Was he trying to contact Sean Ballentine directly?"

"I don't know." She seemed to have nothing else to say.

"How did he die?" I asked.

"He was killed . . . he was brutally killed." Now she came forward and drank the rest of my brandy in one swallow. "You'd better ask the policeman. He'll be here Monday."

CHAPTER FIVE

I called the detective the next day and he did indeed want to see me Monday. Lieutenant Parsons said he'd already contacted Brian; when I offered to arrange a meeting with us both together, he declined. And although he said it was to be entirely at my convenience, Monday was clearly the day. He already had his flight times. Since I was teaching Monday, I scheduled him during my office hours on campus. "Will your attorney be there? Ms. O'Toole?" he asked.

"No, that was my girlfriend being protective. She's a lawyer, but obviously you want to talk to her too, also separately."

"Don't need a lawyer, then?"

"I can't imagine why."

"Well, that's refreshing." Parsons sounded like a guy-ish sort of guy, Monday night football and a few extra pounds after the holiday. He asked me for restaurant suggestions and what a New Yorker might do on a morning free in the City by the Bay. He would see me at three.

Brian couldn't resist calling me a few times over the weekend, if only because he thought the whole thing was exciting. He could, I felt, see it shaping up as a chapter in a bestseller he might write. However, neither of us profited from our collusion, and in fact neither of us thought Bob McNally's search for the logbooks had anything to do with his death. Or as Brian put it: "No historian gets killed over sixteenth-century manuscripts, even by another historian." Kay was the opposite, subdued but eager to talk about anything else. She never offered to come to the meeting as my attorney, either.

On Monday the fog lasted into the early afternoon, then we had a half hour of weak sunshine before it set in again, wrapping the campus in an early, smoky dusk that made everyone of my generation think of Sam Spade and *The Maltese Falcon*. "Dr. Storey?" Parsons asked, stepping through the open door and taking in the industrial, plain metal furnishings of a land-grant professor's office. Parsons wore the worn leather bomber jacket coveted by most men reluctant to abandon their youth, with a white shirt and plain black tie; matching Dockers. Close-cropped greying hair and features consistent with his trade, as I understood it anyway. I'd never been interviewed by any sort of policeman. An extremely noncommittal face and expression, but a very direct stare from eyes the color of the fog outside. He didn't come alone, either. Although Parsons had some extra weight, with him was a man who looked like he did not need a restaurant recommendation, an untidy presence pushing 300 pounds, seeming rather happy, almost eager to be here and utterly without guile, as if the detective had assigned him to distract and disarm me. His features were small within his large face, attractive in the way of *Peanuts* cartoon characters. Parsons introduced him as George Metaxis, a document specialist from the FBI's Carson City office in Nevada. I had to go next door to borrow a chair, and offered coffee. They both accepted, and when Metaxis took his first sip, he said "Peet's," and then: "there isn't a decent cup of coffee to be had in Carson City."

"Welcome to San Francisco," I said.

Parsons took my personal information while Metaxis studied my bookshelves. Then getting down to business, Parsons said: "Tell me about Robert McNally."

I was prepared with Bob's personnel file, which I'd copied and he accepted with a nod. "How did you know him?"

"He was here for a few semesters several years ago. Taught history from all ends of the spectrum. We talked at faculty meetings, that sort of thing. He was a bit isolated, being a temporary employee, but he was interested in his material and liked by the students."

"Why did he have your phone number?"

"Brian Haggerty from Cal—The University of California at Berkeley—said he was coming to see me to give me information on a private collection of manuscripts I'm cataloging. He'd worked there before me."

"The Willems Institute in Berkeley?" Metaxis asked. I nodded, somewhat surprised. "Are you still working there?"

"Yes. I do two or three afternoons a week and I'll be there through next spring, probably."

"What did he want to talk about?"

"You'll get more details from Brian, but basically I think he wanted to tell us about his belief that the collection contained some valuable documents from the Elizabethan period."

"Why wouldn't he go directly to the owners of the collection?" Parsons asked. Metaxis, having sat down only moments before, lifted out of his chair like a small dirigible taking off and walked over to my reference library, which was closer to the door, put on a pair of reading glasses, and carefully balanced his coffee cup on the top shelf.

"According to Brian he was fired from the same job when he was here, and perhaps harbored some ill-will."

"Why wouldn't he just assume you'd find the documents?"

"Well, he never found them, actually. He thought they were hidden somewhere, Brian said."

"Wanted to help you find the secret compartment?" Parsons smiled, but his eyes never left my face.

"Something like that."

"Dr. Haggerty said Mr. McNally told him he had some legal matters to attend to," Parsons said. I found myself correcting him. McNally had his doctorate and would like to be remembered that way. "Dr. McNally, then. Did Ms. O'Toole tell you he had contact information for her client, Sean Ballentine?"

"Yes. We live together. Kay and I, I mean."

He grinned. "She has some client confidentiality stuff going on."

"She's pretty scrupulous about that," I said. "All lawyers are, property rights attorneys more so than most."

Neither man was taking notes. Both were drinking their coffee. And although the questions were direct and Parsons' gaze level, and Metaxis scanned my books as if memorizing them, these actions seemed to be more by habit than intent. They were still law-enforcement types, but on an enjoyable excursion to the West Coast. "Indulge me for a moment. Can you think of any reason McNally would want to call Ballentine?"

"Possibly the same reason he wanted to contact me and Brian. Ballentine is a regent of the university and his family endowed the history museum and two professorships." One of which was Brian's.

Metaxis turned from the shelves. He was holding my copy of John Blake's *The Sea Chart: The Illustrated History of Nautical Maps and Navigational Charts*, just out the previous month and still in its dust cover. He said: "The university and the Willems family were not on speaking terms, your colleague said."

"That was fifty years ago."

"Hedging his bets by contacting you and Ballentine both?" Metaxis continued.

"That would seem to make sense." Parsons' expression was one of mild professional exasperation with Metaxis. However friendly, this was not supposed to be a freewheeling exchange of speculations. But resigning himself he simply asked if I had any idea who would want to kill him. "No."

We talked for a few minutes more, about my background, how I'd come to work for the institute, and a referral to the department chair who'd hired McNally. Then: "We're done for the moment, unless you have anything, George."

Metaxis reshelved the book and came back to the desk. He leaned over and took a very large and sturdy, unmarked envelope from his briefcase. Inside was an oversize ziplock bag and inside the bag was a notebook, a pricey but common leather-bound ledger with thick pages, the kind favored by older academics who can't adjust to laptops. It was placed in the bag so that it was open to a page. Parsons looked disgusted until he realized what it was. He saw me note his expression and shrugged. "I thought for

60

a minute he was going to show you the autopsy photos." What Metaxis was showing me was the page with our phone numbers on it and Ballentine's name and hotel. Parsons stood up and put his coat on and laid a business card on my desk.

There were other numbers on the page that looked like phone numbers with area codes—ten digits. Perhaps a half dozen sets. Metaxis read my mind. "Not actual phone numbers, the rest of them, except a few that are for things like a hair salon in Topeka, Kansas and offshore phone lines in the Caribbean. Any thoughts?"

"No." They seemed like ISBN numbers, publishers' reference codes that also have ten digits.

I raised my eyes and Metaxis actually winked. "Me neither, not a clue." He tore a small sheet of paper from a notebook in his pocket and copied the numbers down. He gave them to me with his card. Call me if you think of anything."

"Do the police have any theories?" I asked. "I mean, was it just an urban sort of crime?" My real question was, one, why were they asking about Bob's academic hobby, and two, why was the FBI involved.

"It's an ongoing investigation, Dr. Storey," Parsons replied. "But I can tell you what was in the newspapers. He was traveling incognito and we didn't know who he was, which is why we released as much information as we did. He was staying in a small but respectable hotel in midtown. Discreet, you might call it, since they waited two days before looking in the house safe. His inside door latch was off, which meant he either opened the door or forgot to close it. Since the door was not forced, we're assuming he let someone in. Urban criminals don't knock, as a rule. And they don't strip the room or their victim of every single thing not belonging to the hotel. He was killed professionally, we think, but not quickly."

With that, they were gone. I turned to my computer. Could you search by ISBN? Of course, you could. I had titles to all Bob's book selections before my visitors had unparked their car. Mostly modern works about Drake (ISBN numbers have only been around for about forty years), all of which were on my shelves, two about Nazi Germany. Exploring the Willems' escape from Belgium, I supposed. I ordered them from Amazon.

"I THINK you should quit your job at the institute," Kay said that night. The fog had thickened into an irregular, but intent Bay Area rain which made a sound like popcorn popping on the cabin top, alternating with a windy silence. I'd made beef and carrot stew, and I was slightly tipsy on the wine I'd drunk in equal measure as I'd added it to the pot. It was a curious, inappropriately ebullient mood for me. I may have been the steadiest man Kay had ever met, but I was rediscovering a sense of adventure dulled by university bureaucracy and a pleasant but predictable life. There was no way I was going to quit the collection. It was the most interesting thing that had ever happened to me, apart from Kay herself. "Why?"

"Ethan, I'm going to be painfully honest with you. I had the idea you might get interested in the collection if I brought you up there and that I might, umm, learn more about it to help out my client. And I thought you needed something more in your life. My little plan. Now we're stuck in a situation where neither of us can talk about it and someone's been killed. I know you doubt that it has anything to do with you, I do too, but . . ." She paused. Kay's pauses, interspersed throughout her conversations at both mundane and significant moments, always caught my attention. Her face was unguarded and profoundly beautiful, something like she looked just after lovemaking. She was figuring things out, making a decision, big or small, and bringing all her womanly skills into uniting both sides of her brain. Now as I looked at her, tears formed in the corners of her dark eyes. "I'm so afraid of losing you." It was what I'd said to her once, and she repeated it sometimes, as a message in our private language.

I wasn't sure how she meant it this time, except as a general plea for the kind of emotional response I never seemed to be able to give. Rather than taking her into my arms, I said: "Let's take a little walk before dessert."

The marina, a well-run place I'd been in since it opened, was on a peninsula that bulged into the bay. A footpath ran out from the marina around the end of the point, a tiny, grassy public park with benches facing the Golden Gate. We'd made this walk many times. The rain had partially cleared the fog. The Gate was invisible, but we could see to Alcatraz and the lights on Treasure Island, and the navigation markers close inshore muttered and flashed. When we stopped, I said: "I'll quit if you do."

She thought about it. "You know I won't, don't you?"

"I know you're loyal, it's one of the reasons I fell in love with you, twice."

She took my hand, kissed it and gave it back. "Is this the new Ethan Storey?"

"I'm afraid so, Kay. That part of your little plan worked."

"Promise me this isn't a midlife crisis adventure."

"I'm past midlife."

"You know what I mean. Promise you won't get involved in anything . . . weird."

I was past that, too. It was already weird. But I made the promise anyway, and we started talking about Christmas.

Between Christmas and New Year's, without courses to teach, I worked steadily at the institute; and despite all the drama leading up to the holidays, it was amazingly quiet. For one thing, both Adrian and Karen were away for much of the time, off in Europe with the Willems, they said in their notes. I was alone with Mike the Samoan, who was never very far away from me, though he did a good job of looking busy. The volumes now, as I completed the "north wall" of books, were predominantly in English, French or Latin; and I was on home ground, as it were, having worked with many of these documents myself: Thomas More's *Dyaloge*, the Catholic League, the 1565 Siege of Malta. All other things aside, this was wonderful moonlighting for a historian.

All other things were not aside, however. In the absence of my employer and associate, I took my lunches in the southern room, where the novels were. Although the light was poorer, it did have the dormer window with its view of the bay, and a table under it where I could sit with my turkey sandwiches and random volumes snatched from the shelves. And the south room was where Bob McNally had made his discoveries. Mike seemed uninterested in me when I was there. I acquired an overview of the European mind between the wars, but nothing else of interest.

I was puzzled not to hear from Brian during this week. I knew he was in town, but he didn't return my calls; a complete role reversal since the weekend before. After New Year's, I put it out of my mind as Kay and I made our yearly pilgrimage to her family's farm in Sanger. We returned on January 4th, loaded down with honey from her father's hives. There was still nothing from Brian, but when we collected the mail from the marina office I found something that could only have one source: George Metaxis, the oversize FBI guy. Unsigned and unexplained, the plain envelope had another page from McNally's journal and an announcement of a historians' conference in Amsterdam in mid-February. The postmark was Bishop, a small city on the other side of the Sierra Nevada mountains not all that far, as distances go over there, from Carson City. That would have been enough of a clue to the sender's identity, but his business card was tucked in as well. My view of this strange treatment with regard to the notebook was that he did not want me to contact him. I had no idea what to make of the announcement for the conference which, as a matter of fact, I was planning to attend.

All of this was too good not to share with Brian. From the marina office, I sent an urgent e-mail, a fax, and left messages on his cell and office phones, and he called me on the boat as we were finishing unpacking. "Before you say anything," he began, "and just so there's no misunderstanding, I've been warned off. So goodbye." He sounded angry but didn't hang up.

64

"I'm getting faster with this stuff," I said, "Let me guess. Your position and most of your grant money was endowed by the Ballentine family."

"I–don't–know–anything–about–that." His inflection was so flat and slow that it would only seem sincere on a transcript. "University legal staff just says stay out of it, for now. Now goodbye for real." He hung up.

"Was that Brian?" Kay asked.

"Yes."

"You didn't talk for long. I thought he was your co-conspirator."

"The university attorneys told him to find something better to do with his time." I watched for her reaction. There was none. "You don't seem surprised."

"I'm not. I tried to get you to do the same thing. And if that's anything to do with the institute," she nodded towards the manila envelope, "don't let me see it."

In my office the next day, bright and early before my first class, I looked over the page from McNally's journal. I'd started thinking it was a diary of some sort because the page had a date at the top. It was just a list of books, some of the novels I'd glanced at in the south room, but the date was June 1993, about the time McNally lost his job. I just had time, over a second cup of coffee, to see what the internet had to say about George Metaxis. He had published two articles in the *Journal of Forensic Document Examination*. In 1999, his name was in the San Francisco *Chronicle* in connection with the arrest of a man trying to establish a mining claim in the Sierra Nevada mountains who turned out to be a mobster of some sort.

The students were tanned from skiing or vacations in Mexico, and most were in their senior year, with the luxury of either goofing off or following an interest they had somehow acquired in the centuries of conflict between Britain and France. We were all in a pretty good mood, and I almost didn't see the department chairman slip in the back. Martin Frost was not a hands-on administrator and I'd never had him in my class before in the ten years he'd been chair. He came up to the front and shook my hand affably, asking about the holidays. We exchanged polite formulas about students and southern California mudslides, and the article Brian and I had written, now in press. He was not a smooth conversationalist, either, but I held neither this nor his distance from the lecture hall against him. Just before I'd met with the police, I'd written him a long e-mail about the McNally business and gotten his OK to share the personnel file. "Ethan, I'd ask you to join me for lunch but I'm off to Berkeley to meet with Sean Ballentine. I think I know what he wants to talk about." Which meant, I supposed, that he already knew.

"The Willems collection?"

"Yes, and thank God not the terrible business with Dr. McNally. Are you aware that the Ballentine family wants to negotiate a purchase of the library?"

"No. But my local contacts have been in Europe, possibly that's why. They didn't confide in me, but they didn't tell me to stop work, either."

"Perhaps you could call the Willems family directly?"

"I wouldn't know how, and they specifically asked that I not do that."

"I see. Well, I just wanted to let you know . . ." he paused now, choosing his words while not meeting my eye, something he *was* very good at. "Our relationship with the University of California in general and the Ballentine family in particular is very important to San Francisco State."

"That's something I wasn't aware of either," I couldn't resist saying. No San Francisco State professor would ever give the UC regents that kind of satisfaction.

"Are we certain that your contract allows this kind of moonlighting?"

"We are."

"Can you see anything you're doing that might affect this transaction?"

"I'm just creating a library database. It's a valuable and fascinating collection, though. If they're buying it they'll probably want somebody of their own, maybe Brian Haggerty."

"All right then. I'm sure you'll find some other way to support your schooner if this falls through. My best to Kay."

At the end of the day, when I went by the marina office for mail, the harbormaster called me over to his desk behind the partition. "You've been an asset to the marina, skipper."

"I'm not going anywhere," I said, uncomprehending.

"Didn't you get my message?" He had the look of a man who suddenly had to do his own dirty work.

"What is it, John?"

"Dang it, Skip, I told you to buy that slip instead of renting years ago. I just sold it for cash, an offer I couldn't refuse."

"Can I counter-offer?" He told me the sum. I could have bought another schooner with it. "Do you have another slip for me?"

"I'm sorry. You'll have to be out by the end of the month."

CHAPTER SIX

I could see Kay through the pilothouse windows. She was not looking in my direction, or she didn't see me coming in the damp dusk. She stood very still, sad or pensive or both, with her finger just touching the tip of her chin. There was confusion and a kind of stern, controlled anger about that gesture; I knew it well. I wondered if she had gotten the same word I had about the slip and our necessary hunt for a new place to berth the boat.

I wanted to be reassuring about dock space elsewhere, but a big old sailboat in the crowded bay was not the easiest thing to park. Ironic, when you think that our home could travel almost anywhere on the ocean planet, in safety and comfort. I turned back to the harbor office, calmed myself and decided to try and get a little more information; I'd just walked away in a huff. The harbormaster was still behind his desk, smoking a pipe and staring out the window with a distraction not unlike that of Kay. I'd known him—his name was John Davenport—for years and we liked each other. He glanced up and said, "I'm glad you came back. I feel badly about this."

"What else can you tell me?"

"I'll make some calls, Ethan, if you like. I know I can get you temporary space at Richmond Nautical Services, probably till spring."

"No, I mean who bought the slip?"

"Oceansearch Foundation, Ballentine family." I paused to digest this. It was a perfectly reputable research organization with a couple of big boats, but as a coincidence it was too much to bear. But why would Sean Ballentine want my boat slip, for God's sake? "Oh, and I forgot to tell you, you had some books in from Amazon."

68

These were the books I'd tracked by ISBN numbers, the books Bob McNally listed on the same page as our phone numbers. Suddenly the mystery at the institute seemed unimportant, now that a dirt clod had been thrown by the schoolyard bully. The San Francisco State flag had flown at my masthead, in that slip, for fifteen years. "OK, just let Richmond know we'll be living aboard, and that I'll do a major haul-out within the next couple of months, but not right away. Hang on to the books for me, would you?"

Kay was just putting the cell phone away when I came down the companionway. "Hold on, captain, it's not as bad as it sounds." She handed me a glass of wine. "I just got off the phone with Sean. It was all a big mistake, he feels terrible and wants to make it up to us." For some reason, and before I knew the details, this just made me more angry. Rather than say something stupid I waited for her to go on. "He'll give us his slip at the St. Francis."

"Oh, and I suppose it comes with a membership in the club." The St. Francis Yacht Club sponsored America's Cup boats. They had dances and drinks on the patio. Everything that floated at its docks was a trophy yacht. You usually had to wait a generation to get in.

"As a matter of fact, yes. He said he'd sponsor us at the next meeting."

OK, time to say something stupid: "Tell him to shove it."

"What?"

"Kay, we're being manipulated. He wants me to help him get at the Willems collection, for Christ's sake. You said so yourself."

"No, Ethan, it's not like that. I mean that may be true, but this is just a coincidence."

I thought for a moment about telling her that the coincidence extended to my department chair having lunch with Ballentine that day. But I could read at least a few of Kay's expressions after all these years. She would stick with her view of events even if McNally had written Ballentine's name in blood on the hotel room floor.

So instead I said: "My father hated that place, you know that. They don't allow people to live aboard, among other things."

"What other things?"

"We couldn't afford the slip fee, let alone membership."

She had been standing; she now sat and smoothed her lawyer's skirt with one hand, then looked up at me. "Maybe it's time we started thinking about moving ashore. Molly told me about a small apartment on Telegraph Hill, ready to sublet, and another in Sausalito."

It was, I suppose, the lowest blow she could have dealt, particularly since she was completely sincere. "Tell me about it."

Missing at first the coldness in my voice, her face became animated, eyes bright and a small smile at the corners of her mouth. She'd obviously been to at least one of them and checked it out. She realized at the last minute that mine was a trick question and now it was her turn to get angry. "Well, what do you want to do? We can't get this spot back, they don't allow research vessels at the St. Francis, either."

"We'll go to Richmond till spring. Something will come up."

If the St. Francis Yacht Club was the cathedral, the boatyard in Richmond was the city dump. Oil tanks, rusting hulks of tramp steamers, unsteady piles of bulk cargo, abandoned warehouses, and that was just the neighborhood. The yard itself had never found a paint can it needed to throw away, a toxic chemical it didn't like the smell of, a broken piece of machinery it wouldn't get around to fixing, sometime. It was also crime infested and noisy all night. I suppose if I'd had time to think it through I might have said the same thing she did next, but coming from her it was devastating: "If you don't mind, Ethan, I'll stay with Molly until you get it sorted out."

Now that my best friend was avoiding me and my girlfriend had moved out, John the Harbormaster helped me move the boat the next weekend. He brought the books from Amazon down from his office along with some other items I'd stored there, and a refund of the slip fees I'd paid in advance. There was no wind, but it was quite chilly with a mist that congealed onto droplets, and we rumbled across the rainy bay bundled up in foul weather gear and taking shots of tequila. When we'd tied up to a sad but still sound dock—one that had done service since they loaded munitions here in World War II—we shuttled vehicles around and said goodbye. I returned to the *Drake* and made coffee on the pilothouse burner. The depth gauge gave me six inches under the keel and not quite low tide. She'd stick in the mud once a month. Nobody ever thought about dredging Richmond Harbor; it was toxic enough to explode if jiggled. When the coffee was ready I opened the box of books. There was one popular modern volume, *The Secret Voyage of Sir Francis Drake* by Samuel Bawlf, but the other two were obscure publications by the University of Iowa Press—McNally's alma mater—about the Third Reich, just before America had entered the war. There was only one reason McNally would be interested in this kind of thing, and I tried to look up Willems in the index. No index. In the introduction, I read:

> *In the spring of 2004, hundreds of thousands of pages of FBI, CIA, and U.S. Army intelligence records related to the Nazis and World War II war crimes were declassified and opened to the public under the Nazi War Crimes Disclosure Act of 1998. 240,000 pages of original FBI files covered categories such as espionage, foreign counterintelligence, domestic security, and treason and included the names of 788 individuals and subjects in 419 newly-opened files. The authors considered the material of sufficient importance to publish it in this format, with the documents arranged only by date and without analysis. We hope this expression of trust in the skills of our colleagues will be redeemed by rapid and accurate accounts of the aspects of the Nazi era which have gone hitherto unknown to history.*

These tomes covered 1936 through 1938. The phone beeped. It was Kay. "You made it all right? Is it as bad as I remembered?"

"It's the world after the Apocalypse, if the Apocalypse had happened around 1950."

She laughed. *Nothing is wrong.* "I spoke to Sean. He says he respects your decision."

Give me a break, I thought.

But I was missing her already, so I said: "Where's my striped tie?"

"In the forward locker along with your boxed shirts from the laundry. I picked them up last Tuesday. Don't tell me you've been wearing those flannel shirts all week."

"Well, yes. I guess I have." We continued in this vein for some time, about what I was eating and how it was rooming with one of your employees. It was calm, cordial, and insubstantial. What we both needed, I suppose. When we said goodbye, I was finally hungry again.

THE NEXT day was Sunday. I drove the truck (Kay had her own car, a Saturn) over to the institute late in the morning and found Karen sitting in the foyer, much as she had been that first day, waiting for me. "How was your holiday?" Her clothes, an ivory skirt and blouse, were as cool as her tone.

"Eventful."

"For us, too. It's time to be candid, Ethan. Let's have coffee before you go to work." I followed her into the kitchen. She and Adrian had brought an espresso machine back from Europe and it gleamed incongruously on the grey soapstone countertop. She started it up and hitched herself up on the counter and said: "The Ballentine family has been all over us, and they won't let the Willems alone, either."

"How was Antwerp?"

"Please, let's not be coy. You'd like to know what we know and we'd like to know what you know. We'd like to know where you stand, for starters."

"I know you were not forthcoming about work done here by Bob McNally, who was at the institute with Adrian in 1993.

Maybe you had your reasons, and now that I've experienced the long reach of the Ballentines, I can maybe understand them. McNally was in contact with a colleague of mine, he wanted to talk, and I didn't tell you about it because he died in New York just before Thanksgiving. Your turn." The machine cycled, and I went to it and filled the two small cups on the counter. There was a small bowl of lemon peel and I added a shred to each cup. Whatever else Adrian and Karen were up to, they ran a class act. And at this point I was inclined to think of them as allies, at least compared to Ballentine, who in the course of a week had broken up my household and moved it to the wastelands of maritime Richmond.

For all its character the kitchen was a grim place; so with an unspoken mutual consent we moved to the dining room and sat at the table, covered against the sunlight—we had sun again, a belated New Year's present from the Gods of California—by a sheet of thick linen. "Well, all right, we did hold back, I admit. But, frankly, we need a declaration of loyalty."

"I'm here. I don't like the way Ballentine operates. The collection is important historically and to me personally. We both know what it might contain. I'd rather find it than one of Sean Ballentine's well-behaved historians."

She thought this through. "Do you know why the Ballentines are so persistent about the collection?"

Quoting from memory a passage I'd read the night before—Francis Pretty in 1579—I said: "'At our departure hence our General set up a monument of our being there, as also of her Majesty's right and title to the same; namely a plate, nailed upon a fair great post, whereupon was engraved her Majesty's name, the day and year of our arrival there.' Ballentine has the plate of brass."

This stopped her. "It's a fake, the one in the museum."

"I think there's another one," I said, cheerfully laying claim to Brian's theory. "The fake was a complex ploy to keep everybody away until the Ballentines had Drake's Logbooks."

"How do you know this?"

"I don't. Call it speculation from someone who knows a bit about the Ballentine family."

"OK, I guess, for the moment. Even though you omitted the part about your girlfriend being Ballentine's property attorney. That's right, isn't it? Ms. O'Toole, the woman posing as your wife when you first came up here? Can you understand how compromised you are?"

I shrugged. "Fire me, then. We both are guilty of a lack of candor, Karen. Kay's not talking to me because of attorney-client privilege and I'm not talking to her because of our confidentiality agreement. So I'm here and you let me in. Let's talk about Sir Francis Drake."

She didn't hesitate, this time. She either trusted me or had poisoned the espresso. She drew a deep breath. "The log books are here, somewhere. They were taken from Drake's ship as soon as it dropped anchor in Plymouth in September of 1580, and Queen Elizabeth immediately banned any publication of the details of his voyage and swore him to secrecy. Drake basically couldn't stand not being able to tell the world anything, so he dropped hints to Flemish mapmakers for the rest of his life. You probably know all this." I nodded. "What you don't know is that the queen never actually commandeered the logbooks, and that one of the cartographers was a member of the Willems family. Karl Van Willems. Drake allowed him to hand-copy the logbooks and to set the type for a book, probably assuming that Elizabeth would relent and it could go to press. She never did. Drake died at sea in 1596, with the logs still in Van Willems' possession."

"Why didn't the family publish them then?" But I had the answer. "Willems died before Elizabeth."

"Willems died in 1602, the year before the queen. Nobody in Europe wanted to cross her while she was alive. So the logs went into the family archives."

"And no one ever knew, apart from the family?"

"Quite the contrary. It was never even a rumor for 300 years. Then the family, which was by then in Luxembourg, started sending out feelers to the academic world that they had this thing. One of the people they approached, maybe the only person in the U.S., was Sean Ballentine's grandfather Curtis, who by then was in possession of a certain brass plate."

"What were you and Adrian doing here, in 1993?"

"Curtis Ballentine died in 1992. Sean Ballentine began making noises about buying the collection, but the Willems family still bore this grudge against the Ballentines over their unfulfilled expectations when they came here to Berkeley."

"No position on the faculty."

"I see you've done a little homework on your own," she said, finishing her coffee and eying me over the rim. "I believe that the Willems told Ballentine that the logbook had gone down with one of the ships that brought the collection here, just to get rid of him. Obviously some books were lost, as well as the catalogue of the collection, on the sunken ship, but the logbooks, or keys to their whereabouts, are here someplace. Adrian worked for Sotheby's and knew the rare book world, I was a starry-eyed undergraduate at UC. We were the team they picked, and we hired Robert McNally to be our sleuth; then we were all let go before we got anywhere."

"What happened?"

"After we fired Bob, a sneaky little opportunist when all's said and done, the Willems family called a halt to the whole thing. It began to look . . . unruly to them. They're an old family and proud, at least the older generation still alive at that time. They weren't about to be hurried. Ad and I went about our careers and came back to continue the hunt last summer, and found our new bloodhound, Ethan Storey."

"Why didn't you tell McNally or me what you were looking for?"

"For one thing, we did need the collection catalogued. McNally got a little further than you are at present, noted that a couple of decades worth of documents were missing, and began fussing around. We probably would have told him, but he found a letter Adrian had written but never sent, to the university, sort of baiting Ballentine. Adrian can be a very naughty boy at times.

"The two families have a strange relationship. The books aren't just on the shelf someplace; we'd have found them long before this if that were the case. There's something else, maybe a key to a locker in the Antwerp bus station." She paused. "It's all great fun, you'll have to admit."

"What happens now?"

"Now we're all above board. It's much more like a business deal. The new Willems is Lucius, middle-aged but sort of euro-trashy; as far as we can tell, he only wants to catalogue and value the collection and then sell it to the highest bidder. If you find out something about the logbooks, the price goes up."

"How long do I have?"

"They're in no hurry. They know what the payoff could be. I have something for you, maybe an incentive of sorts. It's what McNally came across the day he was fired. Put your gloves on."

She opened a drawer in the table and took out an unprotected, single page folio of Jodocus Hondius' broadside map showing Drake's voyage, supposedly prepared to accompany Drake's own account of his travels, never published. I'd seen copies of it before. This one was not a copy. It was hand marked *to Karl Van Willems for the rutter*. "Rutter" was an old Portuguese word for pilot-book, in common use among mariners of that era. The words were followed by Drake's name in its Latinized version. His signature.

Needless to say, the rest of the day was an anticlimax.

I STOPPED off to get a steering-wheel lock at an auto parts store, and a pizza, and it was a little after dark when I walked carefully down the dock. As I passed the boathouse I noticed that the doors were open and that a single figure was sitting at the desk just inside. This was not unusual. The yard seemed to take its role as nautical junkyard seriously, and whatever they thought was valuable was locked down somewhere else. There hadn't been an actual boat inside in many years, not a whole one, anyway. It was a wilderness of tools and tables and shelves of parts catalogues, bins full of bolts—galvanized, no stainless steel here—great spools of rusty cable, everything covered with a layer of wood dust and powdered fiberglass. Maggie, who had run the place since my father's day, kept a neat desk, though, with two comfortable chairs where I had argued over many a yard bill. She frequently worked late, with an old piston-driven adding machine, and liked to watch the sun go down behind the oil tanks on Point Richmond. I stopped to say hello, but it was not Maggie. It was my sometime friend Brian Haggerty, Ballentine professor of European history. "Can I have a piece of that? I'm starved."

"Let's go aboard, for heaven's sake. It'll taste like bilgewater out here."

"I think not. A guy went aboard about an hour ago, and I imagine he bugged your boat."

"How do you know?"

"I suppose there may be a bomb aboard, but it seems unlikely. Everybody thinks you know where Drake's Logbooks are, and they'll just listen in for a while. Then they'll kill you. I saw him, is how I know. I've been sitting here waiting for you since five. Brought some Anchor Steam. I'll trade." He stood up and without much trouble slid the huge doors closed. It was much warmer, and with the desk lamp on the building had a weird, very cozy masculine quality. You could spit on the floor, piss in the drywell in the corner, hack up a steer, weld steel plates or eat pizza. "Sorry to have been so aloof. I heard about Kay, is that, like, a split-up? I always knew she was too good for you."

Brian had more than his usual sardonic edge tonight. He was talking much too fast and had already drunk three beers. There was an open pack of Camel filters on the desk in front of him. He'd quit smoking, except for the occasional cigar, years before. "You OK, Bri?"

He watched me open the pizza box with a vacant stare. Took a single bite of the piece I offered, then put it down and lit a cigarette. "I don't know what the fuck's going on, Ethan. The orders have changed. I'm supposed to sleep with you or something,

77

now. Ballentine doesn't want to wait for the appraisal. He wants you to work for him, steal the logbooks and whatever. He and my lovely cousin will clean up the mess."

There was a lot I could say, but I settled for, "Tell them whatever you have to."

He coughed, put out the cigarette, and began to eat again, this time with more appetite. "Damn sporting of you, especially since you're about to get suspended from your job." I said nothing and he eventually went on. "Here's how it will go down; the classic carrot and the stick. Tomorrow your department chair will put you on paid leave while they study whether you breached your tenure by moonlighting. Now you've lost boat slip, best friend, job. No distractions. All will be made whole when you find the Drake papers, and a huge stipend besides. When you've located the stuff, you're to contact me before you look at it in any way except to verify it's what it is."

"Is Kay in on this?"

"Not to my knowledge, but Ethan, she's completely immersed in this thing in every other way."

"Why don't you tell her what you just told me?"

"She won't believe it, coming from either of us. She thinks Sean Ballentine is wonderful. We've just got to play our parts out, pal. Unless you've got another idea." I didn't. "Look, I told you everything I know, all at once. I was supposed to be more cagey, but I don't like this any more than you. And having spies sent to the schooner, that's creepy. I didn't know anything about that."

"Did you recognize the guy?"

"He's the security guard that works at the institute, started just after you did."

"Holy shit." I was in way over my head. We were quiet for a time.

"Do you think you'll find it?" Brian asked at length.

"They must have searched the house and grounds at some point in the past ten years. They've taken every book off the shelves." But even as I said it, I had the feeling that somehow I had more to go on than anyone to date, between Bob McNally's journal, his choice of books, and my own increasing familiarity with the collection.

"Eventually, the whole thing will be Ballentine's and he can tear the walls off. Until then, just keep pretending that we're in cahoots."

"Come back on board. Let's drink tequila and talk about the 49ers."

He followed me into the main salon and we chatted while I got out my field strength meter from Radio Shack, used to check the transmitter of my VHF radio, and wandered around till I got the needle to move. The bug was a tiny thing, hidden under the chart table, that felt like a wad of chewing gum. I suppose someone sophisticated in these things would have left it in place and just watched what they said. But I was feeling resentful and very clever to have figured it out. I walked up on deck, jumped down to the dock, and super-glued it to the keel of a Monterey clipper on the slipway.

Two questions persisted. I was maybe the only person who could ask both, which was some consolation, but I didn't know the answers. First, why did the Willems collection feature so many documents relating to the coast of California, highly technical sailing directions all at least a century old? And why did Bob McNally want books on Nazi war criminals? When Brian left, I gave him those two books and asked him to scan them for me, so I could deal with the lack of an index.

CHAPTER SEVEN

I woke to the sound of what I thought was heavy rain. But winter, apparently, was suspended for a while. It was chain rattling down from the high-prowed Monterey clipper that just launched, with new bottom paint and a listening device attached to its rudderpost. They anchored noisily and I could hear them talking about heading home.

I watched the fog clear, working through my second piece of cold pizza and drinking coffee. San Francisco Bay fog is a multiple personality, from dominant and all embracing, through coy and flirtatious. This was one of its best moods, when for some reason fog burned off from below, lifting its skirts to show off a day of warm sun, under a diaphanous white ceiling like a wedding tent. The phone rang as I was cleaning up. Kay? No, it was the History Department chair. "Good morning, Martin," I said cheerfully. No point in making it easy for him. "To what do I owe this pleasure?"

"I wanted to get to you before you came all the way in. The attorneys want to review whether your moonlighting violates your contract."

"It's only a violation if it's clearly not in the interest of the university."

"Quite so."

"And which university might that be?"

"Let's be professional, Dr. Storey. You'll be on full salary while this is resolved." We went over who would best finish up my classes, which T.A.s would be available to do all the real work. No point in letting the students suffer the agony of losing touch with History. When we were done with this unpleasantness, I found myself curiously complacent about my immediate fate.

80

It was as if I'd done something exceptional and was facing dramatic consequences. It was as if I deserved an award. I decided on a day off.

I drove the truck into Berkeley, parked in the space reserved for visiting professors and identified myself at the office. They gave me a little chit for my windshield. The long arm of the Ballentines hadn't reached this far, yet. But the family was all over the historical collection, starting with its name on the Ballentine Museum of California, an odd hexagonal building in the northeast corner of the campus. Most of the architecture of the older Berkeley buildings was an attempt to look like an ivy league, established eastern university; this looked like a cross between a Navajo hogan and a Greek temple. But it had been carefully and strongly built, and other than burnishing the copper dome every few years, it had been spared the disfigurement of earthquake retrofitting. I'd been here countless times and never paid much attention until today. There was a lot of money in California, of course, but not that much old money. Inside, a massive portrait of Curtis Ballentine, looking like a Southern Pacific railroad baron, gazed down inspiringly at the collection of students lined up for early morning classes. It was the same at State: these morning classes and seminars were almost all comprised of overachieving Asians, clean and well dressed. When it was my turn I asked where I could find Drake's Plate. "It's not really Drake's, you know. A famous prank."

"What do you call it then?"

"The Great Drake Hoax. It's in the gold rush section."

It was a small room on the fifth floor, and odd that I'd never seen it before. It was touristy and trivial, by and large, with dioramas of claim jumping and false mining claims, and a new exhibit about James Marshall's hidden mine, rediscovered in 1999. But it was a lovely space, with floor to ceiling windows opening onto a balcony draped with bougainvillea, eager to bloom. These were open now and from here, with the morning fog a memory, I could see the similar dome of the cyclotron that anchored the Ballentine Berkeley labs near the crest of the

81

low hills. All the heavy duty physics had moved away, but the thousands of tons of concrete underneath was not going anywhere. With the perception of a man with time on his hands, I realized that the two buildings, museum and cyclotron, were very much alike.

When I saw the plate I was surprised by how unconvincing a forgery it was. The rectangle of metal was headed "Be it known by all these present," a phrase not really in use at the time and there were, in fact, not many present when Drake did or did not land to career his ships in Drake's Bay. It just sounded old. The chisel used to indent the letters was about the size of a large screwdriver head—they surely had better tools—with the edges sheared. Both ways, it didn't work. Elizabethan shipboard smiths were better with a hammer and chisel than the chisel used here, and good enough so that they didn't need to use shears at all. It was signed "Francis Drake." He wasn't knighted until he got back, but it seemed a little lacking in the passion for titles at the time; it needed something like "Governor General of New Albion." And the metal was wrong: surface corrosion too uniform, among other things that even I could see. Claimed for the queen, blah, blah. Things like this never, ever read like they were trying to make themselves clear to discoverers centuries later.

A voice behind me stopped my Monday morning quarterbacking. "Good morning, Dr. Storey." I turned. "I'm Sean Ballentine. I believe we've met at some university function or other and your lovely wife is on my legal staff." He was as I remembered him, only more so. Instantly recognizable as a generically handsome man, longish face formed below light green eyes, expensively but casually dressed in a cashmere sweater under an Armani jacket. Hair blond, fading into red, well coiffed. I thought if I smelled him up close, it would remind me of polo ponies in wet grass. "What brings you to Berkeley?"

If the man hadn't already done everything he could to manipulate me, I might have hesitated to find the right words and lost my temper in the process. But being jobless on full salary does wonders for your spontaneity. And I knew something. Don't ask me how, unless it was the perspective of history. These people, the Ballentines of the world, don't command respect. Their wealth and power are not limitless, although they think they are. My university would take me back and Kay would come home. He wanted me to serve him because at some level he knew I was brighter and better than he was. "Enjoying myself on paid leave," I said.

"Busman's holiday?"

"Drake is a hobby of mine. My father named his boat after him and I've a special interest in this thing."

"The plate?"

"I use it as a teaching tool. Don't believe anyone entirely, even your professors."

"What do you think of it?" He gestured toward the case.

"I'm amazed that this fooled as many people for as long as it did."

"California was advertising itself in the early part of the twentieth century. The plate, and naming the bay after Drake, were all manufactured in the service of selling real estate through the romance of the place. My grandfather was no exception. Tell me, do you think the plate exists? As a historian."

I wasn't going to rise to that bait. As a historian, I was in a unique position to drown him in misdirection. "A man named MacDonald found it in 1954 on Kuiu Island, at 57 degrees north latitude." That was, in fact, my opinion of the matter a few months back. "We at least know that one was in Latin." I couldn't actually remember, but I said that MacDonald had thrown it out by mistake. "These things have a tendency to disappear," I added, now actually enjoying myself.

"And be refound," he smiled. We could have gone on in this matter for some time. I was still prepared to play this game like a gentleman, up to a point. But then he said: "Sorry the St. Francis Yacht Club didn't suit your needs. How is Kay liking her new apartment?"

I felt my pulse race. If Kay had found a place of her own, it was news to me. This whole conversation was just a test for me,

I concluded. But he couldn't possibly have known I'd be here and he was winging it in a chance encounter. *Get him off balance; you're the one with nothing to lose.* I said the first thing that came into my head. "She was long overdue for some closet space." Then without pausing I gestured through the windows and said: "The museum and the cyclotron were built at the same time, weren't they?"

"Yes, in 1939."

"They look a lot alike."

I only wanted to break his stride, but the remark made him pause. He took a starched white handkerchief from his pocket and blew his nose unnecessarily. Men like Ballentine rarely had to blow their noses. He seemed uncomfortable. "Damn allergies. I think it was intentional, the museum and the lab. Looking forward, looking backward, that kind of thing. I've enjoyed talking to you, Ethan. Good luck on the Willems collection. A wonderful opportunity for you." He said goodbye, turned abruptly, merging with a crowd of schoolchildren, which tossed like wavecrests on a stormy sea. The year 1939, I thought, had been a busy one for the Ballentines. I would check later, but I knew I would find as much Ballentine money in the cyclotron as in the museum.

I retrieved the truck and worked my way north toward the institute, thinking of all the poisonous things I could have said to Sean Ballentine instead of being so damn passive-aggressive. Lack of passion was one of the things Kay had come to dislike about me. As I passed along the bottom of the hills, through the land of untenured teachers and perpetual graduate students, tasteful brownstones and stucco bungalows, the cell phone rang. It was George Metaxis. "Sorry to bother you, may I call you Ethan? Do you remember me? FBI? Calling from Nevada?"

"Of course."

"Did you get my announcement of the conference in Amsterdam?"

"Yes, I was planning to go."

"Good, good. I'll be there myself, you know. We can chat about Sir Francis Drake, and I understand someone from the Willems family will be presenting a paper."

He spoke to someone beside him, a chortling term of endearment as to a child or a pet. It was evidently a parrot, because a moment later I heard a loud "GOODBYE NOW." Followed by: "There was one other thing . . . pardon my bird Merryman, please."

"I suppose I should ask if this is official."

"Well, you know I'm not an agent, so there's that."

Yes, document specialist, as I recalled. His reply was sort of goofy, yet after the complex but shallow mind games of Ballentine, Metaxis in the desert, a harmless fat man with a quick but disorganized mind and a parrot, was a vast relief. "Good enough for me, Mr. Metaxis."

"George." Behind him the parrot said GEORGE. "Do you know the man who found the fake plate at Point Reyes?"

"William Hallowell?"

"Yes, that's it. His son is a Vietnam veteran at the Yountville home. Do you know where it is?"

"Napa Valley."

"Yes. I wanted to talk to him while I was there, but he was medically indisposed. The doctor says he's fine now and a visit from someone would do him good." I said nothing and he went on: "I'm interested in the plate, unofficially." So is everybody else, I thought. "Since you're there, and working in this area of inquiry, you might want to visit him yourself. You could just say you're a friend of the man who called him about his father and the plate."

I pulled the truck into the Shell station on the corner of The Alameda and Hopkins. "You're asking me to interview him about Drake's Plate?" I started pumping gas into a tank just half empty. I was going to Napa. "This is a rather odd request."

"I suppose so. I only called because I thought you might have a historical interest, and if it was convenient to go, ask a question for me?"

"And that would be?"

"What happened to his father's taxi business, after 1933? Goodbye now."

THE YOUNTVILLE Veterans Home was something of a Napa Valley institution, if only because it occupied the single most expensive piece of real estate in the area. Perched like a Spanish military mission on a ridge that protruded out into the valley from the coast range, it looked like a movie set from a distance: from its lawns you had the carpet of vineyards below you, at this time of year and in the bright sunshine swathed with yellow ribbons of mustard, as far as you cared to look. Domaine Chandon, the champagne vintners, occupied the base of the ridge on land leased from the home, and gave the old soldiers a fancy lunch a few times a year. Metaxis had said the man's name was Timothy Hallowell, former Army Specialist Fourth Class with a metal plate in his head, former selectman at the town of Point Reyes, unmarried, prone not to combat flashbacks, but to periods of profound, empty, almost catatonic inactivity which were thought to be more neurological than psychological.

I'd called ahead and he'd seemed delighted I was coming, asked about George Metaxis, and invited me for lunch if I would take him off campus, as he put it. He met me in the lobby of one of the residence halls, most of which still had the whitewash and red tile look up close, but which inside were simply efficient and comfortable. "Storey," he said. "I know that name. Knowledge without connection, my curse. Never mind. Where shall we eat?"

We went to a little French bistro in the town which I'd read about in the *Chronicle*. He ordered paté and cornichons and I had steak tartare. Tim was completely in the moment, asking me about my job as if he were considering a second career, the politics of teaching, and my family situation, while we waited for the food. He had a shaved head that somehow suited him and a leather snap-brim hat which he removed indoors. He had a lean, smallish, unwrinkled face with a small mustache. He wore prim

86

spectacles while reading the menu, which he removed and put into a leather case that matched his hat; he carefully unfolded his napkin on his lap and unconsciously tidied up the floral arrangement in the center of the table. "Sorry to be so obvious. Exhausting to be a gay man among battle-hardened veterans, don't you know. All of us have to work at it. I don't really mind, it's like living in a foreign land and honoring its customs. But it's a relief to have a nice lunch with a San Francisco academic." The food came and he buttered a piece of bread with care and considered the choice of paté. When he'd made his selection he looked directly at me and said: "All right, have your way with me, Dr. Storey."

"Did you know about your father and the plate before George Metaxis contacted you?" I asked.

"Well, it all happened ten years before I was born. It was a very small sort of notoriety, but we lived by Drake's Bay and every few years someone would want the tale told. But Pop was not one to indulge his fifteen minutes of fame. He never talked about it, at all. As a teenager I may have asked the Pop-I'm-doing-a-project-at-school kind of question and I may remember him saying something like, 'All I got out of that business was a bad case of poison oak.' He wouldn't be pressed, and as a child of the sixties I just thought of Sir Francis Drake as another white imperialist who slaughtered indigenous peoples."

"He wasn't. He was maybe the only character of his era to stand the test of modern political correctness. Treated even his enemies with dignity, hated tyranny and was clever as a fox."

"You don't say." A light went out of his eyes. "Excuse me while I go take a pill." He was gone quite a while. Then he came back, sat down and said: "A thin thread of care from the Veterans Administration and the State of California is all that holds me above a walking coma. Where were we?"

"What did your father do as you were growing up?"

"For a living? We were the richest people in Point Reyes, thanks to his chauffeur business. He went from a single Oldsmobile to a fleet of Lincoln Town cars, wine country tours, special

87

dignitaries from the San Francisco Airport. He did a brisk and very successful business serving the affluent of Marin County."

"Did he ever have any contact with the Ballentine family?"

"Not that I'm aware of, though the foundation supplied him with a steady stream of business, and paid for four vehicles reserved exclusively for their use."

"Have you ever seen the plate yourself?"

"No."

I showed him a picture postcard I'd bought in the museum. He barely glanced at it. He seemed very tired, and though he'd arranged his place setting as a kind of display platter for the paté, he'd eaten virtually nothing. "Looking back now, what do you think of the story?"

"It's odd that he wouldn't talk about it, I suppose, but it's even stranger that he'd clean out his trunk in Corte Madera and throw the junk into the creek. I mean to say that he'd never put anything in his trunk that would need to be thrown away. He was fanatically neat about his vehicles. You could have surgery in a Hallowell limo, my mother used to say."

I drove him back up to the home. He changed his snap brim for a baseball cap and thanked me very formally for lunch. He asked me for a business card with my cell phone number and promised not to call just to flirt with me. "I'm not a needy man," he said, squaring his shoulders as he walked in. With Specialist Fourth Class Timothy Hallowell, the bad taste left by Sean Ballentine was banished for the day.

Metaxis called me before I left the grounds. "What did he say?"

"Don't you have a job, George?"

"I could ask you the same question."

"I was suspended from teaching under pressure from the Ballentine family so, no, I don't have a job."

"Oh. Touché. What about the taxi business?"

"I think it was bankrolled by the Ballentine Foundation."

"So we have the finder of Drake's Plate, who loses the thing only to be refound years later by someone else who brought it to Berkeley, getting money from Curtis Ballentine. So?"

88

"So I think the elder Hallowell found the real plate, and the second time it appears it was replaced by a fake."

"Interesting hypothesis."

"I have to know if this is an official inquiry or just a hobby for you."

"Why?"

"Because the Ballentines tried to plant a listening device on my boat yesterday. This is getting more difficult for me."

"Still fun though. Did you save it?" I said I'd thrown it overboard. "Too bad. Federal law prohibits that kind of thing, I understand. Is there anything else you'd like to tell me?"

"I'm pretty clear on a couple of things. Everybody thinks I can find the Drake Logbooks, and after a little coyness on the part of all parties, that's what I'm doing in the employ of the Willems family. Ballentine is frantic to get the documents, which would establish the validity of the plate, which I believe now they must have. For some reason the two families—the Willems and the Ballentines—can't deal directly with one another. Ballentine has been putting pressure on me to be his spy."

"What did you say?"

"I think I just confused him." I paused. "You haven't answered my question, George. What's the FBI's interest?"

"I can tell you that I have an assignment that may or may not be related to Drake's Plate."

"How about Robert McNally's murder?"

"I'll see you in Amsterdam, Ethan. Goodbye now."

I was mulling this over as I crossed the Napa River on the graceful white arch of the bridge a half hour later. I opened the window and smelled the underlying, surging growth of California spring in the midst of winter. The phone chirped. I closed the window and there was Timothy Hallowell. He sounded much more lively. "My memory comes and goes and sometimes delivers an old one so complete it's like watching it on *60 Minutes*. I have no idea what this means, I couldn't have been more than six years old or so. The only reason I remember at all is that I thought his name was *'Tell me a story.'*"

"Who?"

"What was your father's name?"

"Thomas Storey. His friends called him Tommy."

"Tommy Storey. Tell me story. Call it fate or coincidence and I know you're not gay, but he visited my father several times in the 1950s." I couldn't think of what to say. "For what it's worth, he seemed like a great guy and Pop liked him a lot."

CHAPTER EIGHT

My mother died when I was a toddler. Tommy Storey had been a loving but no-frills single father, as reserved as he was gentle. He hugged me after infancy only twice in my memory, at Mom's funeral and on the day of my Stanford graduation. But he filled the house with wonderful things to read, saw to my needs with an often furrowed brow, and would show up for every event that marked my passage, even some I had not invited him to nor informed him about. As I entered my teenage years and showed every indication of becoming a man not unlike him, he allowed a distance to settle between us, filled with the things we both enjoyed (working on the boat, primarily) as opposed to things which had content, like his work. I never knew what he did exactly, but could see myself doing something like it. I certainly never heard him express an interest in Drake's Plate, but he spoke of the explorer often enough, from childhood tales of semi-piratical derring-do to object lessons on courage and perseverance. In the pre-internet days after he died I looked at his publications in the library at Cal. He ranged over a much wider area than I did, from Billy the Kid to St. Boniface. Heavily into nautical history in various forms, focusing on shipbuilding and nineteenth-century fighting sail. But nothing on Drake. He left to his son the field of the early exploration of North America.

In returning from Napa to the Bay Area, one has to reach a decision as to whether to head for Mount Tamalpais or Mount Diablo—San Francisco or the East Bay. Without thinking about it I headed down the westerly course, towards Kay. My upbeat mood of the morning had been a false one, and as the afternoon dragged on and the traffic congealed around me, I became in my own eyes a man with a lot of problems to sort out and not much with which to sort them. Kay was a good sorter; she was my lady; we'd been apart for a few days and it felt like months. It was time for us to try and be honest with each other again, starting with Ballentine's statement about her new apartment. As far as I knew she was still staying with Molly in San Francisco. She had mentioned something about a sublet on Telegraph Hill, I recalled, that might be it. She did not answer her cell and she wasn't in the office. When I got Molly on the line, she said that yes, Kay just found a place in Sausalito and was eager to show it to me. She gave me the address in just the nick of time for me to drop off Highway 101 before I had to commit to the Golden Gate Bridge.

Sausalito is a primal green hillside with an impenetrable warren of twisting streets and houses hung below the roads; in many places you parked on a pad that looked in attic windows. All seemed relentlessly charming and artful, though the artists had long since abandoned them to young entrepreneurs with deep pockets and strong calves. The addresses were hard to read, and though it was only four PM the fog had returned to (or never left) Sausalito and everyone was driving with their lights on. But I found the place easily enough by the Saturn, parked with just enough space beside it for the truck. She had left the parking lights on, something she did when distracted. I unlocked the door with my key and shut them off. I stood for a moment, now chronically unsure of what I was doing. It was almost like I was meeting a stranger for the first time; impossible to imagine her in a domestic situation other than the galley, the forward cabin, or the main salon of the *Drake*, her office or one of our favorite restaurants. We hadn't even been to Sausalito since she'd quit her job at the firm there, years before.

There were tiny orange lights that outlined the stairs and the railing down to the door, which in these sorts of houses is always on the side, since stepping out the front meant a drop of anything up to thirty feet. I paused at the platform in front of a teak door, greyed to a rich granite color, almost white. The house was an arts and crafts bungalow reimagined as a treehouse, solid redwood where it wasn't glass. Across the landing from the door was a terraced garden, hidden from the road by a high camellia hedge and sculpted with boxwood and low rock walls sprouting lavender and sage. There was a small bench and a chair, and on the chair was the Maeve Binchy novel she'd been reading, last seen on the chart table aboard the *Drake*. I instantly recognized the scene, without her ever having been so specific, as what Kay had wanted all these years, and experienced a moment of profound regret that she'd had to get it on her own. Still I hesitated. I couldn't remember whether I was mad at her, she at me, or something in between. I had an absurd thought: *I'll hire Kay to sue San Francisco State over my illegal suspension from teaching. We'll see who's breached their contract.*

The landing was positioned so that I could see into the front room and out through the front windows. Standing and looking out the window was John Peters, a cup of something hot in his hands, watching the lights come up around Richardson Bay. I suppose I would have recognized Kay's lover anywhere, even from this angle. He was a few years older and just a little thicker through the waist. Kay came up behind him and touched his shoulder, a sheaf of papers in her hands. He turned to take them from her, set his cup down and saw me. He must have said something, but his lips did not appear to move. Kay froze. She was wearing a black silk blouse and a simple gold necklace I'd given her two Christmases before. I could sense her taking a deep breath, then she came to the door. We stared at each other for a moment and she seemed to want to say something. But after a moment she just took a step forward and threw her arms around me, trembling. "Please," was all I heard except perhaps the words, *there's nothing*. I started to pull away and she hung on harder. I put my hands over hers and forced them off.

"Don't," I said. "Don't say anything, don't do anything. Don't call me." I walked up to the truck and drove away. I saw her briefly in the rearview mirror, fists clenched as if she wanted to hit something.

MAGGIE, THE Tugboat Annie of the Richmond yard, was still in the shop, welding a custom rudder gudgeon in clouds of acrid smoke and sparks. When she saw me walk towards the boat, she stopped what she was doing and came out. It was full on dark by now and she came up close before saying, "You all right, Mr. Storey?"

"Sure, Maggie. A little tired is all."

"You look more like your father every year."

"Thanks."

"You want us to haul you tomorrow?"

"No."

"Well, you'll have to anchor out till we get at the next guy in line."

The turning basin was nearly empty, its surface festooned with reflections of the orange arc lamps from the tank farm on the other side. "Work my lines, would you Maggie?"

I went aboard, turned on all the running lights and the spreader spots and started the engine. I gave her a minute or so to warm up and went on deck to take the lines from Maggie, who was still wearing her welder's mask tipped up on her head. I dropped *Drake* into gear and the old pier moved astern. But I didn't anchor. Instead I turned down the long waterway leading from Richmond Inner Harbor to the bay. The old port slid by us, displaying the kind of turgid, obscure beauty you sometimes find in film noir, overlapping patterns of harsh light and shade, mysterious shapes that could be anything the mind might make them. I turned northeast toward the Richmond Bridge, dousing the spreader lights, and entered the Sacramento Ship Channel just off The Brothers Lighthouse. The bay became San Pablo after that and the land fell away on both sides. It was only foggy in Sausalito, it turned out. The channel was narrow but deep, and since the tide was high and slack and the bay flat, I could vary a few degrees off course if there was no ship traffic. I hadn't eaten since the steak tartare with Tim Hallowell and I was surprised to find myself hungry. I stood at the galley counter and watched through the porthole. There were almost no lights visible, no boats at all. I made two sandwiches that would hold up well against strong drink—cheese, pickles, and sliced onion—and back at the helm had one with Jim Beam and club soda.

By eleven PM I was passing under the Carquinez Bridge and then the long, straight passage up the straits, past the town and bridge at Benicia, probably the effective upper limit of San Francisco real estate barons, and into Suisun Bay, with its primeval, brackish marshes still intact, broken only by the railroad tracks. Things became progressively wilder after that, with the exception of the colony of mothballed military ships which would never sail, but would float till they sank or were cut up for scrap. It was poorly lit and gave the impression of a small city on a flat featureless plain, abandoned by once industrious citizens. Between here and Sacramento was the true Delta country. California's only big rivers, the Sacramento and the San Joaquin, had been laying down canyon silt from the Sierra Nevada for long enough to produce dozens of islands, many of them lower than high tide, habitable only in shacks on stilts, some precariously farmed, others an impenetrable jungle of brush. The river branches and sloughs between them were bordered by giant reeds; even in daytime you could lose your way, seeing nothing from deck level, and grounding the boat in the soft mud. In summer there was a human presence defined by jet skis, and a few landings with redneck bars and greasy fried fish.

I turned the GPS on but didn't need it. My father had taken me to a particular place many times, by a route known only to the two of us: south from the main channel around Decker and Twitchell Islands, reverse course briefly and head north into the nameless dead-end sloughs that had no soundings, even on the best charts. Dad had discovered that there was a naturally scoured route along the northern shore, just enough for us to get by in a spring tide (which was running now). I'd never tried it in the dark, of course, but buoyed by rage, adrenaline, caffeine, and the Jim Beam I made it, parking the fifty foot schooner in a basin only half again as wide. When I left, I'd have to haul the bow around manually, by lines from shore. These lines I now rigged, to stout cottonwood trees, by rowing them ashore in the inflatable dinghy. Another tether, a well-set stern anchor, and the boat was safe from anything but curious vandals. It was unlikely they would arrive until summer was well advanced. I sat for a while in the darkened pilothouse, feeling sorry for myself and wondering what I was up to, besides something like a sick dog hiding under the porch.

Eventually, I showered and lay down in the pilot berth. The owls hooted steadily, calibrating the passage of the night, until a brief rain silenced them at dawn. I might have slept for a few minutes, because it was light when I climbed out and ate my second sandwich with a cup of tea. What would Sir Francis Drake have done, I wondered? This line of speculation got me going. It took me two hours to button up the boat, connecting my theft-proof solar panels to the batteries, closing the seacocks, putting plywood screens over the pilothouse windows. I filled a suitcase, a canvas bag with ship's papers and my own (passport, insurance policies and the like), and a paper bag with perishables from the refrigerator and freezer. When this was done I dug the small outboard out of its brackets under the cockpit seat and mounted it on the back of the inflatable. Then I padlocked and chained everything in sight, stepped down into the dinghy and motored south.

I had just enough gas to make Eddo's Harbor, on the San Joaquin River across from Sherman Island. The launch ramp was deserted except for two cats playing under the eucalyptus tree, but the red, weathered shack was as I remembered, and the Bud Light sign was on. I went in and had a second breakfast of scrambled eggs and corned beef, and when it came I called Karen Molina at the institute. "Where have you been? I thought you'd be here yesterday."

"Sorry, Karen. I was arranging a short sabbatical. I'm working for you full time until the cataloguing is complete."

"That's wonderful. When will you be back?"

"I'm going to find a place to stay nearby in Kensington, then I'll be by."

"Don't be ridiculous. You can stay here, if Kay doesn't mind. There's the extra room. Anything else?"

"Can you walk outside and call me on a cell phone?" I stood on the dock and watched the red-winged blackbirds arranging their world of cattails and controversy until she rang. "Fire Mike the security guy. He works for Ballentine."

She didn't ask how I knew. She just said, "You've been busy, haven't you?"

"I should be in this afternoon." Eddo's took cash to store the dinghy in the locked enclosure where they kept the dumpster, padlocked to the fencepost so it wouldn't be hauled away as trash.

It's NOT particularly easy to get anywhere in those parts, but I caught a ride into Antioch, the train back to Richmond and a cab to the boatyard to get the truck. When I arrived back at the institute, the car belonging to Mike the security guard/spy was gone, replaced by Adrian's MG. Karen met me at the door. "Hullo, Ethan." She examined me the way women do sometimes. *What's up with this one?* "Have you given up sleeping?"

"Just until we find the logbooks."

"Leave your stuff here, then. Adrian's waiting for you upstairs."

Adrian sat hunched over the bench, his nose nearly touching his work. He was as tall as he was thin, and he looked like a stick bug feeding on leaf nectar. "Back in harness?"

"Let's do it."

He paused, though, straightened and stretched, several joints popping gently as he did so. "What keeps you going? For me it's money, not the paltry hourly rate, but my percentage of The Big Find. What about you? The laurels of academe?"

"Seriously, no." I could see no reason to even start this conversation. "A niggling sensation that the logs exist, it's like an itch I can't scratch. They did not go down with the torpedoed part of the collection, and we'll find them if we keep our heads about us."

"Right, then," he said simply and turned back to the books he was looking at, carefully half-opened and covered with Saran Wrap.

"Adrian, would you mind telling me about the letter you wrote to the Ballentine Museum?"

"I never sent it, you know. Did the late Dr. McNally tell you about it?" He didn't look up.

"He had a Xerox. He showed it to Brian Haggerty at Cal the week before he was murdered, and asked him to check and see if it had ever arrived. So yes, I know it was never received. That's why I'm asking."

"I'm not the only one around here with mysterious motives. Take yourself, for example." He now turned to face me, but his tone had not been defensive. He seemed more amused than anything else. He gestured to the books before him, which I'd catalogued weeks before, and raised both eyebrows.

"Cook's *Voyages*," I said.

"Yes, a complete set of all three, contemporary tree calf, spines with embossed gilt ships, occasional foxing. An absolutely exquisite set. B. L. Rootenberg will sell you a lesser version for about $75,000. McNally and I, and now you, were asking the same question, really. Why did this Luxembourger sprinkle his collection of respectable European books with these travelogues? Did you see the map signed by Drake?"

"Yes."

"That's what did it for me, that and the old California coast piloting manuals, which have no value unless someone was comparing a verbal description of the coast with something a sailor had written. Somewhere along the long line of this Willems dynasty, they began collecting books that to an antiquarian like me, seem to orbit around some central document.

"I wrote the letter in a moment of complete naiveté. It seemed silly not to bring in the university, with all their resources. Karen nipped it in the bud, and put me in the circle that was privy to the fact that the Ballentines and the Willems had known all about it for many years."

"Except where the logbooks actually are."

"Quite right. I was a bit miffed that she and the family waited to tell me. I felt better when they treated you the same way, and paradoxically better still when she brought you in, too. Now we just have to find the damn things."

They'd made a few changes in procedure since they'd cancelled the security service that morning. The most valuable volumes I had catalogued, and Burke had valued, we now carefully boxed and arranged to be picked up for shipping to a humidity-controlled vault facility in British Columbia. Captain Cook would be accompanied by Frederik de Wit's *Nova Totius Americae Descriptio*, published in Amsterdam in 1666. "It'll help to have the shelves a little clearer."

"I suppose. Any other ideas?"

"I think, Adrian, we just forge ahead with what we do best."

"Mess about with old books?"

"There you go."

The rest of the afternoon and the next three days were an oddly consistent run of volumes on Renaissance science: the third edition of Bartoli's *L'Asia descritta,* a Latin version of Euclid's introductory astronomy text, published in Messina in 1558, a 1545 illustrated alchemy textbook, and on through the minds of our elders, and the hands of their publishers. Though the room made up for me was comfortable, it felt claustrophobic and I slept badly; but in the hours awake I did not toss and turn, but simply rose and walked the few steps to the library. I went back to work, raw history—devoid of students and deadlines and university politics—a kind of balm. Karen was not there that night, but the three of us ate breakfast and dinner together. I finally met the cook, who was an amiable Philippina nurse moonlighting from the intensive care unit at Alta Bates Hospital.

Her mother had been a cook for the Willems, when the family had last visited in the 1970s.

On the first evening, Karen, Adrian and I went down to the basement (California houses almost never have basements) to a small jewel box of a wine cellar. Karen, taking the key from a long necklace of silver chain, unlocked it with a little flourish. "Lucius, the current prevailing Willems, said we could start raiding the wine cellar when the assessed value of the collection passed $500,000, which is where we're at as of the *Voyages of Captain Cook*. How about a 1971 Margaux? Adrian?"

"About $200," Burke said.

We drank the wine with a pea, pumpkin and ham soup with croutons. Karen and Adrian were witty and very comfortable with each other, deferential and courteous to me. I had never really thought about liking them; now it seemed I'd liked them both right from the beginning.

OVER THE next week, I lost track of the days. Kay did not call, Brian did not call, Metaxis did not call. There was a message to contact the attorney that represented faculty in disputes with CSUSF, which I ignored. The next Sunday I took a day off to check on the boat. I picked up the dinghy at Eddo's and motored up. Bilges dry. Boat undisturbed except for raccoon tracks all over the pilothouse roof. On the way home I began to think about the other room, the one with the collection of fiction, where I'd eaten lunches in the natural light from the dormer window. If the institute had been a real home, and the books more contemporary, I would have thought it a curiously eccentric pursuit, without real interest or merit, After all, they had been collected when the books were current, of no real historic value. Could they be a sort of bibliographic camouflage? They certainly should all be looked at, if only to verify they weren't false fronts or something.

Karen found me there when dinner was ready that evening. I had made a terrible mess, finding only one item of any note at all. It was a short history of the institute itself, written in French and published in 1940. As far as I could tell, it was a self-serving memoir of the family's flight from the Nazis and the high hopes for the collection in the new world. There was a photograph of the institute in happier times. In sharp black-and-white, and in excellent repair, the house was almost unrecognizable. The trees were carefully trimmed, and a lawn advanced out from the steps to meet the driveway. There was a large sign in French and English over the door and boxes of bright flowers at all the windows. "What on earth are you up to?" Karen asked. She took the book and flipped more pages, finding a young Kurt Willems, the father of her contact in Europe. "He was just a young man then. In later pictures around the house he looks much more handsome. You men are so lucky in how you age. Come along for dinner. I have you to myself tonight."

She had set a table by the fire in the sitting room, where she'd offered me sherry on that first afternoon in the fall. "It's my cooking, I'm afraid." There were two omelets set out on the Willems china, dusted with paprika, and salad with small strips of smoked salmon. A three candle Baccarat crystal candelabra reflected its own light and that from the fire. Karen had set her hair in the polar opposite of its usual brush back, and now that it framed her face I could see a few wisps of grey. She had dressed in a style not completely her own, and though I had been attracted to her before, she now gave the impression of attention going the other way, carefully dressing up for a history professor: an antique brooch, a blouse beaded with a floral design and a long, cream-colored skirt. "I should have dressed for dinner," I said.

"You look fine," she said. "You always look fine. How was your day off?"

I told her about my day in the Delta. It had been cool, the water leathery brown with sediment from the recent storms. "You keep your boat way up there?"

"The Ballentine Foundation bought my slip in San Francisco. I had to put it somewhere safe till I can find another spot."

"I know you're a crackerjack historical sleuth," she said, though I couldn't think of anything I'd done to deserve the title, "but why do they think you're so important in all this?"

"I hadn't looked at it that way."

"But you should. It's not just that jerk Sean Ballentine. McNally wanted to talk to you. He's never come forward to talk to anybody else in the ten years since we fired him. The Willems seemed to know you as a historian, when I called to see if I should ask you to work here."

"The day before I moved in, I visited with the son of the man who first discovered the plate, the one we now think was real. He remembered meeting my father."

"Was your father a Drake scholar?"

"A great fan of the man, but it was news to me that he was doing research on the plate."

"I should look in the files, see if there was any correspondence with any of the family."

We were finished with dinner, but neither of us was interested in getting up to go through the files or anything else. I didn't want to be seduced, that was how Kay and I had started. I wanted more control this time. But, utterly unpracticed, all I could say into the candlelight and silence was: "You look like Meg Ryan."

"A half-Portuguese Meg Ryan who dyes her hair." She was waiting for me, but when I stood up she met me half way. "Your room or mine," she said.

WHEN WE lay side by side on her bed, tingling and damp with sweat, she was quiet for a time, then said, "Don't shoot me, but I'm going to have a cigarette." She stood naked by the window, a swath of moonlight lighting her from breast to hip, and blew smoke into the air above the back garden. I was in a moment of visceral tranquility, waiting for some moment of perception that would not come. What came instead, slowly but completely and in the span of time it took her to finish, was the photo of

102

the institute we'd been looking at when she called me to dinner. "Come with me," I said. "I just thought of something."

Something in my tone made her smile and reach for her robe. I pulled on my pants and walked down the hall to what I'd come to think of as the Lesser Library. I turned on the lights and walked to the table where the history of the institute lay open to its photographic profile in 1940. "Notice anything?"

"Flower boxes?"

"No."

"Roof doesn't sag?"

"You're getting warmer."

She said slowly, "There are no dormers."

"Nope. When I first came here I assumed that there were two and that the one for the rare book room was removed to seal it up. But this one was added. Take away the sixty-five years, and every other detail is exactly the same." We turned two of the lampshades to shine on the space below the window, and without saying anything else began to remove the books from the shelves below the window. It was classic plaster and lath, by the look of it, identical to the rest of the room. There was a heavy amber paperweight on the reading table behind me and I rapped the wall solidly, in a straight line from left to right, including a foot or so of wall on both sides.

"It's not hollow," Karen said. It took me a minute to realize what she meant. "It should be hollow."

CHAPTER NINE

Karen made coffee and came upstairs with two cups in one hand and a regular telephone in the other, which she plugged into the wall. There was a hammer and a screwdriver in her pocket, which made the robe sag to one side. "What time is it in Antwerp?"

"I think about noon."

She called a number there, then one in Paris that led to a bright conversation in fluent French with someone who was not Lucius Willems. "We can't really start taking walls down without his approval."

"Agreed."

"I suppose it's only fair to wait for Adrian as well. He doesn't have a cell phone and he never answers at night. Antiquarian book dealers will be the final hold-outs." We were sitting cross-legged in our robes in the disorienting, improvised spotlighting. At three AM, without makeup, she looked pretty good. She read my mind. "Do I pass the wake-her-up-in-the-middle-of-the-night test?"

"You're a beautiful woman, Karen."

"What's going on?"

"What do you mean?"

"You know what I mean."

I did, even with a priceless artifact possibly only a few feet away. "I saw Kay with an old lover."

"Just together?"

"He was with her in a place she's renting. They were having drinks."

"Hardly *flagrante delicto*."

"She was never supposed to see him again."

She considered this. Karen was not unlike Kay, in this respect: she was loveliest when thinking. She pulled the robe around her, sipped some coffee and said: "Have you ever been unfaithful to her? I mean, before . . ."

"No."

"You obviously love each other. It was coming off you in waves last fall when you first came here. I was terribly envious." She paused, rubbed sleep from her eyes, and yawned. "Perhaps you should give her another chance."

"I gave her another chance."

We sat waiting for the phone to ring until my back hurt. "I want to go back to bed with you. The logbooks have waited 400 years. They'll keep."

She smiled. "I'll bring the phone anyway."

It was more this time, by being less. I was as soft as she was, in most senses of the word; she guided me to parts of her I'd missed before and I could taste and touch them at my leisure. And when she came I felt her deep, strong contractions in the palm of my hand, arousing me to the point where I could enter her for form's sake, at least.

When we woke, Adrian was standing in the open door. "What's all this in aid of then?" I rubbed my eyes. It was the best five hours of sleep I'd had in a month. Deep down, it felt like Christmas morning.

Karen sat up. "The dormer was added to the roof after the institute was founded," she said.

"Pardon?"

"Go look for yourself. The book is on the floor under the window. *L'Institut Willems*. First photo."

He was gone. By the time we were dressed, he was back. "Did you call Lucius?"

"I can't find him."

"What makes you think . . ."

"It's not hollow. The dormer has enough space below it to form a cavity, but when you rap on it, it's solid."

"Shall we have a go with an ice pick while we're waiting? Tiny holes, just to check."

We agreed this was a good idea, but there was no ice pick in the Willems Institute. Adrian made us toasted cheese while Karen and I walked a block to the True Value in Kensington; then, they had to journey into the hardware archives to find such an arcane instrument. It was the last day of January, with a brisk southerly wind under an untroubled sky. The bay, where we could see it below us between the houses, was the color and texture of sweet pickles. We had tea and Irish cheddar melted on toast on our return, eating while we drove the ice pick into the wall at various points. We drilled holes in a straight line, six inches apart, and six feet along the wall, before probing. The pick went through plaster and sometimes lath, but then slid clean up to the handle, except directly below the window, where it hit something impenetrable just beyond the plaster.

"This is driving me crazy," I said.

There was a brief call around eleven, the secretary saying Willems was skiing in Switzerland and insisted on his privacy. Karen uttered what seemed an irrelevant request: "Please tell Herr Willems we need him to authorize funds for house repairs." When she hung up she glanced at both of us. "Code phrase."

"You guys are good," I observed.

"We've been at this for ten years, Ethan."

By this time it was early afternoon and we worked without lunch in the other wing of the library, cataloguing and packing books for the scheduled pick-up by the Canadian storage company. Karen stayed in the dormer room, on the phone frequently by the sound of it. Things were moving. The shippers came at dusk. Just as they were leaving, a black Cadillac Escalade came up the drive. "Willems' attorney," Karen said.

"First rate chap," Adrian added.

The lawyer was a small man with curly hair, almost like a watch cap. He exited the vehicle with a briefcase and a camcorder and bounced up the steps. "I hope that wasn't Sir Francis on his way to some vault in Canada," he said. He politely

106

introduced himself to me and asked for identification, and for some reason wrote down my driver's license number. Then he went back to the SUV and returned with a reciprocating saw, still with the price tag attached. When we were all seated at the somber dining room table, he brought out two identical documents and gave one to Karen and one to me. "Obviously, we have the green light to open the wall. Adrian, I have some bad news for you. Mr. Willems doesn't want you here."

"Whyever not?" But he didn't seem entirely surprised.

"Because of the letter you wrote to the Ballentine Museum."

"That was a long time ago, and it was never sent," Karen protested. "He's been trusted ever since."

"If I may speak plainly, it seems a bit spiteful to me as well. Our client's family has a long memory for such things. You're not dismissed or anything, just barred from the big moment."

Karen said: "I'm going to call him directly."

Adrian stood. "Don't be silly, my dear. As long as I'm in for my portion, let's let it go. I shall go home, have a splendid dinner which I will not taste, a night in a comfortable bed where I will not sleep, and I'll be here with my tongue hanging out tomorrow at seven." He turned and left. Strangely, there was an air of relief about him, more than resignation.

When he was gone, the lawyer said, "The documents are confidentiality agreements."

"I already signed one," I said.

"Slightly different. These deal with disclosing whatever happens when we open the wall, not just what we find."

The document, which was in three languages—all of which I could read, fortunately—said just that. I signed, Karen did, and we filed upstairs. "Dr. Storey, can you use one of these things?"

"My father and I used to give each other power tools for our birthdays."

He nodded. "I feel I know you already. I did the background check on you." He handed me the reciprocating saw. Just let me get set up." He fussed with his camera arrangement, announced the time, date, and who was present, and nodded to me.

It took about a half hour to cut out a two foot square of wall. There were no studs below the window, but I had to be very careful not to make contact with whatever was back there. It was also very good plaster and it held together in a single piece until I was all the way around. I would have paused for dramatic effect, but it fell cleanly away in a small puff of white dust. I stopped so the lawyer could reposition the lights. We were looking at a metal cube, possibly tin, that completely filled the space. The end facing us appeared to have the edges soldered together. Hermetically sealed, 1930s style. Gloves seemed irrelevant. "Everybody ready?" They nodded. I reached in and pulled out the cube, which slid easily onto the floor. The top was gone and the cube empty. At the bottom there was a layer of small paper shards, like paint chips. "Oh, well," said Karen.

"Could you get me a hand lens from the other room?" When she came back with Adrian's jeweler's loupe, I had a closer look. "It's parchment," I said.

WHEN THE lawyer had packed up and departed, we bagged the manuscript crumbs and sealed the cube in plastic wrapping. With everything back in rough order and both of us nearly speechless with anticlimax, she said: "I think I'll go back to my place." Karen had a condo in El Cerrito as well as her room here.

"I'll be here if you change your mind," I said, trying not to sound needy.

She looked at me like a critic might look at a painting: *Now why do I like this particular thing?* She had a habit of inspecting me in that way; and now that I'd noticed it, I could recall experiencing the same thing all the way back to the first time we'd met. In reply she kissed me on the cheek and sang a fragment of song into my ear: *"You make me feel like a natural woman . . ."* Carole King, I remembered.

When she'd left I walked around both library rooms, still tidying up. These were rote actions: backing up computer files, updating the catalogue with the few things I'd not quite finished, answering the forwarded mail that had piled up for me. I was off the magical mystery tour for the moment. Time to pay the periodontist. There was a letter from SFSU, saying that pending final approval by the faculty senate, I was welcome to come back. More bills. Boat catalogues. My bursitis was acting up, as it tended to when low-pressure systems moved through San Francisco. I was very disappointed, of course; the discovery, in my current view of things, would be an end to all this, a start to returning to the familiar. While I made myself a salad in the old soapstone kitchen I had to deal with the lack of resolution, and also the realization that maybe there was no going back, logbooks or no logbooks. Then, in hindsight, it seemed too easy, anyway. Hidden behind the wall, for God's sake.

But on the other hand, there *had* been something there. Under the hand lens there was a just discernable hair follicle pattern (parchment was made from animal skin). Parchment production declined with the advent of paper in the 1500s, but when used it's been a boon to historians, durable for centuries as long as it's kept dry. The question was why the contents had been moved. There seemed only one scenario, though it hardly explained anything. The 1939 Willems had arranged the hiding place, the box to protect the logbooks, and someone had changed their mind, removed it, and carefully restored and re-plastered the wall.

For the moment, I let it go. I'd been in the old house for ten days and nights now, probably a longer stretch under one roof than anywhere else on dry land for several years. And though I'd been too busy to notice it, falling asleep moments after shutting down my computer every night, I'd acquired an affection for the old place. There was something in every room to admire, something old to touch, something intriguing. In the dining room there were framed proverbs in ornate Arabic calligraphy and Chinese on the walls, and the delft plates and cups Kay had admired so much. The floors under the oriental rugs were wide, random hardwood planks; hard to imagine obtaining them locally, they must have come over with the Willems. I knew it was still windy outside from seeing Karen to the door, but it was warmly, serenely silent in here, except for the ticking of the mantelpiece clock. I'd looked behind it earlier: ANTWERP, 1929. I stopped thinking of everything as a potential clue to Drake's Logbooks and just enjoyed myself walking around with a brandy like I owned the place. I suppose, in a sense, I did.

I found stamps for my letters and was about to walk to Kensington to mail them in spite of the wind when it occurred to me to call Brian Haggerty, who I hadn't talked to since the night in the Richmond boatyard. He'd taken McNally's WWII books to have them scanned. When I found my cell phone I realized I'd had it turned off, probably for days. The last five calls recorded were from Brian. It was after nine by this time but obviously he wanted to talk, too. "Brian, it's Ethan."

"Where have you been?"

"I moved into the Willems Institute about ten days ago. And no, I can't talk about anything. Why were you calling?"

"We have to talk. Would you meet me at the Jupiter in fifteen minutes?"

The Jupiter was a student hangout west of the campus, the kind of place only serious college towns have. A stripped-brick interior. A United Nations of beers, discussions of Kierkegaard at the next table, laptop screens crawling with lines of code. It was bustling as it always was, but he'd found a table in the loft upstairs. He saw me and waved over the railing. He looked more together than the last time, but rather stern. "Sit down and welcome. Enjoy your last minute as a sheltered academic." He'd already ordered for me, something molasses colored that tasted like toasted barley and honey.

"Say what?"

"This is the last of our little chats, for one thing. You'll understand when I tell you. I brought those books in to the library scanners, but it took almost a week for them to get around to it. When I came to get them, they had it on a hard drive. While I was waiting for them to burn me a CD, I scanned for Willems." He sipped his stout.

"And?"

"Nada. Just a reference to the collection being impounded."

"So . . ." Then it hit me. "You scanned for Ballentine."

He nodded. "Two hits. In 1939, the year Willems came over with his books, Ballentine wrote a letter offering unrestricted use of the cyclotron to the U.S. government."

"I'm not that surprised. Uncle Sam was coming anyway. But why would that merit a mention in these files?"

"Because it referred to advanced weaponry based on particle physics."

"And?"

"And he shouldn't have known that. Niels Bohr had just published his theory of the compound nucleus. It wasn't until a series of experiments in Germany were made public later that year, splitting the uranium atom, that anybody in the nonscientific world had a clue." I raised an eyebrow. "I asked somebody in the physics department. Anyway, that's when they started watching him, though nothing came of it, obviously; but it got him on somebody's list. Curtis Ballentine seemed to have more knowledge of what was going on at the cyclotron than a simple university benefactor whose primary interest was supposed to be history."

"How do you know this stuff?"

"I printed the other one. I'm glad I did. I never got the CD or the books back. I had to enter them into the library database to get them scanned, so they looked like recent acquisitions. They were all gathered up by someone from the University of Iowa, where they were published. Recalled, they said, by the government, which had not adequately vetted them for national security concerns. No harm no foul, they said basically, but they politely asked that the books go back and electronic copies be destroyed. The library complied."

"That seems very strange. I ordered them off Amazon."

"You and about a thousand other people, apparently. But that's what happened. Librarians are very compliant about security issues since the Patriot Act."

"I don't see where this is going."

He handed me a piece of paper. Typewritten in the stodgy fonts of the 1930s. It was a portion of a very long list of drafts—the page was headed "1938 Fund Transfers, Axis-Controlled Institutions"—from a Belgian bank wired to account numbers in the U.S. The amounts were substantial; the numbers were identified by a single name. Three of them were Curtis Ballentine or members of his family. "Who sent them?"

"The University of Antwerp, former home of the Willems collection."

Stout on top of brandy after a night of passion and a long day, but I was suddenly up to the hunt again. "Wait. Willems was paying *Ballentine*?"

"I'm glad you're as surprised as I was. You know a lot more about the relationship between the two families by this time, but if Willems had Drake's Logbooks, the money should have been going the other way."

I had an uncomfortable thought. "Did the library inform Sean Ballentine about the books?"

"I don't think so. He can hardly be aware of library acquisitions by tenured professors. If they had, I'd surely have been fired by now, if he knows anything about this. This is all as close as I want to get, Ethan. We're even now. How about something to eat?"

We shared a basket of onion rings. Surprisingly, I was still hungry and Brian was always hungry, so we ate in silence. For all Brian's attempts to wash his hands of the Drake business, I knew he was thinking about it and would never let it go. Sooner or later he would want back in. So when he paused to speak, I thought it was about the collection. But he said: "Do you want to know that I've talked to Kay several times?"

I felt myself turn stonily sober. "What does she want?"

"She wants me to talk you into letting her explain. She gave me the lowdown on what happened. You should do it, pal, talk to her, if you want my advice. She totally freaked out when she

112

tried to find the boat, thought you'd taken off again, like you did to San Luis that time."

"I took the schooner up the Delta for the winter."

"Yeah, well, I guessed you were at the institute, saw your truck parked there. Told her you hadn't sailed off to Tahiti. So I've done my duty."

I thought of several things to say about Kay, but what I said was actually about him. "You're a good friend, Brian."

"What are you going to do now?"

"About Kay?"

"About anything."

"I'll go back to SFSU—they're through investigating me—as soon as I've finished up at the institute."

He walked me to my truck. It was after eleven, the town quiet except for a distant siren. "Can you tell me whether or not to scan eBay for the Drake Logbooks?"

That was the only possible way he could ask it and allow me to answer. "No priceless artifacts ever show up on eBay."

"Well put, Deep Throat."

The fire trucks were just wailing out of the station at the corner of Marin and Martin Luther King. I slowed to let them past, but I caught them from behind a few blocks later, pulling the steep grade up Arlington. At times like this it always seems like your own house is burning, then you tell yourself no, what are the chances? The water from the hoses was already running down towards me, and though the smoke was blowing away I could see its thick trunk, surrounding a core of flame and now loud enough to challenge the sirens. The street was blocked by the police cars I'd heard earlier in Berkeley. I turned around, parked, and walked up through citizens in their bathrobes watching the spectacle. The very first one I passed was saying, "That old eyesore; always did give me the creeps." There was no other ugly building on Arlington besides the institute. Fifty yards away there was another cordon around the engines, and even from here it was obviously too hot to approach, the structure fully involved, flame from every door and window, a smell stronger and stranger than wood smoke. A smell dark and sharp, like bitter chocolate. They were hosing in huge, high-pressure arcs, half of them spraying adjacent structures. Then I called to one of the firemen that I was staying in the house. "Is there anyone else inside?" he called back.

"No."

"Is that your car?"

I saw it, its own pillar of flame, something small and practical, Toyota Corolla.

Karen's car.

CHAPTER TEN

There was nothing they could do; the building had already collapsed in upon itself. I stayed and told them what I could about Karen, then stood dumbly, immobilized but shivering. I was there until they reeled in their hoses.

For the last two hours before dawn, the setting gibbous moon looked oversized, orange and deformed. I walked the streets of Berkeley until daylight came, a sultry yellow haze through the inversion-trapped smoke. When I was tired enough I walked back past the collapsed walls and leafless cedar stalks of the black hole on Arlington, once the Willems Institute, which twenty-four hours ago had held much of the remaining important things in my life. The books had continued to smolder for many hours after the engines left. There was no one for me to call, nowhere for me to go, but I felt oddly focused in the moment. I was not, of course, the victim, and I didn't feel like one. That would be Karen Molina, the sweet, bright woman who wanted me to give Kay another chance. I thought of Karen with piercing guilt and a gathering, but tightly bound rage. She'd come back to spend another night with me and died in a fire that was unquestionably arson; and now McNally's death, Kay's betrayal, the trivial losses around the boat and my teaching position were placed, not in chronological order, but in a pattern of increasingly deadly intent. At each step I was changed by the events, trimmed down and hardened like an athlete. Now I knew that I was at the center of things, and if they were going to turn around me, I'd be the one to decide the direction of the spin.

The arson investigator at the scene of the fire had requested politely that I walk in front of his Labrador, who apparently didn't smell evaporated gasoline on me. They both lost interest quickly, but he asked that I stop by the Berkeley Police Department first thing in the morning. At six-thirty, I returned to the truck for an hour's nap, ate a Power Bar, and drank a can of warm Pepsi before driving to the station. The investigator was still polite, thorough, and uninformative, and didn't really listen to my simplified version of what went on at the Willems Institute. But now he was no longer disinterested and watched me closely. "You knew Ms. Molina, right?"

"Yes. She was my employer, in a sense."

"Know anyone who'd do her wrong?"

"No."

"This is a fire of suspicious origin. The owner's attorney told me just ten minutes ago that there was very substantial insurance coverage."

"For what it's worth," I said, "I don't think that family needs any money."

"What about this Englishman, Burke?"

"He and Karen had worked together for many years before I showed up."

"Any romance there?"

"I think he's gay."

"Between you and me, the guy is totally messed up." I said nothing and he went on. " 'Inchoate with grief' as our university friends might call him." I wasn't sure that was the word he wanted, but I got the drift. "You'd think he started the fire himself." I made no comment.

When we were finished he gave me his card. I now had three in my wallet: his, George Metaxis, and Parsons, the policeman from New York investigating McNally's death. I bought a cup of coffee from the machine in the hall and checked my phone. Sometime that night Kay had called, but my cell had been in the truck. Her message: *Just call and tell me you're all right.* I did so, intending to respond just to that. She answered immediately, her voice hoarse and muted as if she wasn't breathing properly. "It was Karen Molina that died," I said. "I was out drinking with Brian."

"Oh, God. What are you going to do?"

116

I knew exactly what I was going to do, but was not about to tell her. Instead, I said: "Kay, you need to leave those people. Find yourself some other client." She was silent just long enough for me to hang up and not feel I was being gratuitously cruel.

I parked in a tow-away zone in front of a store along Telegraph that sold work clothes to students who wanted to look blue collar, the only one that was open at that hour, and bought two pairs of jeans and shirts. Money was suddenly an issue, and short term cash could be a problem. I decided I wasn't going to be staying much in hotels while I sorted things out, so I checked the locked bins in back for my slightly mildewed sleeping bag and aired it out. At the twenty-four hour Safeway, I filled the cooler with cold cuts, bread, cheese, and cheap beer. I had a small camping stove in the back along with the bag I'd taken from the *Drake*, and some forgotten, but now handy, gear: a tent, a paint-spotted Gortex parka Kay had insisted I throw away the year before, an unopened jar of instant coffee, snow chains. I parked again on Shattuck and went into the Wells Fargo Bank where Dad had insisted I get a safe deposit box just before he died in 1990. There wasn't much there, but enough savings bonds to keep me in funds for a while without engaging my Visa. There was also his old watch, a TAG Heuer nautical chronograph which I'd never thought to wear. I quietly removed my Casio and exchanged watches. The Heuer was as big as a silver dollar, heavy on my wrist. It was self-winding and started running almost immediately, as if it had been waiting for me to come get it.

There was no such thing as instant cash for savings bonds, but I made arrangements for a deposit into my checking account. Then I walked a block to the public library and used their computer to book a flight to Amsterdam from New York on February 14th, the day before the conference started. I gassed up the truck, bought a map of the U.S., and headed out from Berkeley, against the traffic on Interstate 80.

I WAS glad of both the parka and the tire chains because Donner Pass over the Sierra Nevada was a near white-out of wet, driving snow. It didn't freeze much but piled up rapidly, the kind of snow that looks great behind weather people when they report from the summit. Across the Sierras and into Nevada; at midday I could open the windows for awhile to purge the cab of its smell of smoke and ash. I spent the night at a public campground in Elko, Nevada, where I could shower and change into my new clothes. The weather had followed me east, but passed me by as I slept; and when I woke late, there was full winter desert around me, brimming with a hard, bright sun. It was in the fifties with only a patina of snow, from which lupine bloomed the color of claret, and there was a pervasive scent like turkey stuffing that I recognized as sagebrush. I dropped down to Highway 50 at Ely, many miles out of my way. I told myself I wanted to avoid Salt Lake City, but in truth I wanted to avoid everything, and 50 was America's loneliest road. You are in a greenish-brown bowl, gently sloping to range after range of barren hills, burned black by the summers. This was not a drive so much as a catharsis, and I wandered across Utah, then north into Wyoming before I stopped again, this time in a grove of blackthorn and skeletal cottonwood on a dirt road just off the highway. There was no snow, but it was so windy and cold in the tent that I pushed on shortly after two AM. I chained up again for the Continental Divide and stopped, finally, at a Motel 6 in Laramie for a shower and a few hours sleep.

My phone was still in business, and over a breakfast sandwich in my room I called Des Moines to see how many McNallys were in the book. Cell phones don't quite work that way, and the system connected me with the first Robert McNally listed. A woman answered, a voice at the upper end of the register, peaking almost into silence when the Midwestern inflections kicked in. But she sounded all right, a sort of glad-you-called tone that would encourage telephone salespeople. Maybe everyone in Iowa answered the phone that way. "My name is Ethan Storey," I said, and: "I'm a history professor from California State University." I'd had occasion to track down leads to the past, not the Elizabethan past but the kind of history people sometimes hired me to do, bits of family sleuthing. Most respondents are surprisingly receptive. At one end is: how threatening is a history teacher? At the other: am I interesting to history?

But this was far from how she responded. Her voice dropped, her words came slowly with more warmth and less automatic cordiality. "I know who you are, Dr. Storey. You were a friend of my husband's. I'm sorry we never met in person. Robert thought highly of you."

"I'm coming through Des Moines on my way to New York," I said, "and wondered if I might stop by and chat. I'd probably be in your area late tomorrow afternoon."

"Please come by for supper. We're on Woodland. It's just off 235." She gave me directions, and said, almost to herself, "I'll make fried chicken. I haven't done that since Robert died."

The radio held little of interest across the Great Plains, and the plains themselves were expanses of snowfields and farmsteads, but I had emerged from my post-traumatic stress to start thinking this through again, this time with more clarity. I had set things out in a sort of historian's outline when somehow Verizon found me. It was George Metaxis. "Hullo, Ethan. I know about the fire. Where are you?"

"Somewhere in Nebraska."

"You should have stopped by in Nevada on your way. We have a lot to talk about. Was anyone hurt in the fire?"

"One of the curators died. Karen Molina. Please don't tell me you have a dossier on her."

He thought for a moment, during which time I plugged the cell into the cigarette lighter to charge. "Headed for Iowa?" he asked finally.

"I want to talk to Bob McNally's wife. Did the FBI interview her?"

"There has never been an active FBI investigation, not into McNally anyway. I just came along with Lieutenant Parsons as a loaner specialist in documents. In a sense I'm not involved,

119

though I tried to stir things up when I found those 1930s payments from Institute Banks in Europe to the Ballentine family. Did you get that far?"

"Yes."

"To be frank I . . . I'm following this in my spare time, so to speak. That's why my contact with you has seemed a bit informal."

We each waited for the other to go first. I could hear his parrot muttering to itself in the background. I had nothing to lose and everything to gain from this exchange, so I said: "McNally was killed because he knew something, not only about Drake's Logbooks but about something else. He wasn't going to help me archive the collection. He wanted to warn me about something. Me personally. Listen up, George: it was clear to me from my interview up at the veterans' home and my conversation with the institute staff that the Ballentines had stage-managed the finding of the plate, hidden the real one behind a decoy, and had been after the logbooks, had known for fifty years that they were linked to the institute."

"I'm with you."

"Hang on, because this is what you don't know. We found the place where the original documents, the logbooks, had been hidden." I described the empty tin box and the parchment shards.

"When was this?"

"Just hours before the place was set on fire."

"What?"

Something occurred to me. "Are you taping this?"

"Oops. I should have told you. Want me to turn it off?"

"No, somebody needs to have this on record. Adrian Burke, the appraiser, left the house just before we broke through the wall. He had every expectation that the documents would be there. I'm guessing he reported back to Sean Ballentine—had been his inside agent all along—and they burned it down. The Ballentines now seem to want to have the documents destroyed, if they can't have them."

"Whoa, Nelly. Let's go backwards a sec. You said McNally wanted to warn you personally. What did you mean?"

"I mean that I was chosen from the start, and carefully manipulated to take the assignment as archivist, maybe by both families. Nothing else really explains things, from McNally to Hallowell."

"Hallowell, the son of the man who found the plate in Point Reyes? What does he have to do with it?"

"My father visited his father several times."

"But you didn't know any of this?"

"No."

"But an outsider might think otherwise." It was not a question. "Your father left papers, surely."

"My father died intestate and left me with a watch, a boat and some savings bonds."

"Does that strike you as curious?"

"If I died tomorrow I'd be just like him, minus the savings bonds. Articles in historical journals, a watch and a boat. But yes, it does strike me as curious. He was not a particularly secretive man, just rather uncommunicative."

"All right, then. I like where your head is at. What's your plan? Leaving California was a good start."

"There's only three places I can go to get closure on all this. McNally's widow, the police in New York, and the Willems family in Antwerp."

"I think I can help."

"I don't want your help, unless it's information."

He responded with another question. "You'll be at the conference in Amsterdam, then? A sort of working cover story?"

"Yes."

"It would not be out of place for me to say be careful?"

The parrot said, "Goodbye."

I CAMPED out again in a rest stop near Lexington and stopped for lunch just into Iowa at a diner, to wash in the restroom and put on the other set of clean clothes. Des Moines was snowy but thawing in the late afternoon, a reassuring, no-nonsense Midwestern city settled into winter. The house on Woodland was an early twentieth-century craftsman bungalow, which would not have been out of place in Berkeley, but probably cost a tenth as much, and whose broad, pillared porch might actually see use on a long summer evening. It was immaculately restored, cream white with a brown trim. Even with the snow the yard looked tailored, its shrubbery under protective bonnets and the mailbox painted to match the house. Mrs. McNally opened the door, drying her hands on a towel. "It's Helen," she said. "Come sit by the fire, you look tired from your drive." It was obvious from the first moment that Helen McNally was comfortable in her life and in her home, and that she would dictate the terms of our encounter. She was a graceful fifty, plump in a natural way with weight that would have to be starved off if she wanted to lose it. She had very pale skin and short dark hair that curved slightly at her temples. She'd put on lipstick and watched me through glasses which she frequently took off and let drop on a chain around her neck.

The fire was in a modern woodburning stove, set into a tiled hearth, the room lined with family photographs. It was slightly dark but immaculate and cheery, like Helen herself. I removed the old parka and sat in what must have been McNally's chair, because when an ancient tabby jumped up on my lap, almost immediately, she said: "Would you mind? She misses a man's lap. That's where she and Robert would sit for hours, in their own little world." I said I didn't mind. The cat began to purr and drool slightly. She brought me a bourbon and water and sat opposite me. "Dinner will be ready in a half hour. How was your drive?"

We had a half hour of the most normal conversation I'd had in months: weather, Iowa drivers, her job as a nurse. They had no children. She'd been married to Bob for thirty years and they'd lived here for all that time, though he was often away on his stints as a wandering professor. She visited him once when he was in the Bay Area and she commented on San Francisco's

122

hills and Victorian houses, taking the ferry to Alcatraz, having chowder in a bowl made from a loaf of sourdough bread, the de Young Museum and the redwoods on Mount Tamalpais.

Dinner was a comfort food miracle: besides chicken that seemed to both float lightly and anchor soundly, there were mashed potatoes and gravy, home-canned butter beans, hot biscuits, apple pie. No wine, but beer in a long-necked bottle beside a heavy chilled mug. Helen ate little, though her plate was as full as mine, and when she deemed I'd made enough progress she said: "Robert said you were the only one who treated him professionally." I could barely recall speaking to Bob McNally at all. "It meant a lot to him. More chicken? But . . . I don't think you came to Iowa to express your condolences."

"Have the police in New York told you anything about the investigation?"

"The lieutenant calls every once in a while, but it sounds more like he's investigating me."

"What do you mean?"

"I don't mean they think I'm a suspicious character. They were worried that something might happen to me, related to his death. There was a break-in here about a month ago and they were very interested. But I think it was just kids. A broken window, middle of the day. They didn't take anything but the TV, certainly nothing from Robert's study."

"Do you know why he went to New York?"

She took the worn linen napkin from her lap and spread it carefully beside her plate, as if to signal that, for her, the eating part of the meal was over. "Robert was a much more complicated man than people thought at first, than I thought at first. He had this Midwestern life of work and play, wife and home. I know he always wanted a university position and he was very disappointed that it never happened. But in a way I wished he were more conventionally depressed by his life."

"In what way?"

"For a long time I wondered if he had a lover; it seemed he was keeping a secret that big. A secret that kept him going

123

through everything, even ending up as a high school teacher when he wanted to be an Oxford don. When I just decided he loved me and adored me—it can take the longest time for a woman to trust that that's true—and he didn't have a mistress, I was grateful enough not to question what he did with his researches, as he called them."

"You had no idea?"

"He had a very good explanation, Ethan. It was a general interest in Elizabethan England. He told me wonderful stories from the period, about Robert Dudley and the Queen, about Henry the Eighth, about Mary Queen of Scots. We traveled to England once by ourselves and another time as chaperones for the high school senior trip to Europe. He was a wonderful tour guide. No place we went had any tourists. It was all little villages and crumbling walls and tiny libraries. He made it all come to life, every battle, every conspiracy, every doomed love."

"He seemed like a happy man. Why do you think there was something else?"

"Because he was killed, and because you're here." I began to speak, but she held up her hand. "I'm not at all sure I want to know. Maybe you can tell me some day, but not now. You look very tired, anyway." In truth, I could barely keep my eyes open. "Where are you staying?"

"I'd planned to keep going. I'm on my way to New York."

"No, you mustn't. We have a spare room here. Go get your things."

It was very cold outside. When I glanced in the cooler, thinking to bring the perishables inside, I noted that the ice had refrozen along with everything else. I drove the truck to the next block behind McNally's house as a rather crude, paranoid precaution and to protect the reputation of the widow McNally. When I returned she was waiting inside the door. "My, you do travel light."

She led me upstairs. The guest bedroom held a small cherry four-poster bed with an antique quilt over thick wool blankets in the University of Iowa colors, hardwood floors with braided rugs, and more quilts on the walls. The small window across the room was now thickly frosted and reflected the bedside light like stained glass. She showed me the tiny bathroom and gave me clean towels and soap. I showered quickly and found pajamas, McNally's obviously, on the bed. I put them on and climbed in. When I was about to turn out the light, Helen entered in her bathrobe, with a soft knock and another blanket. She sat down on the end of the bed and looked at me appraisingly. "Your beard needs trimming," she said. "If you're here tomorrow, I'll do it for you." I said nothing, embarrassed by the intimacy. She sighed. "But I expect you'll be on your way. Thank you for coming, Ethan. If I leave the door open, Sally will want to come sleep with you." The cat.

"You can leave the door open, Helen. Thank you for dinner." She patted my foot under the covers and left.

It was Sally, and not Helen, that came in just as I was falling asleep. The cat spooned into my back and we both slept until light poured through the double-paned windows. It was almost 10 AM. I left the cat still asleep and brushed my teeth. There was no sign of Helen. After I packed and dressed I went downstairs to the kitchen, where another small wood stove burned in an otherwise stylish, modern kitchen, with the granite counter-tops Kay so admired when we toured open houses. There was a speckleware pot of coffee keeping warm on the stove, along with a plate of biscuits warmed from last night. Jam and jelly in Ball jars on the table, set for one. I sat down to eat and found a note from her under one jar, and under the note a key. *Please take a look around Robert's study, the key is to a place behind the bookshelves to the right of the desk. You're welcome back any-time. For what it's worth, and you may know this, I forgot to tell you last night that Robert was going to try and visit you in Cali-fornia after he got back from New York. Affectionately, Helen.*

I ate slowly, staring at the basement door opposite me, waiting for insights and feeling only that last night had closed a few of my wounds. If I was on the same side as Helen McNally, I was doing something right. When I was finished, I cleaned up and put the dishes in the drainer. The door to the basement was unlocked and the light came on automatically when I opened it. The basement office was brightly lit with fluorescents and, though with only one tiny window at ground level, it had the same sturdy, safe feeling as the rest of the place. McNally's files were in hardwood cabinets on one side of the desk and a bookcase was on the right. The famous 1580 full-size portrait of Sir Francis Drake was over his desk, the one with the wise and cunning mariner looking stiff and foolish in his courtier's clothes. The desktop had nothing on it but a decorative blue ceramic lamp. I looked in the file cabinets and desk drawer, but there was little there that seemed out of place for an ordinary man who took most of his commitments in life equally seriously: charitable contributions and work for his church, car maintenance records and tax returns, student records and papers.

The key was not to a compartment that was really secret. The bookshelves were obviously on tracks, slid easily to one side, and there was a conventional, though locked, closet door with a recessed latch directly behind them. I began to doubt what I'd been nearly sure of last night—that the break-in was directly related to all this. When I unlocked the door another light came on automatically, and I looked at books that any savvy historian would want under lock and key. A few early Shakespeare folios and a first edition of Gibbon. There was also, I noticed, a small cardboard box with soft-core pornographic movies, and a mahogany box that looked like it might contain very large, very costly cigars. I took it out with me and sat in Easy Bob's chair. When I opened the box, two things made me go as cold as the Iowa morning. One was a letter, undated, to my father at a post office box in San Francisco. The other was the sound of footsteps in the living room, just above me. It was a well-made floor and I only caught the footfalls. But they were heavy, uncertain and there was more than one set of them. I glanced up the stairway; the door was closed. I killed the desk lamp and the fluorescents by unscrewing the bulbs, and pawed around until I found the phone.

I brailled my way through 911, though there was a little light creeping in from somewhere outside and my eyes were adjusting. "There's a break-in in progress at 3546 Woodland. I live next door and can see two men moving around inside that have nothing to do with Mrs. McNally. She's at work." Then I hung up, pulled the phone on its long cord into the closet and pulled the door almost closed. Knowing Bob through Helen's eyes, I tried the first number on the speed dial. "Mercy Hospital."

"I need to speak to Helen McNally. It's an emergency." They were in the kitchen now and I could hear voices. One said, *Of course we checked the basement last time.* The door opened and a hand reached for the light switch which was not there. It made a few ineffective swipes before I heard, and the visitors heard, the sound of police sirens. *Pretty good response time,* I thought, absurdly calm. The hand disappeared and about thirty seconds later, the footsteps. At the same time Helen came on the line. "Helen, it's Ethan."

"What's happening?"

"There were two men in your house a moment ago. I called the police."

"You're in the basement?"

"Yes. Listen Helen, do you have any other place you can stay?"

"My sister lives in Davenport, but I can also sleep in the hospital."

"Please don't come home until the police figure out what happened."

"Do you know what's happening?"

"No, I don't really know. But I will."

"I guess I'm changing my mind from last night. Please tell me as soon as you can." Nurses under pressure, I thought. She was not unsettled.

"I promise. Is there another way out of the basement?"

"The tornado door. It's on the other side of the bookshelves."

"Goodbye, Helen. I'm sorry."

"It's all right, Ethan. You're an honorable man."

I stuffed the letter into my pocket, grabbed the box of videos which Helen was never meant to see, cranked the door open, and was through the snowy yard to the next block, where the truck was parked, before the police could arrest me or anybody else.

CHAPTER ELEVEN

I rejoined I-80 north of downtown in time for the last of Des Moines' orderly rush-hour traffic. It took that long for my window to defrost and for my chest to decompress. The letter McNally had stolen from the Willems Institute files was written to my father the year I had graduated from Stanford. Nineteen sixty-nine was the sort of year one generation didn't speak to the next very much, and I had been no exception to the rule. I had no idea what the letter might contain, or why McNally had taken it. The first line or two was text referring to previous correspondence, including a power of attorney for the Willems family made out to him, and receipts for certain items borrowed from the collection and returned in chronological order beginning in the late 1940s. The author was expressing his thanks for all Dad's help. The letterhead was that of the law firm that had dispatched the lawyer the day we opened the wall, the day of the fire, but the attachments had several imprimaturs. It was several pages long and the type small and blurry enough to be impossible to read without my glasses; but evidently it was a summary of all his contacts with the institute since the 1930s. I was not going to look at it until I had time and place under control again. Meanwhile, I just drove east, putting anonymous distance between my truck and Des Moines.

But I could think about it. My father had been born in 1903, which would have made him a new Ph.D. and teaching assistant at San Francisco State, then just getting its history department organized, when the Willems collection arrived. This was a relationship that had continued through the 1950s, when he was visiting the Hallowell family in Point Reyes, to 1969 when the letter was written, and probably longer. He had never said anything to me about it, but then, I myself had signed two confidentiality agreements with the institute and Dad took property rights for data or records very seriously. And it wasn't the only thing he never talked about.

I was stopped by the Illinois State Police near Morris, a town on the banks of the Illinois River. It looked like a routine interstate stop—something like expired tags or a broken taillight—I wasn't speeding, and by that point was ready to find a diner with good overhead lighting. But when I started to pull over into the breakdown lane, the officer signaled for me to take the next exit. He passed me as I did so, and in the mirror I saw that there was a second car behind me. I slowed, braked and slid down the ramp and into town with my escort.

Morris was a little like everything else had been since Nebraska: old, cold, solid. Its main street had a reassuring Midwestern undertone, two-story brick structures with shops on the bottom floor and high arched windows at the top. The kind of place with angled parking spaces never full, and cafés with the name of the original owner. We made a few turns in convoy and turned behind a granite building, Greek revival, with two perfectly spaced trees flanking the entrance and a sign that read GRUNDY COUNTY COURTHOUSE. The whole scene had the feeling of illustrations in a civics high school textbook. I sat until one of the officers came and tapped on the window, his partner behind him. The weather was cloudy, the air moist and still. His breath made a misty shroud between us. "Leave your engine running and exit the vehicle, please," he said. Given the past few days, I felt more relaxed than stressed by this episode. I was in Illinois, in the hands of the state police. The safest I'd felt in days.

But when I stepped out, he immediately took my place and drove the pickup toward a garage at the far end of the lot. "Come with me, please," the other said. I went inside the courthouse with the three remaining troopers, up a flight of stairs and into what must have been a judge's chambers. It was furnished with heavy hardwood furniture and law books, a library smell of polish and bookbinding and old leather, not unlike the institute. It was very warm. I took off my parka and he gestured for me to sit on a leather couch, with a low coffee table made from a half barrel that was branded GEBHARD BREWERY 1866. "What's up?" I asked.

"We'll be sorting things out shortly, sir," one of them said.

"Would you like coffee? I think there are some doughnuts downstairs, also," said another.

I reflected silently that I'd only made more progress in the current conundrum by asking questions. But now didn't seem the time, and it was obvious from their tone that they hadn't a clue why I was here, either. "Yes to both."

Ten minutes later they brought me two jelly doughnuts and a cup of a coffee-like substance, and answered my inquiries about the truck and its contents with assurances so devoid of content I asked if I could leave. To my initial surprise they said OK. Then I realized that they had no agenda, were acting out someone else's plan, and that the purpose of the stop was just this, ten minutes to search my vehicle. It was downstairs at the curb with the engine running. George Metaxis sat in the passenger seat, and when I got in he said: "Let's go get lunch. NYPD is waiting for us at Mary's Diner."

"What's this about?"

"Come on, a little food and we can be gentlemen about the whole thing."

"How did you find me?"

"Well, I knew you'd be on I-80 out of Des Moines after you called the cops, and I was pretty sure someone, not us, put a tracking device on your truck even before you left Berkeley. We had a chance report from the credit card you used last time you stopped for gas; then it took us awhile to find your frequency and set up scans along the interstate."

"You found me in about four hours. You can't even do that with terrorists."

We sat for a moment while I tried to sort this out. Metaxis watched me patiently, then said, "I'm sorry, Ethan. Just trust me for a few minutes. I was once as confused as you are about all of this, but not after reading the letter." He nodded toward the dashboard.

"I haven't had a chance to read it all yet."

"I didn't think so. You'd have called me if you had."

I put the truck in gear and we drove back downtown through the grey streets to where there were two Crown Victorias with U.S. Government plates parked in front of a café which, though brightly lit, had a CLOSED sign in the window and was nearly empty. The New York policeman named Parsons was sitting there, at the table farthest from the door, with some recording equipment, a wireless computer and printer, and a bowl of something into which he was crumbling crackers. "Hello, Lieutenant Parsons."

"Call me John. There's chili in that big pot on the stove. We had to buy the whole thing, and it's pretty good." I declined and sat beside him. Metaxis helped himself and sat across from us.

"Why not the police station?"

"They were not comfortable with a federal operation that we couldn't explain to them. We got use of their garage, the highway stop, and ten minutes of your time," Parsons said.

They fell into the silence of men eating, as if they hadn't spent considerable time and money tracking me down for no clear purpose. But that was it, of course. They did have a purpose. Metaxis had said nothing when I pocketed the letter before we left the truck, and now I put my glasses on and read it. "Herr Professor Storey," then reviewed all the transactions between the institute and my father, most of which were books he had borrowed and returned with short memoranda on their contents, but two were the powers of attorney that he had been granted by the institute. One was to negotiate the terms and specifics of renovation of the original building, adding the dormer and air-conditioning and dehumidifying equipment, in the 1950s; the other to commission the radiocarbon dating equipment at Stanford to determine the age of a document. This was in 1969, just after such equipment became available at major universities.

The document was referred to by a Willems collection catalogue number, even though there was no catalogue: that's what they'd hired both McNally and me for. The letter went on:

Should the item referenced above be at any risk of discovery by any person not of our mutual acquaintance you are hereby empowered to remove it from the Institute and move it to a safe location. You must not communicate its whereabouts to anyone until the undersigned or his direct heirs ask you to do so. Your service to our family for two decades has been appreciated and we hope adequately compensated. We assure you that, when we are able to make the books available to the larger academic community, you will have sole rights to their analysis, and full exclusive rights to publish, for two years. A copy of this letter will be on file in the collection, and we will notify our attorneys in the United States about its existence, though you will need to allow them to review it if they deem it necessary. In the interim, I have asked the firm to remove all correspondence and other items bearing your name from the Institute files. These actions have been forced upon us by B., as you know well, but please be assured that they are unlikely to approach you personally. We have been as discreet on your behalf as you have been on ours. Congratulations on your son's university degree from Stanford.

It was signed Manfred Willems. I looked up. They were watching me. Parsons said: "Know where your father kept his life insurance, your birth certificate, the family silver? Ever seen a sixteenth-century parchment on the kitchen table?"

"I didn't know anything about this. He lived on the boat from, I don't know, 1965 or so. There was nothing in his papers when he died. The only things in the safe deposit box were this watch and some savings bonds."

"How did he die?"

"A stroke. I found him the same day it happened. He just put his head down on the chart table and died."

"Was there a chart on the table?"

"I don't remember. It was fifteen years ago."

"Difficult not to believe you in the circumstances. Do you think of your old man as somebody who might have accepted such a strange assignment, and kept the secret until he died?"

I thought about it, but not for very long. "Yes," I replied.

"How can you be so sure?"

"Because it's exactly what I would have done." For other sons, it would have been hard to be so sure. But I was not anyone else's son. I was Tom Storey's son. "Why didn't anybody find the letter?"

"There was no real search by the Des Moines police," Parsons said. "The first break-in was amateurish and cut short, much like the one this morning. At that point last fall they weren't sure McNally had anything of interest for them; they were just tying up loose ends. They've been much more focused on you, ever since you walked in the door."

"Who is 'they'?"

"This might go better," Metaxis said, "if we just give you a briefing of the unclassified parts of this thing."

"Can you tell me something first?"

"Sure."

"What about Kay? Is she all right?"

"Your friend is a sharp property attorney who was hired by the Ballentine Foundation last summer. Their headquarters are in New York, by the way, and they do a lot more than provide grants to historians. There were extremely complex provenance questions about Drake's Plate—the real one, not the one in the museum. It turns out that they made life difficult for themselves by camouflaging the real plate with a fake one. Ownership is now in question. She was in New York when McNally was murdered. But she knows less than you do, much less than you will in a few minutes. Apparently, she resigned from their legal team within the past few days."

"All right. Go ahead."

Metaxis went on: "The Ballentines had been negotiating with the Willems since the plate was recovered in 1933, for the purchase of the Drake Logbooks. When Manfred Willems and his family fled Antwerp with the collection, Curtis Ballentine helped them get started with the institute and all was set for a full accommodation of the two families: Manfred getting his professorship, his collection in its own university building, the presentation of the logbooks, the validation of the real plate. But there was a serious complication. Did you know that the collection was technically impounded by the U.S. Government?"

"I had heard that was all a mistake, that the seizure was because the collection was thought to be Danish and the government wanted to keep it out of the hands of the Germans, who'd just invaded."

"No, although the U.S. government still gets Holland, Belgium, Denmark and Luxembourg confused. I'm not sure I could locate them on a map, myself. They were impounded—but this meant seized in place, at the institute and under lock and key—with no possibility of access, even to the Willems themselves. It wasn't part of any attempt to keep Danish assets safe. It was because Manfred Willems, though a worldly, gentle, apolitical academic in most respects, was a Nazi agent." Metaxis stopped for a moment. "Did you order the books with the ISBN numbers recorded in McNally's journal?"

"Yes."

"Anything strike you?"

"Am I trying to guess something you're not supposed to tell me?"

He and John Parsons conferred without speaking. Difficult to imagine why a hardened NYPD detective would have a professional relationship, including visual shorthand, with a loose canon FBI document specialist, but there it was. "That about sums it up," Parsons finally said.

I began: "I had the War Crimes Disclosure book scanned, then searched, for either family name. I just found this out before the institute was torched, but there was some money paid from the Willems Library in Antwerp to the Ballentines. I think in 1938, the year before they came to California."

"And you inferred?" Parsons asked.

"In the last two minutes, I inferred that Willems was paying Ballentine for services rendered to the Third Reich."

"And those services might be?"

"Access to information on the cyclotron he was financing."

They both nodded. "Good guess," Metaxis said. "Since it was still a private research facility at the time, this was not strictly speaking espionage, but it got McNally thinking. He followed the same lead you did, before the books were published. He was under contract to the University of Iowa when those files were made public."

"Why did he have the book numbers, then, if he'd already seen them?"

"Same reason you did. The documents couldn't be rapidly searched until scanned, and they couldn't be scanned until published."

I thought of Bob McNally, a failure on his own terms, blessed by having Helen and perhaps trying to prove to her he was everything she believed him to be. He has a few months in California at SFSU as a substitute, moonlights as the institute's scholar. He gets an inkling about the presence of the logbooks from Adrian Burke's letter, and learns about my father's involvement from the letter to him. Then, in some capacity for the University of Iowa, he comes to understand that Ballentine is mentioned in the FBI files. In other words, he was, perhaps six months ago, in the same stage of partial enlightenment that I was, sitting here in a diner in small-town Illinois. "Did McNally come to you, to the FBI?" I asked.

"He was to meet with us the next day, the day after he died."

"Why did he have phone numbers for the Ballentines?"

"Oh, he called them. We're reasonably sure about that," Parsons said.

"How?"

"That's how they knew where to find him. We don't know why he called."

"I think I do," I said. "The same reason he wanted to talk to me. He wanted to get his facts straight; he wanted to work as close to primary sources as he could. At the end of the day, he was a historian doing research on documents and artifacts." Parsons looked skeptical; as a cop he suspected, I was sure, a case of attempted blackmail gone horribly wrong. Metaxis just nodded at me. He understood the curious passion of McNally, me, my father, and at some level the Willems family, with their secrets and their books. I was suddenly hungry. It was mid-afternoon and I hadn't eaten since McNally's kitchen, having skipped the doughnuts at the police station. I slid out of the booth and went behind the counter. The diner's working stage was as clean as an operating theatre, and I had yet another feeling that this was part of the country where things just didn't get as messy as either coast. The chili was pretty good, too. When I returned to the table, I said to Metaxis: "And?"

"And the letter you found, and the empty hole in the wall at the institute, tells us that your father became a sort of emergency custodian of the documents and moved them somewhere. It's our guess that in the 1970s or thereabouts, Thomas Storey moved the documents, and if he told the Willems, they seem not to know where they are."

"Why would the Ballentine family want them destroyed today if they wanted to buy them for most of the twentieth century?'

Parsons' turn. He was straightforward and unequivocal: "Because starting almost immediately after the institute was declared the Willems' free property again, they were blackmailing the Ballentines, or so we think, because they played ball with the Germans in the early days of uranium enrichment. They may have bundled some of that, some proof of collusion, with the Drake manuscripts, though I'm just guessing. And the part of this that I don't know any better than you is the connection between all of this and the FBI's investigation into security breaches at the Ballentine Nuclear Laboratory right up to last month."

Metaxis looked as blank as he possibly could. "I only know what I read in the newspapers," he said unconvincingly.

This was all I was going to get. "What would you like me to do?"

"We think you should go to Amsterdam and talk to Lucius Willems, just as you've been planning. We'll take your truck and its transmitter and send it on a wild goose chase. In fact, we'll book you a new flight and cancel your old reservation. I don't think you're in any danger for the moment; after all, they think everything burned up in the fire."

"What about the break-in this morning?"

"Well, they were following you, I suppose, because they never got it straight what you and McNally were up to. But at this point, I think you must be just a loose end for them. That appraiser wasn't there, but he knew you'd found something. He was their inside man. He reported back, the institute was torched. Who else was there?"

"Karen Molina and the California lawyer for the Willems."

Parsons said to Metaxis, "We should have a word with him." He turned to me. "So they think the documents have been destroyed?"

"The Ballentines do. Maybe the Willems, until they heard from the attorney, who told them nothing burned but a million dollars in other manuscripts and a tin box."

"Look, Dr. Storey, we can't make any guarantees and we can't tell you any more than you already know. So we have to ask you: what do *you* want to do?"

"I want to finish this thing. I'm assuming that the only way to do that is to keep on until there's no place left to go." They looked like they wanted to talk to each other, so I got up and went outside. I pulled everything except the groceries out of the truck, and walked around the block; when I came back there was a printout with my new reservations—Chicago to London to Amsterdam—and a brief listing of everything they knew about contacting the Willems family, names and numbers all over northern Europe. There was another number on a yellow post-it.

"This one is for emergencies," Metaxis said. "Can you remember it?"

"Yes."

"There's a transit bus to O'Hare that leaves in an hour, from across the street."

"I have one other question. Did the Ballentine family somehow engineer the recall of the FBI materials, the World War II files published by the university?"

"Nope. We were starting to catch up with them by that time. The volumes were re-classified as secret by Homeland Security because they were part of an ongoing investigation."

"Whose investigation?"

"Ours, of course."

CHAPTER TWELVE

Parsons walked me outside, past the truck and through the curbside slush to the bus station. It was warm and slightly steamy, like the diner, and empty except for a mother with a sleeping baby, strapped to her front in a carrier. She was asleep too, I noticed, one perfect auburn curl dipping to a perfect cheekbone on a face that made fatigue look like a spiritual experience. Parsons, without Metaxis overshadowing him like a moving piece of architecture, seemed more mobile and more human. He sat beside me on a plastic chair, where we both faced the front and could see Metaxis' bulk through the frosted windows across the street. He seemed to be sitting absolutely still. "I better tell you some things," Parsons said.

"OK."

"Chief George and I are way off the reservation. This whole contrivance of tracking you down he did entirely by bluff and by understanding enough about radiotelemetry and computers to start his own espionage outfit. The Bureau sent him to assist with McNally's murder investigation and analyze the notebooks. You know he's not an agent."

"Document specialist, I think he said."

He nodded. "The FBI effort is capable of getting a book recalled, but that's not where we're at. We don't really know what's happening in Washington."

"Why not?"

"Apparently, his security clearance doesn't stretch that far. They—'they' being the Department of Homeland Security— think this whole Francis Drake business is just static. Their main interest is in the lab."

"What about the lab?"

He regarded me with a combination of consternation and disappointment, like he'd confided being gay to someone who didn't know what the word meant. "The Ballentine Labs. The superlaser? Missing computer disks? Gates unlocked? What we were just talking about? I thought you taught there at the University of California."

"San Francisco State is a different institution," I said, though they both seemed a lifetime away at this point. "But I know what you mean." The Ballentine Labs had retained the name of the great family that endowed them but, as far as I knew, they had no role anymore. But the labs were in the news a lot over the past year, security problems and unaccounted-for materials, suppressing whistleblowers, the full catastrophe of academia-meets-the Pentagon. "What's your role?"

"Metaxis' keeper, I guess you might say. I was the investigating detective on McNally when the Bureau took it over. His boss asked my boss to have me follow him around."

He was silent for a minute, seemed to want to say more, so I prodded a little. "You're OK with that?"

"God, yes. This is a dream case for a cop, Ethan. Brutal murder by a person known to the victim, mysterious documents, rich and powerful families. Also, I've applied to the Bureau and this will be a big boost. But I'm a career law enforcement guy. My Dad was a cop like yours was a professor. What that means is I know my stuff as well as you know yours, and I know how lost I'd be trying to work your side of the street. I'm more than a little worried about you. Neither NYPD nor the Bureau proper would send a civilian out under these circumstances." He took a package of antacid from his shirt pocket, unrolled a tablet and placed it on his tongue, in a ceremony long practiced. "Don't try to do anything more than go to your convention or conference or whatever and look up the Willems family and see what they say. I think it's still plausible that you're just interested in the book collection and exploring some family history; maybe you want to keep your part-time job. Something like that. Or better,

141

tell them you want to explain about the fire. Have they tried to contact you?"

"No." That surprised me, now that I thought about it. "But how would they do it? I don't have any address apart from the institute, and my cell phone would be a hard number to get."

"There'll probably be something at your university office. Do they know where you are?"

"I suppose if someone called the history department, they'd find the conference dates on my computer."

"OK. Maybe they'll come to you. At this point it might look worse if you just dropped out of sight, so to that extent I'm comfortable with it. But that phone number you memorized is just a way to get hold of us. There's nothing in the way of support for you from us from this point on, so don't do anything but socialize, listen carefully, and report to us when you get back. No following people. No listening at doorways. No trading information."

"Got you."

At the door to the station he turned. "I think your dad and mine would have . . . had some things in common." After a brief pause he thought of something else. "You'll have plenty of time at the airport. Shave off your beard."

I fell asleep in my chair considering fathers and sons. And when I slept I dreamed. I dreamed of Dad and Kay, who had, of course, never met in real life. The dream started confused and fretful, with the three of us aboard *Drake* going much faster than boats could, and ready to broach in a following sea, with me at the helm. Then, they both started saying words of reassurance that I could not understand but that had the desired effect. I woke ready for what came next, which was the bus to O'Hare.

Chicago's international terminal was a good place to refit. In the three hours before the Amsterdam flight, I called the Berkeley bank that was cashing in my savings bonds, transferred the funds to my checking account, bought a suit and a suitcase to put it in, a turtleneck and spiffy leather jacket to wear on the plane, got my hair trimmed and my beard shaved, and had a T-bone steak and a martini. The security people had to have a small sidebar conference when I showed my passport as ID. "You are this person," they finally said, and let me through. Waiting to board I thought about Kay, and her incomprehensible words of reassurance in my dream. It would be fair to say that the woman was and always had been an enigma to me, maybe more than most women are to most men. Could I love the woman still, when she had . . . had she betrayed me? Recalling the scene through the window in Sausalito made my hands itch to throttle both of them, but at the same time I could imagine her so sure of her own faithfulness that she'd meet Peters, and work for someone whom I despised, blissfully confident that she could work out a last-minute rescue mission at a time and in a manner of her own choosing. The memory through the window was replaced by the Kay who rowed a slab-sided, leaky skiff off the bar at Port San Luis with a thermos and sandwiches, and tied up to a mooring ball in an exposed roadstead to wait for the chance of my arrival. In the face of her courage and complexity all I could think of was Kay as a Wild Animal of Unknown Species, who could save me or eat me for lunch. As they boarded my flight, I remembered an exchange we'd had once. *I'm not sure I'm capable of playing my part in the relationship.* Don't worry, she said. *I'll wind up playing all the parts anyway.*

METAXIS AND Company had reserved a room for me at the Winston Hotel. I'd been in Amsterdam twice before, when the same conference had been held, but it had always been at the Grand, which fronted on the canals with a certain architectural gravitas and historical charm. The Winston Hotel proudly announced itself as a two-star, but the first to offer specially designed artrooms and, it added helpfully, immediate access to the red light district, within convenient walking distance. Metaxis: when I saw the room I had a deep and unsettling insight into the character

143

of the man I was beginning to regard as my own private government agent. It was small, stark, with meticulously replicated fifties-type motel furnishings, painted in shades of grey (an artistic statement called the Greygarden room), implacable, existential grey. I could almost hear Metaxis say 'might as well have some Amsterdam fun while messing around with murderous arsonists and academics,' but stopped short of imagining him here with a pair of seriously saucy Dutch prostitutes. When I checked in, I thought to ask if a Mr. Metaxis was due anytime soon. He was due the following day.

I'd arrived the evening before the conference started, too jet-lagged to sleep; and when I'd changed into my suit, I took a tram from Central Station through streets with unpronounceable names and walked across the bridge from Dam Square. It was raining, a typical northern European, fine-grained, world weary rain that felt like it had persisted since the East India Company sent its ships lumbering down these same canals. These were the color of prune juice under the streetlamps, mildly disagreeable as canals go. But I knew Amsterdam, and in spite of its tendency toward urban decay, I liked it. At night it is not defined by rain or anything else. I had a carafe of Syrah and a fondue in a café and walked toward the Grand, beardless and bold, with a feeling of being on familiar turf. The Grand is in the old Dutch Admiralty building. From the courtyard, looking up to the floodlit tympanum, it was strikingly like the Willems Institute in proportion and design, but on a massive scale. Where the chimneys rose in the institute, the Grand had floodlit weathervanes in the form of gilded ships, swinging in the wind and dripping pearls of water into the night sky.

The conference was a yearly gathering of the gracefully named "Society of Euro-American Historical Archaeology." My fellow professionals from around the world, united by eccentricity, obsession, and poor grooming, wandered about or stood in small groups. No one recognized me without my beard, but I did many of them: Prentice-Smythe from Trinity College, Dublin,

144

shaved head and ascot. Louise Brigham from Duke, an expert on textiles and the tiny animals that eat them, stirring a drink with her finger and talking to a sturdy looking Dutchman I remembered as an authority on sixteenth-century canon. As much as I found the company comfortable and comforting, I enjoyed the anonymity. I signed in, but pocketed my name tag. There was a message from Brian Haggerty saying if I got in tonight to look for him in the bar.

I found him holding down half a plush beige sofa, spilling crumbs of some kind from his hand onto one of the Arkedan rugs. They were of reds and blues that glowed like jewels, and gave the lobby the feeling of a mosque for rich sheikhs, who also liked an occasional brandy. There was no bullshit from Brian this time. He was not falsely contrite or sardonic, and lacked his usual perpetual attitude of being ready for prime time. He was all by himself, defined only by an expression of slight wariness that had apparently kept people away: Brian normally worked a room like a politician. When he saw me it changed to relief, after a momentary hesitation for drawing facial hair on the person that approached him. "Jesus, Mary and Joseph. Am I glad to see you. Where have you been?"

"I left Berkeley the morning after the fire. I went to talk to McNally's widow."

"Did you call Kay?"

"I left a message for her just before I left."

He rubbed his eyes. "What the fuck. Tell me it's over."

I thought long and hard before answering. I trusted Brian, but not his judgment. "It's over. The Drake Logbooks burned in the fire."

"Are you sure? Did you see them?"

"Just a glimpse. The parchment wrapper with Drake's seal."

He was silent for a long time, grieving a historian's grief. Then he sighed. "All right." He ate a peanut, dropping two more on the rug. "I have my explanation of why Manfred Willems was sending money to the Ballentines. Want to hear it?"

"Sure."

"It was to get it out of the country in small amounts before they fled. Sound good?" I nodded. "Then, collection impounded. Then, the families dicker for a generation about the price of the logs. Problem is, the Willems don't know where the logbooks are, maybe something happened while the books were locked up, and for the past ten years, anyway, they've been hiring people to look for them. How did you find them?"

"I found an old picture of the institute that didn't have the dormer. It was hidden in a welded tin box behind the wall under the window."

"And now it's over. Sean actually called me the day you left and apologized for all his shenanigans. They're planning to release the real plate from storage sometime in the spring. He wants me to write this up as a sort of *da Vinci Code* kind of true-life drama. The cruel passions and greed of two generations, and in the end it all comes down to old wiring and a house with a humidifier but no sprinklers. You should really write this, obviously, but I've got better access to the Bs. So why don't we co-write?"

The old Brian had returned. "Sure," I said.

"And, let's get you and my cousin back on the same boat. Kay quit the Ballentines, you know. She's applied for an instructor's job at Boalt." Boalt was UC's law school. "Promise me you'll call her again. She didn't sleep with Peter Peckerhead."

"I'll call her. I just can't think of what to say."

"She almost came, you know. Here. I told her to give you time and space and credit for knowing you had something special in her. Is that true, by the way? Me, I can't imagine being married to her. She's my crazy wife on steroids."

"I'll call her."

"Good. She gave me something for you." He opened his briefcase and removed a manila envelope with my name on it in Kay's hand. "I suppose it's personal," he said. When I took it but said nothing he added: "Then again, maybe not. She said it was an unintended gift from the Ballentines. Which if I

146

know my cousin means she took it without asking, and my guess is that she sent it as a peace offering. Any idea what's in there?"

"No. Not a clue."

"Well, let me warn you, I just can't take many more late night phone calls from the O'Toole side of the family." He ate the rest of his peanuts, drained his scotch and began chewing on his ice cubes. He took a conference program out of his pocket and put on his reading glasses. "By the way, why did you go visit the widow McNally?"

"I don't know, really. To pay my respects. Something like that. I was the only one who paid him much attention when he was at State. I had a lot to think about, plenty of time, and a secret desire to cross the northern tier of America in the dead of winter."

"I met him once, I think. Maybe even here at SEAHA." His eyes ran down the page. "What a pathetic bunch of losers we are. Did you see Louise Brigham, still stirring her drink with her finger? Ferocious lesbian, you know. Must be some sort of secret code gesture. Hold up, now."

"What?"

"Check tomorrow, just before lunch."

It was a lecture on some aspect of the business dealings of the Dutch East India Company with their outpost in Batavia, bearing on colonial administration as a function of trade policy. For a moment I wondered how I could ever have been interested in such things. But I was, of course, and even more so when I read the presenter's name. Lucius Willems, Assistant Curator, Antwerp Museum. Had Metaxis known about this? Is this why he sent me the announcement back in January? "Have you ever heard of this guy?"

Brian already had his computer out. "I'm going to google him. Get me another drink, Ethan, and one for yourself on my tab." I went to the bar, got another scotch for Brian, and a Perrier and lemon for me. When I returned, Brian took his glasses off and said: "He's not a published scholar, as far as I know. And he's not a curator, but is chairman of the Board of Directors for the museum."

"Anything else?"

"He is one of the Willems clan whose house burned down last week, that much is clear. And this should tickle you. He's also chairman of a syndicate to promote a Dutch challenge to the America's Cup."

"A wealthy young heir to the family fortune with time on his hands, is what it looks like to me."

"Coincidence?"

"I don't think so. Someone mailed me the conference program announcement anonymously, just after New Years."

"Why wouldn't he just call you? You were working for him at the time."

"I don't know."

Brian waved a waiter down and asked him if a Mr. Lucius Willems was staying at the hotel. The answer, a few minutes of ice-chewing later, was negative. "This is great. The story isn't over yet."

"No," I said. "It isn't."

I HALF expected to find Herr Willems waiting for me, chatting with Metaxis in the lobby of the Winston. Though it was well past midnight, the lobby was full of people who could not have been Willems or Metaxis. None were over twenty-five, all were conversing in a variety of languages at high volume with no apparent listening going on. After a moment of despair for the future of the European Union, I went upstairs and fell asleep with my clothes on.

When I woke at three AM I ordered coffee and hot milk. You can get anything anytime in Amsterdam. I wrapped my hands around the cup for the warmth, and watched the strange doings at Central Station outside my window until I got the courage to call Kay. She drew a breath. "Hello, Ethan."

148

"Where are you?"

"You go first."

"Amsterdam. At the SEAHA conference."

"Have you talked to Brian?"

"Yes. He threatened to kill me if I didn't . . ."

"Take me back?" This was headed to awkwardness, by my compass. But Kay steered by a different star and went on after a very long pause. "I'm a silly, stupid girl and also an unemployed attorney living out my security deposit in Sausalito. Where did you put our sailboat?"

"Up in the Delta for the winter."

More silence, but it had acquired a character that was mostly timing, like two people chatting while half asleep. "Ethan, I'm sorry about Karen Molina." Somehow, Kay knew. In that moment, though, I wasn't ready to open up to her. I remembered how she seemed to know everything I didn't, realized that I'd been hampered since the beginning of this thing, hobbling through it, without her beside me. "Did you get the envelope?"

"Yes, I've got it right here, but I haven't opened it."

"Well . . . I'll wait."

The contents were about twenty double-space typed pages, clogged with footnotes, entitled "An Assessment of Drake's California Voyage." I read the first paragraph and instantly recognized my father's writing style, not by the text but in the reckless intensity of his footnotes, where for some reason he felt he could write without the discipline of the main text. And if I had any doubt, there was a stamp on the last page EX LIBRIS THOMAS STOREY. However, this had never been published as far as I knew. It was a discussion of the navigational texts of the time, and some of the early narratives which dealt with Drake's crew's small boat trips up narrow passages to determine whether they were rivers or part of the sea. "Where did you get it?"

"Let's just say I thought you had a right to see your own father's work. Was he involved with the institute in any way?"

"Apparently. But not with the Ballentine side of it. Did you read it?"

"Yes. Pretty dry stuff unless you read only the footnotes. I wish I'd met him."

"I do, too."

"I just figured out that it's three-thirty AM there. Why don't you call me after you've gotten some sleep?"

"Kay—"

"Don't say anything, my love. Just that you'll call. I'm in your life for good, Ethan Storey, so just deal with it."

"I'll call," I said. I read the paper three times with a gradually increasing sense of familiarity with what he was saying, and a feeling of getting close, very close to understanding what it really meant.

CHAPTER THIRTEEN

I slept until nearly eleven, local time, and when I left the hotel
the street corners already smelled of French fries and may-
onnaise, a ubiquitous and uniquely Amsterdamian outdoor
snack. This was my breakfast, as I decided to walk all the way
to the Grand. The rain had cleared and the sky was a thread-
bare blue, the air blustery. It was only chilly around the edges
of the wind, when I crossed a canal or negotiated a roundabout,
but the world and its weather still felt more intrusive without
my beard. I walked the cobbled streets and thought about my
father's article. First, why was it never published? It was obvious
that he had access to the logbooks or other supporting information: navigational notes on charts or journals written by Drake's
officers. So he'd begun to organize and make sense of the frag-
ments of history that passed through his hands. It was more
than a temptation for a historian working with primary sources:
not to do so would violate his nature. But on the other hand,
it was not unusual for historians working for private collections
to be restricted from publishing for a time, and he was certainly
legally bound in that sense.

Second, how had it crossed over into Ballentine territory?
A little easier, there. Karen Molina and Adrian Burke had come
to work at the Willems Institute in the early 1990s, a few years
after my father died. I knew from the documents McNally had
sent to Brian that Adrian was already making overtures to the
Ballentines as early as 1993. He might have sent Dad's research
as a kind of teaser. Hell, McNally could have done it. Or, come to
think of it, my father himself.

Third, why had he chosen this particular subject? Drake
was, of course, obsessed by the Strait of Anian. In those days,

the unexplored was only known by the names people called it, and the effect was to make it magical and real. The Kingdom of Prester John. The Fountain of Youth. El Dorado, the City of Gold. All fantasies to us now, but to them worth lives and fortunes in the pursuit because *it was believed they must be there.* I suppose a modern equivalent might be life on other planets. But Drake was no aimless wanderer, no stargazer. He was first and foremost a seaman and a navigator, and if he was going to look for Anian there was a method to his obsession. Sailing the coast of the Pacific Northwest even today needs skill and focus, it being a bleak and unwelcoming expanse of exposed shore, ferocious rivers, shifting sandbars, rain and fog. Any river could be the start of the passage, any bay. Each had to be explored, along with any tributaries. The test was simple enough. You rowed inland in the pinnace until the water changed from salt to fresh, at which point you knew you weren't connected to the Atlantic Ocean. If you tasted the water for, say, a week, and made ten miles a day and the water was still oceanic, you'd certainly be on to something. The issue then became remembering how you got to this point, and how to get back to it with a bigger fleet and earlier in the season. Drake was in a tearing great hurry with winter coming on.

Dad would, of course, have read the logbooks and known that they contained proof that the plate was left along the coast of California. At some point he would have realized, because of his interviews with the family (the Hallowells) of the initial "discoverer" in Point Reyes, that the plate was not only real, but was in the Ballentines' possession, hidden behind the forgery. The original plate could have been found anywhere, come to think about it, and the whole part of the story where Hallowell found it in Point Reyes was probably a complete red herring.

As I entered the Grand and looked up at the admiralty symbols, I knew with a sudden certainty that the plate had been found, or something significant had happened, at the furthest point the explorers had penetrated upriver—the delta of the

Sacramento–San Joaquin rivers that empty into San Francisco Bay. It had been left where the Northwest Passage was believed to be, claiming the land for Queen Elizabeth. Finding that spot was the reason for the paper Dad wrote, and why it had never been published, and why it had been sent to the Ballentines. Thinking about it in this light, it didn't really take the intercession of either Karen or Adrian. Dad might have written it and sent it at the behest of the Willems themselves. For now both families could tie together the logbooks and the place where the plate was found. Now both knew what the other had. And now began at least two decades and two generations of bargaining over the deal.

Lucius Willems, Assistant Curator, Antwerp Museum, was beginning his presentation as I walked into the lecture hall. He was a surprisingly young man, younger than Sean Ballentine, but with an air of the self-contained dignity and the reasonableness of wealthy European academics that comes from not having to compete for tenure. He wore a very well-cut grey suit and had hair the color of the canals, the color of undrinkable coffee. Beyond the elegance there was a sign of softness about him, visible even from the back of the room. He had a very pale complexion and was slightly overweight. If he was a sailor, he just paid for the boat and came along as passenger. Was this the man I was working for? He was introduced by the session chair as grandson of the famous Manfred Willems, the man who had hired my father, whose monographs on medieval tapestries had been published while he was living in America.

This was actually something I didn't know about Manfred, and since Louise Brigham, the lesbian textile specialist from Duke, was handy in the back row, I sat down beside her, went through a moment of the didn't-know-you-without-your-beard, and asked if she knew anything about the middle generation of Willems. Like many historians, she had a phenomenal memory for dates and details, though she probably lost her car keys as often as the rest of us. "I want to listen to this, Dr. Storey," she whispered.

"Just the abstract version is OK."

"Manfred's son Kurt was killed in 1990. A break-in at his home, I believe. Never published, and neither has Lucius."

So Lucius was the last of the clan; the man for whom I'd been working. It seemed odd, I suppose, that he hadn't looked me up; I'd been pre-registered since December. Especially after the fire. But then, I hadn't looked for him either, and I wasn't staying in a place where academics lodged. I was not particularly interested in Dutch East India Company trade policy, so I glanced around to see who else was there. Brian, of course, toward the front. I saw George Metaxis helping himself to pastry. Our eyes met, but there was no information exchanged. A few more people I knew. Willems stuck to his twenty minutes in a professional manner and took few questions. This was the last paper before lunch, and as he made his way through the crowd toward the back of the room I was able to follow him outside, where a car, a black BMW, was waiting. On impulse I did what Kay might have done in this situation: I flagged a cab and asked the driver in English, German, and French to follow him. "I guess you're serious, then," he said in perfect English and with no hint of surprise. Amsterdam cabdrivers have seen it all.

Just outside the city the canals became healthier, an oceanic blue that rippled in the wind, set between banks of rushes or plowed fields. They now seemed the substance of the landscape, with the road and buildings the afterthought. There was just enough traffic—mostly buses and light trucks—to make it unlikely we were detected; but I was not stalking the man, I just wanted to talk to him. When his driver pulled to a stop on a side road, I had the cab stop at the corner. I sat for a few minutes, rehearsing what I might say. Then I asked the driver to wait so I wouldn't get stranded, pulled up my collar against the chill and followed, but only for a few steps. The side road went directly down to the canal, where there were a few leafless plane trees and a landing which ran along the canal edge for fifty yards or so. The BMW had dropped him and gone, but there was a Porsche Boxter parked on the gravel. There were three or four barges there, but not much doubt about where Lucius Willems had gone. The barge last in line was a broad old lady of the canals, refinished in brightwork so well varnished it glowed like a piece of fine furniture. She was double ended with a fine cutaway, and though the vessel had been built as a barge, she was a sailboat, with a mast and a gaff rigged sail tightly furled. Right now it was all in a neat bundle ready to set, but the mast and spars could be pivoted to the horizontal on what low-bridge sailors call a tabernacle. As I watched and thought about what I wanted to accomplish here, two men left the cabin. One was carrying an empty canvas bag, as if he'd just delivered something. My breath caught in my throat when I made the figure out, by its reddish blond hair, to be a rather poorly dressed version of Sean Ballentine. The other looked like someone else I knew, but at this distance and bundled against the cold, I couldn't be sure.

He looked like Adrian Burke.

I hopped back into the cab and asked the driver to take me back to the Grand. "That's it?" he asked. "End of the line?"

"No," I said. "Beginning of the end, maybe."

THE LUNCHEON meeting on "Renaissance Inks and Writing Implements" was just coming to its conclusion. Brian was there, spilling out of the dining room with the rest of them. I had a moment of feeling estranged from them all, as if I was no longer a member of the tribe, no longer a student of the past. Brian came up to me and said, "Where'd you go? There was a note for you on the bulletin board." He handed me a folded piece of notecard with a Dürer engraving, the one with the rabbit, on the outside. "Lucius Willems is sending a car for you after the session today."

That's what it said. "You read the note?"

He seemed offended. "Why not?"

I thought of a use for his implacable nosiness. "Could you do me a favor?"

"Sure, if you tell me where you went."

"Later. For the present could you call around to the conference hotels and see if a man named Adrian Burke is registered?"

"The other guy working at the institute. OK. But just tell me this." He wrestled with his question, then gave up and just asked: "This is still going on, isn't it?"

"Brian, the fire at the institute was arson. The arsonist is here in Amsterdam, I think."

"Fucking no way."

"Get a grip, Brian. You're playing a part in Act Two. I'll be over at the business center."

He swallowed a question and darted away toward the registration desk. Willems was sending a car for me at four, when the session ended for the day. That gave me about ninety minutes. I debated calling someone. But after websurfing the year 1990 with the hotel's computer, I instead sent an e-mail to myself, Metaxis, Brian, and Kay with the following message:

Based on what I've found in Amsterdam, I believe that both the Willems and the Ballentine families wanted the logbooks destroyed. Both my father and Lucius Willems' father died in the same year, 1990, and everything that has transpired since has been a conspiracy between Lucius Willems and Sean Ballentine to find them. They continued the feud as a sham, largely to keep the collection and the institute itself from any kind of public scrutiny. My father had been the last person to know their whereabouts, once Manfred had died, and I was the obvious person to know what he knew. I believe he removed them from an older hiding place in the institute building to another spot, possibly to protect them,

himself and me. He never told me anything about any
of this.

I thought, but didn't add, that he'd left me a clue.

Brian stuck his head in the door of the computer cubicle and said that Adrian Burke was registered at the Royal Dutch, as well as at the conference, and to let me know there was a driver asking for me at the front desk. "Brian, if I don't call you in two hours, ring this number," I gave him the one Parsons had given me in Illinois. "And get a message to George Metaxis that I haven't checked in yet from a meeting with Lucius Willems. I expect we'll be on his boat. Also try to get a message to Metaxis here. He's at the conference and staying at the Winston."

"Anything else?"

"Check your e-mail."

I bought a scarf in the hotel shop against the deepening chill, checked for phone, wallet, passport, and money, couldn't think of anything else that would do me any good, and walked with the driver through the courtyard to the waiting vehicle.

They'd moved the barge. It was another half hour farther away in the opposite direction, toward the port. On a previous trip to Amsterdam, I'd thought about a canal voyage with Kay on a rented barge someday, and I could guess generally where we were headed. From near Central Station, you could take a boat that drew less than nine feet all the way to the Port of Amsterdam without dropping your mast. The port itself was the usual modern mess of container facilities, bunkers, and commercial berths, but there was a marina near where the harbor gave way to the North Sea Canal.

The driver introduced himself. He was an elderly man who had worked for the Willems for many years, and when I told him my name, he said: "Excuse me, sir, but I think I knew your father."

"Were you ever in the States?"

"No, it was usually in Antwerp or Luxembourg. Not often, but I remember him well. He died, did I not hear?"

"The same year as Kurt Willems."

"And now you are visiting the son."

We wound our way through a rain forest of container loading cranes. They were all working, though it was nearly dark by now. Their lights, swinging overhead, made the shadows of trucks and rail cars undulate, and the industrial landscape seem inhabited by spirits, or running on speeded-up film. The car was soon through it.

The Dutch don't seem to care for big things, and when we left the harbor and turned onto the marina grounds, everything returned abruptly to human scale, with tidy cottages and patient perennial gardens waiting for spring. It was curious to think of marina developers recreating a Dutch village in Holland, the way Californians did Cape Cod, but that's what they'd done. It only lacked a windmill. The slips were the treated concrete favored in Europe, about half full, and the dock area was flooded with acid-blue lights like a prison yard. But at the far end by the seawall, and nearest the fairway leading to the North Sea, a gated private dock had been constructed in wood and was lit with gaslights. There were only three yachts: two obscenely tarted-up cruisers that looked like small ocean liners, and the barge, named the *Essa* I saw now, tied off at the far end. We drove all the way up to the boat and a little carpeted stairway leading aboard. I thanked the driver and he smiled in return.

There was a tiny businesslike cockpit, with a wheel and an open companionway through which I could see someone moving below. I knocked on the cabin top. "Dr. Willems?"

His face appeared at the bottom of the companionway ladder. Up close, Lucius Willems looked smarter and tougher. His hair was receding front to back, in the manner of people who are clever enough not to care much about it. He'd changed from his suit, and what I'd taken for a certain chubbiness looked more like the compactness of a middleweight. But most of all his face gave him away: grim and set, skin tight rather than smooth, almost devoid of expression, but simply and unthreateningly strong. "Permission to come aboard?" I asked.

He regarded me with no emotion I could decode. "But of course," he said.

In five steps down the companionway ladder, I entered the world according to Willems, an extraordinary little salon filled with pale light and the most exquisite furnishings. The bulkheads and overheads were painted a muted yellow, the deck beams white. To port there was a table spread with starched linen, a silver warming tray over a soft yellow flame, a breadboard with the blackest of black breads, tubs of butter and what looked like herring. To starboard was a leather couch and chair, and a keyboard on a pedestal. Almost every vertical surface held a painting or a small framed piece of tapestry, each with its own tiny pinlight. It had the same aura of elegance and intellect that the institute had, money in the service of mind. Willems was dressed in comfortably baggy grey wool slacks and a sweater. After we shook hands, he went to a small cupboard forward, took out a glass and decanter, and held them up for my inspection. "Jim Beam?"

"My father's drink," I said. "Did you meet him? Your driver did."

"Only once. I wasn't born when he visited us regularly, but I certainly knew who he was, as I do you." He poured a shot into the amber cut-glass tumbler and handed it to me. He put the decanter away and poured himself a glass of wine from an open bottle on the table, then moved to the couch and gestured for me to sit. A second gesture, paired with a nod, took in the boat. "What do you think?"

"A *volksbarge*? Not Dutch built but Swedish, I think, early twentieth century."

He nodded approvingly. "I'm a terribly spoiled man in many ways, and what I could call luxury yachting is one demonstration of that. Let me tell you about the boat, since you're a sailor yourself. Eighty years old, double planked with English oak a full eight centimeters thick. Custom built for my grandfather. I daresay your father sat where you're sitting a number of times. The leeboards are mechanical now, but it still can swim in just a foot or two of water. Rolls Royce diesels for which we would have to have parts made if they broke down, but they never do. Sails like a ship on tranquilizers, but speed is only appropriate to certain things. Did you notice the name?

"*Essa?*"

"No, that's our port of registry. The *Golden Hinde* is her name. Drake's flagship. Let's do some small business things and then a little light meal, yes?"

He handed me an envelope. Inside was a cashier's check issued by the Bank of the Netherlands made out to me for $50,000. The message was obvious. "You may have overpaid me for a job I never finished," I said.

"You've been through more than . . . I expected you would. Also, much of the collection made it to the Canadian storage facility before the fire, along with your electronic archives. It's still a very valuable collection and, of course, now completely archived. May I?" He stood and went to the table for large, delicate bowls in the same pattern as the ones Kay had admired at the institute last fall, when we first walked in the door, a million years ago. He served bowls of soup from the chafing dish. It was onion soup with a thick layer of gruyère cheese. He passed me a bowl and a slice of black bread. I was surprisingly hungry for a man in my position, so close to knowing the answer to everything, so close to being the only one who did. "At your leisure, might you say what you thought of the collection? As a historian, I mean."

"You know my father never spoke to me about the work he did for your grandfather?"

He just looked at me in response, signaling a skepticism we might as well both acknowledge up front. "So I came to the work without preconceptions." No point in not being honest, but I wouldn't belabor the point since he wouldn't believe much I said on this subject. "It struck me as curiously random, even given how it arrived in the States and the loss of the original archives. There was enough nautical material, mostly nineteenth-century coast pilot stuff, to make me curious about other hobbies your grandfather may have had. And there was a chronological gap in the collection around the latter half of the sixteenth century. Some portion had been surgically removed. I knew the story about the loss of half the library on the Atlantic crossing, but this seemed an odd chunk to be missing, with volumes both before and after on the same shelves.

"Then the novels in the north wing of the house. It was simply not scholarly. I came away with an impression of a wealthy dilettante who had all of his pleasures on the same level with no compartments. A man not unlike my father, except for the wealth part. A man for whom passion is equal to intellect, albeit in a man otherwise disciplined."

He ate a few spoonfuls before answering. "Well put, Ethan, if I may call you that."

"Now, will you tell me what's going on?"

"Sean Ballentine told me you'd been doing some extracurricular investigating. If I promise to fill in all the gaps and correct your mistakes, will you tell me what *you* think is going on?"

"The Ballentines found the plate in the thirties. I'm not sure how, but they knew the supporting documents, Drake's Logbooks, were in your collection. They created a fake plate and a fake site of discovery, which they wanted deliberately exposed to keep other scholars disinterested. They were very successful. It's been a favorite of pseudo-historians ever since. There hasn't been a doctoral thesis on Drake at either Berkeley or my university since that time. There were payments from your grandfather to the Ballentines just before he came over, and that didn't make much sense, though perhaps he was trying to get cash out of Europe any way he could. After the war, when the documents were released from government control, my father was hired in

161

a professional capacity to keep the Ballentines at arms length and organize the collection in some way; and I believe one of the things he organized was concealing the logbooks in an architectural detail, a dormer, when the building was renovated in the 1950s or 60s." Lucius was taking detailed notes between sips of wine. "How am I doing?"

"Pause and eat. Your soup is cold." He rose and poured my soup back into the chafing dish, stirred it, and ladled out a hot portion. These were not, I reflected, the actions of a man who intended to tear my fingernails out tonight. "You are correct. You may be wondering why we never just sold them the documents at some point, at any point, in the next forty years." He paused. "Have you any hypothesis?"

"Well, I know that that my father visited the man who supposedly found the plate, and that might have been to keep him from saying anything by showering money on his family. At that point, he must have become a sort of confidant to Manfred and a go-between with the Ballentines."

"They became friends, of a sort, yes. But I think your father was . . . luxuriating in the collection and in no hurry himself. He was the only one; it was his private library. Of course, that still doesn't answer the basic question."

"Do you know?"

"Yes, I do." He finished his wine and crossed the cabin to sit on the leather settee. I turned to face him and waited. He closed his eyes for a moment, then said: "My grandfather was a Nazi sympathizer. There were certain experiments then being conducted in a laboratory, a particle accelerator financed by the Ballentine family, and he was approached by a German physicist at the same time the Ballentines came looking for the Drake papers. I'm not sure of the details, but I know that a condition of the exchange was not really monetary, and involved access to some research papers before they were published, and some that were not published at all. Sean Ballentine, Senior and Manfred were, to put it simply, spies. One the agent and the other the master.

162

Manfred was allowed to flee Belgium essentially as a ruse by the occupiers. The American government suspected something, but could not find anything incriminating, and of course, the subsequent longstanding estrangement of the families helped cover things up.

"But the relationship continued through the war. When Germany surrendered, it came to an end, of course, and the collection was technically released from impoundment. But by that time, the relationship had essentially changed."

"How so?"

"The Willems were impoverished after the war, when Manfred returned to Antwerp. He demanded a stipend from the Ballentines, grant after grant, year after year, secure in the knowledge that he had both the Drake documents and proof that one of the great California families had tried to give the Third Reich the secrets to the atomic bomb. He blackmailed Sean Sr., and now the money flowed the other way. Your father knew nothing about this. But both families trusted him; he acted in a very private capacity; he was well paid. He had almost forty years to come and go freely at the institute and probably had every expectation of being able to publish, eventually, when the deal for the Drake Logbooks was finally struck."

"Go on."

"My father Kurt told me all of this at a time when we were back on our feet with our ill-gotten money and my father's hard work. He was a banker; the history gene came out again in me. He told me all of this right here on the *Hinde* and that we didn't need our American benefactors any more. He told me he was ashamed, and that the collection was mine to do with as I pleased, and even if I wanted to finally sell the logbooks I could.

"Of course, I wanted the discovery, not the money. The luxury of our generation, I suppose. I went to the States in 1986 and explored the collection for myself. I did not find the logbooks of Sir Francis Drake. I visited a professor named Thomas

Storey in San Francisco who I knew had played some curatorial role for us, though the collection, the institute itself, had been in the hands of a management company for many years at that point. He said he had helped Manfred out many years before."

"What else did he say?"

"Nothing, really. We talked of boats, I recall, and I had my first taste of Jim Beam. I returned to Belgium, and after your father died I began to employ a series of professional historians, the most recent of whom is yourself."

"How did you get my name?"

"As it was explained to me by the woman who died so tragically, you simply happened by one day."

"Did you think I knew where the logbooks were?"

"I still do, though it hardly explains your straightforward hard work right up until the fire. In your position, knowing what I thought you knew, I would have waited around for a week, gone to the cupboard and shouted 'Eureka!'"

"Were you actually considering selling the collection?"

"Yes, though not to the Ballentines. I was hoping to offer it to the University of Antwerp, where it would no longer be private and would be returning home." There had to be more, and after a long moment, during which time he stood and poured bourbon into his wineglass, he said, "I had visitors this afternoon. Sean Ballentine the Younger and Adrian Burke, who was working alongside you at the institute, technically my employee."

"Had you met either of them before?"

"Ballentine, never. My father and I spent our lives trying to forget the Ballentines, both generations. Adrian, I had talked to by phone. He never called after the wall was opened, or since. I think I know why. I think he told Ballentine that the logbooks had been found."

"And Ballentine burned the building down."

"Yes."

I was wrong in what I'd e-mailed earlier. It was all Ballentine, all of it. "Why, for God's sake?"

164

"I assume he thought the logbooks were about to be dis-covered and wanted them destroyed. He knew he would never have them from me. I have never responded to any of his enqui-ries." His composure was intact, but he drank in the manner of someone about to lose some of it. "I must tell you the rest. I must tell you what Ballentine believes to be true. After the fire, immediately after the fire, he knew that the container you found was empty. I suspect my attorney. He knows that your father was involved with the families for many years. He knows that the original hiding place was known only to your father and Manfred. He has concluded that the only one who could have moved the contents is your father, and that you know where they are now."

"What did he want from you?"

He waved his glass around. "This, this meeting, some money from me to you, a quiet meal. He wanted me to find out. He thought your father's allegiance to my grandfather might be the key. He thought you had come to Amsterdam to tell me."

"He knows I'm here?" In all my quiet life, I had never known real physical fear until that moment.

"Not exactly. I moved *Hinde* this afternoon. Dr. Storey, Ethan, if you know you must tell me."

"I don't know."

"Then talk to him. This is a dangerous man, I think, but he can be persuaded, surely. This bitterness cannot lead to violence. The fire was just a tragedy. They didn't know Karen Molina was there. There can be no threat of physical harm to you, can there, if you negotiate?" *That's what killed McNally*, I thought.

My phone went off, and I stepped into the cockpit. It was Metaxis. "Wherever you are, they know it." At the far end of the pier, two cars were approaching. Their headlights were out and they were moving slowly. "Get out of there and meet me in front of the U.S. Embassy."

Underfoot, the Rolls Royce diesels throbbed to life. Lucius Willems was by my side, then past me, untying the dock lines. "It might be a while," I said to Metaxis.

165

"I'll wait," Metaxis answered. "Better yet, keep your phone on. We'll find you." The progress of the monster barge was slow. Which was good in a way, because for a while they didn't know what was happening. Then the lights came on and they surged forward, and I thought an agile man might just be able to jump aboard, but they were too late. Not out of earshot, though. Lucius, still the rational man, called out: "HE KNOWS NOTHING!" at the top of his voice.

But I'd lied to Lucius. I did know.

CHAPTER FOURTEEN

Willems called a taxicab from his cell, and when we eased into the fuel docks on the other side of the fairway it was waiting for me. In the twenty minutes getting across the harbor we passed under the bow of a bulk freighter, so that it would have been hard to tell from our point of departure exactly where we were landing; not only that, but a fog sidled in from the North Sea and was so thick by the time I stepped off, that the cab was barely visible and had to flash its lights to get my attention. Willems said only: "Please be careful. I doubt we'll meet again." We shook hands, each unsure whether the other was friend or foe or something else, both bound by decency and a sense of finality. I watched him for a moment, backing the dignified old craft away from the pier and into the mist. All very film noirish, and it was about to get more so. When Willems had asked where I would be going, as if the cab company had put that question to him over the phone, I told him the American Embassy. But after I'd settled in the back seat, I checked that my passport was in my briefcase and as the cab moved off I said, "Schiphol Airport," and when we got there I left my cell phone on the seat.

There was a flight to San Francisco with a stop in New York, and, as an uncrowded KLM red-eye, all it took was money to get on it. Before I boarded, I visited the bookstore and found a guide to San Francisco that had a large, foldout map of the Bay area. The aircraft pressed me back, rising into the night sky. I was a free agent again: I didn't want anyone to know what I was up to, not even Kay. During the first half of the flight, I took Dad's article and spread it out on the tray table for the unoccupied middle seat, got a blank yellow legal pad from my briefcase and made a crude compass rose on it. If Drake's lieutenants had started from the Golden Gate, the *Golden Hinde* would have had to anchor somewhere in Richardson's Bay, now Sausalito, where there was some protection from the northwest wind, water of a reasonable depth and decent holding ground. I recalled that some historians, engaged in similar efforts, applied a correction to old compass courses to correct for changes in the magnetic field (and hence magnetic north), something on the order of fifteen degrees, but I couldn't recall whether it was east or west. Using the compass rose and the narrative's description of distance traveled, I began plotting their course, one with an easterly correction, one westerly, on separate sheets of paper, starting from just inside the Golden Gate on the north side. For the length of the lines I used their time measurements (variously a day or half day, or occasionally the length of a tidal cycle), and multiplied this times an average speed of about three knots. Having used the same scale on the paper as the map from the guidebook, I could then hold the map with the yellow course plotting sheet superimposed on it up to the reading light and see them both at once.

One sheet put me squarely in a part of Solano County now covered with wind farms where the sea never went, the other where I knew it did. Given the right tidal moment, a mariner arriving at that point would still find the water to be salty, and Drake's men believed they'd found the Strait of Anian. They were in fact at the lower end of the delta of the Sacramento and San Joaquin rivers, and though a future adventurer might travel on in the hope of finding eastern Canada in a while, they'd ground out on the gravelly flats and willow groves of the Sierra Nevada foothills. Gold they might have found, but not the Northwest Passage. Returning to Drake and claiming success, the captain would exit the Gate and find the best spot nearest the entrance to careen his ship and stake his claim for the Queen: Drake's Bay.

I didn't stay on board for the second half of the flight. I got off in New York, had my passport stamped, and boarded a domestic flight to Portland, Oregon. I slept on that leg, but never deeply, and thought off and on about my mother. I never knew her. She'd died of leukemia in the house in Alamo when I was two. There were pictures of her, three of which had made the transition to the boat when I sold the house: one at the wedding, she looking shy and pleased, the professor in the uniform of an army captain, nonetheless besotted. Another of the three of us: Mom now wan and sickly, but still with a luminous expression, now directed to me; Dad more dignified. My expression is best described as oblivious, a term which suited me still. The last was a picture of Mom breaking a bottle of champagne on the bow of a small skiff he'd built for her. There were no girlfriends for my father after she died, at least none that I was aware of. Of course, he'd managed to hide his connection to the Willems for most of my life, and all of his. He spoke of her very rarely, and at an early age I stopped asking about her. But as with everything, his silences meant a lot, for the few times he began a sentence with *your mother and I* . . . he would look at me obliquely as if searching for her in me, and his confused, inarticulate loving for us both flashed bright and brief as a strobe.

Portland was rainy and grim and I moved, jet-lagged, through airport business like an automaton. But when I'd rented a car and made my way down the Willamette Valley, the open landscapes of the Northwest purged me of Amsterdam, the Willems, and the Ballentines, the FBI and the NYPD. Even of Kay and Brian, and what I would be putting them through. When I was back in California, on I-5 following the Shasta River south, the sun came out. The profile of Mount Shasta was covered with an antiseptically white marble of new snow against a blue sky that was almost black by comparison; I was restored in my resolve. It was five more hours to Sacramento, where I turned the car in at the airport, shuttled into town and picked up the Amtrak train to San Francisco, disembarking in Martinez and reversing direction by bus out to Antioch. A cab took me the rest of the way to Eddo's Landing. It seemed improbable that anyone could track my movements any farther than the rental drop-off in Sacramento. And unless Willems had tricked me into swallowing a transmitter, abandoning the cell phone in Europe had ended any chance of remotely finding me this far off the grid. Nobody knew that I had food, shelter, clean clothes, cash, Jim Beam, a twelve-gauge shotgun, and transportation to the ends of the earth hidden in the depths of the Delta. Unless, of course, the boat had been stolen.

I rescued my dinghy from behind the dumpster, filled the tank for the outboard and had coffee at the café. It was twilight before I started out on the water, in a deep, still calm between the ranks of the giant reeds. It had been a heavy rain year, and the channels smelled of musk, and the sharp, flat scent of the granitic sediments that wash down from the mountains on their way to California's beaches. As long as there were navigation marks, most of which were lit, I was moving along well. Although I'd found Dad's hideaway in the dark the last time, at water level and without the *Drake*'s navigation systems, it was like trying to find a book in an unlit library. I was prepared for it to be troublesome, even to stay out until dawn if I had to, and I just poked into every slough that seemed promising, trying to keep track only of where I'd already turned off main and into side channels so I wouldn't go round in circles. I had a flashlight aboard for just such occasions, Dad's old flashlight from his army days as a matter of fact, restored by me many times as a kind of heirloom. So I didn't have to go all the way to the end of every one. But I had lost count, and the batteries were low, before I thought of killing the outboard and listening. I heard the owls almost immediately, and followed the sound with an increasing optimism. There were not that many places with enough high ground to support owl-bearing oak trees, and at three in the morning, *Drake* showed her varnished stern in the light from the torch, just before it went black.

I tied off the dink, pulled myself up her topsides and looked around in the light of a quarter moon. Stem to stern: a mourning dove had started an early nest on the bowsprit; there was a pile of raccoon droppings at the base of the foremast; the after spring line had chaffed itself through, so we were likely aground; the raccoon himself was aboard, washing a fish in water pooled over the cockpit drains, which had been blocked by oak leaves. He just looked up at me in a raccoonish way and went back to his business. The Contra Costa County Department of Waterways had labeled me an abandoned vessel, so said a faded yellow notice tacked to the taffrail. Below, the battery monitor lights blinked a low voltage warning, and before turning anything else on I started the engine, its sound enough of an annoyance to send the raccoon over the side. I lit all the kerosene lamps, then sat on the companionway steps for five minutes, letting the boat settle around me. The pumps cycled, but didn't run for long. Only rainwater in the bilge. The cabin smelled faintly of old boat and old man.

When the electricity and propane were back on, I scavenged for dinner. Without getting into the deep stores, which I'd have to do tomorrow, I found a can of black beans and one of crushed tomato, combined them in a saucepan and added a teaspoon of dried coriander. Some Triscuits in a sealed plastic bag were OK, and I could scrape the mold off a wedge of cheddar. With a stiff Jim Beam and Vivaldi on the stereo, I was home. By the time I'd eaten there was hot water, and there was also enough battery juice restored to shut the engine down. I aired the bunk sheets, showered frugally and climbed in. I was exhausted and comfortable, but I could not settle. I kept thinking about the photos of my mother that had come unbidden into my thoughts on the flight. At length I got up, turned the lights on and looked at each in turn. Funny thing about old photos on the wall. Become blind to them through perpetual presence, and rediscover them some other day. I was as emotionally touched as if I'd never seen them. In this moment of clarity, I noted the patch on Dad's uniform sleeve in the wedding picture. He always said he'd worked as a quartermaster in the Pacific. Nothing to tell, really:

a bout of dengue fever and he was invalided home after a year. The patch was quite clear, crossed lighting bolts over a Roman numeral two.

Being back in my world also meant that I had access to the rest of it. I turned on the computer and woke up the satellite link. Then I made a pot of tea, and found a website that displayed the U.S. Army uniform patches of World War II. My father, I learned long after the tea had gone cold, had been a captain in G-2, military intelligence. Then, I slept. Right out of my jet lag, right past high noon, and only woke when the sun blasted down through the skylight. I was sore down my right side from having slept there without moving, and the rest of me was stiff from airplane seats and long drives. Nonetheless, it felt a little like Christmas morning; I had only, now, to unwrap my present. The one from my father.

First, some tools. The oars from the dinghy were unsuitable for my purpose, but a spare grounding plate the size of a thin paperback book—oval in shape, and tack welded to an old, galvanized keel bolt—gave me a perfect hand shovel. I removed the grill from the skylight. It was quarter inch steel mesh designed to keep pirates from boarding when the glass was opened. It would do duty as a screen for the soil; I was leaving nothing to chance on this excavation. Then, I dealt with the boat, since I wouldn't have another suitable tide for twelve hours. Put simply, I had to manually turn the *Drake* around, because the boat was an unpredictable beast in reverse gear and getting out of the narrow passage that way would be a series of groundings. I replaced the line that had parted, and rigged a cable between the cockpit winches and the shore. The winches were massive bronze drums eight inches in diameter, oversized even for a vessel of *Drake's* displacement, and could probably pick up the entire ship, though they'd rip out of the deck first. The line ran from the stern of the boat to a tree forward of the bow on the opposite shore, so when

I cranked her off the mud the stern came free, but the boat was still partially aground up front. Having gone this far, I decided to complete the necessary turning maneuver before accomplishing my primary mission; so with the boat diagonally across the slough, I repositioned the line on shore and pulled her all the way around, pivoting on the stationary bow. Finally, almost an hour later, the cable, now set on the anchor winch at the bow, pulled us into deep water and pointed us in the right direction. I was bathed in sweat by this point, though the day was cool and cloudy. I needed a break.

Dad, though never a true mariner in the cross-the-Pacific sense, was always prepared to do so. There were plenty of vacuum-sealed day ration packs, with everything from beef stew to apple cobbler, and he renewed everything periodically. It was kind of a hobby; we'd regularly eat these on our short cruises when we could just as easily have had fresh food. Some of the stuff I was looking at was from the late 1980s and in very heavy vacuum pouches, in turn within other pouches, each of which contained three meals for two people. I'd never brought myself to throw them away, even when Kay tried to get me to do so. But they were fine, as far as I could tell; and the one I opened, pea soup with chunks of ham, laced with a good port wine, made the cabin smell like a bistro. There was even a small pouch of pipe tobacco. When I had eaten the soup, I sat in the cockpit smoking his meerschaum and, waiting for food poisoning. But after I finished the pipe, I only felt nourished and ready for what came next.

I rowed ashore with my shovel, my screen, and a bottle of water. The oak tree and his old fishing lure were still there as they always had been. I took a few photographs of the site and then I sat cross-legged directly beneath the lure and began to dig. The topsoil was surprisingly dry and screened easily. This part was just a reconstruction of the hole itself, not its contents. I did not expect to find anything in the top layers unless it had been dug up, disturbed by the movement of the earth, or come

173

apart in pieces. In the top foot, there was a quarter and a fork and a tangle of fishing line. I kept the hole about two feet on a side, so there was plenty of digging to do. I was only eighteen inches down when I began to lose the light. I went back aboard for the kerosene lamp and another bottle of water. More discoveries: a key to our storage locker in San Rafael, I thought, and a foil package wrapping. Then nothing until I hit it: solid, flat and level. About the size of a cooler, I thought as I dug around it; then I realized to my astonishment that it *was* a cooler, not something in welded stainless steel; and when I pulled it free, I found that it was red with a San Francisco 49ers logo. I knew this cooler better than I knew the locker key. Dad and his faculty friends were always tailgating before games, the only social function he ever hosted.

But I was not nostalgic: I was excited to the point of nausea. My father had found this spot based on the directions provided either in Drake's Logs or those of his officers, and revealed in the article on the upstream expedition that he wrote but never published. He'd moved the materials from the institute, sometime in the late 1970s, and re-excavated it a couple of times to make sure it was safe. But the cooler seemed almost irresponsible. It was not airtight and only barely watertight. The seams weren't even reinforced or taped in any way. I was not going to further imperil the contents by opening it up on the shore by the light of a live flame; so I carefully wiped it clean, backfilled the hole and pulled myself along the cable to the boat, where I tied a safety line around the cooler before lifting it aboard. It weighed about thirty pounds and the contents did not rattle or shift.

I didn't have enough light below decks for photography, and I debated waiting for morning for about ten seconds before deciding that this wasn't a historical moment as much as it was an intensely personal one. So I set it on the salon table and opened it. There was an internal cover or plate pressed down upon the actual contents, a plastic panel glued solidly all around.

I'd have to cut it free. I got the box cutter out of the tool drawer and set the blade for only a tiny increment of depth. Tracing and retracing a line around the sides got me through this without going deeper than necessary, but I didn't lift until it was entirely free and could be removed all at once. I readjusted the lights, mopped my sweaty face with a towel and pulled it free.

The vacuum plastic bags inside were actually bags within bags, but they were just translucent enough for me to sense the contents of the topmost: a volume leather bound and about two inches thick, bound on one side by some type of leather cord, substantially larger than modern logbooks or ledgers. On the outside of the outermost bag was a label in my father's sturdy block capitals:

> BKFST: GNOLA
> LUN: MAC CHEESE
> DIN: ETHAN'S SURPRISE

I sat back on the settee and wept, sobbing into the night with no sense of grief, exactly; just the sense of a terrible, terrible father-shaped hole in my life.

THERE WAS no question of opening the bags. They needed to be in a first-rate university laboratory, preferably under a hood with sterile gloves. They should be scanned and photographed in place before any possible contamination. I was about as tempted, I suppose, as I had been as an adolescent with my first *Playboy*; nothing seemed quite as important as seeing Drake's Logs. But I was not a boy; I was a professional historian pushing sixty and I knew my duty to my craft. I had not thought much beyond this point, in any event. I couldn't imagine just turning in for the night, though I was exhausted. I sat staring at the cooler and waiting for inspiration and eventually it came, a series of thoughts as logical, linear, and satisfying as any I'd had in days.

I had no cell phone, but the radio was working and I called John Davenport at my old marina office, using his amateur radio call sign and a frequency he monitored for offshore networks used by cruising sailors. He was frequently there, harbormastering into the night, a bachelor more at home in his tiny den than anywhere else. He passed along messages, made arrangements for repairs and berthing, and offered advice to the dwindling number of ships at sea that had no satellite phones.

The frequency was quiet except for the background atmospheric noise that sometimes allows you to predict the weather. But good ideas have their own magic and he came back almost immediately to my call. He asked where I was and how I was doing. I told him I was on my way to Baja and that losing my slip was the best thing that had ever happened to me. "Life's funny that way sometimes. What can I do for you?"

"Cell phone problems. Could you call Dr. Brian Haggerty at his home and ask him to call Kay and tell her I'm OK?" He said sure, and I gave him Brian's number. "Then one other thing. Tell him that Dr. Robert McNally will look for him tomorrow noon at the southwest corner of the anchorage for the mothball fleet in Suisun Bay. He'll know the boat to look for."

"McNally, tomorrow noon, the graveyard fleet. Anything else, skipper?"

"Nope."

"Keep going and don't think you have to come back, Ethan."

"Copy that. *Drake* clear and out."

I checked the marine forecast, which was bad enough for me to turn on the weather fax and see for myself. Clouds stacked from the Marin Headlands across to Hawaii. Within the low, the pressure was below anything I'd seen recently. This was an El Niño year, with a dry early fall, turning very damp with violent storms in the spring, and here was one. I didn't want to be in the Delta waterways with a balky fifty foot, full keeled boat. A lee shore and a levee breach could land me in someone's rice field. By the forecast, though, I had just enough time to get to

176

the mothball fleet and down to the bay proper. I could anchor in Paradise Cove off Treasure Island, which was built for the 1938 World's Fair. They'd tacked it to the back of Yerba Buena Island and formed a harbor with good sand and excellent protection from a southerly wind. I thought about calling Kay, but they'd shut down the radiotelephone link last year after losing out to cell phones. It didn't matter; I could row ashore and call from a phone booth—assuming they still had those—and we'd have our reunion in Paradise Cove.

I repacked my own treasure and lay down on the settee behind the table, waking to the sound of a fine rain, swishing the surface of the water like a broom. I started the engine and made coffee. On deck the wind was still westerly, a good sign, and the general conditions were not scary at all. It was about 0800. I changed into my foul weather gear. Allowing myself an extra hour to get to the rendezvous, and not hungry for break-fast, I cast off the lines, cleared the slough and turned south-west, tidying the deck and tying some loose gear down against the blow. In the long straight stretch north of Port Chicago, I pulled out the storm trysail, feeling a bit foolish running hurri-cane canvas up when I could have dropped anchor and rowed to a Starbucks.

The mist and drifting rain changed direction several times by mid-morning. There was a strong ebb tide under me, so I knew we were moving in the right direction; but *Drake* didn't like shallow water under these conditions any more than I did, and she steered like an opinionated quarter horse as I tried to stay in the channel. When it widened and with time to kill, I lashed the helm to turn us in a wide circle while I made a sandwich. I was about to come back on deck when the VHF broke squelch to call my ship. It was Brian Haggerty, on a handheld radio somewhere ahead of me in the mist. Bless him, he was not chatty in this situation; he just gave me his coordinates to enter into my GPS. I did so, and I activated the autopilot to take us there. I picked up the red cooler and climbed the companionway steps.

177

On deck again, I swung the boarding ladder over the side. We were still a couple of miles from Brian, so I had time to contemplate how I'd handle this in a rough and confused chop, with two boats and one of history's most valuable artifacts. In the end I decided the cooler was too bulky for the job. I took the small sail bag which had contained the storm trysail, and which was about the size of an airport carry-on—thick Dacron with a long string closure cord—and put Dad's vacuum-sealed packages inside, along with a life belt to make sure it floated. Then back to the helm. Ten minutes later I saw the stark, businesslike superstructure of a Liberty ship, its slab side faded grey and streaked with rain. Against it in silhouette was Brian and someone else in a Boston whaler. The someone else could only be Kay O'Toole, and my heart sang. She was wearing a ridiculous Gloucester fisherman's hat I'd bought her years ago. We were within hailing distance when the first squall hit and I maneuvered to windward of him as best I could, backing the trysail and effectively stopping the boat so he could come under my lee. He managed this in a seamanlike manner; but from the helm I couldn't quite see him at sea level, and my first sign of success was Kay coming up the ladder with the grace of a cat. She kissed me and took the wheel. I grabbed the bag and leaned over to look down at him. Before I lowered it into his arms I shouted: *"University of Iowa Library, Brian. Go there directly, to Des Moines. Don't talk to anybody till you get there. Just get ashore and go."*

"What do I tell them?"

"A gift from Bob McNally," I said, not shouting now. He heard me well enough.

CHAPTER FIFTEEN

We shared another long kiss while the storm gathered itself around us and *Drake* drifted dangerously close to the WWII transport *Desmond O'Grady* and its dozens of companions, through which the waters of Suisun Bay churned and frothed. I put the engine in gear and took it up to the red line until we were in the main channel. Kay watched Brian's progress through binoculars—the wind had blown the fog away—and said: "He made it ashore. There's a low stone jetty over there and his car was parked above it." She lowered the glasses. "Well, here we are. You did it, no thanks to me."

"My father always used to take us up the Delta in the winter to a spot that had water deep enough and a lot of privacy. It also corresponded to the rough endpoint that Drake's men reached in the search for the passage. There was never any idea that the plate was left there; it was just his sense of . . . irony?" I allowed a little for leeway—the wind's annoying attempt to push us sideways. Before me, Suisun Bay went the color of silly putty with the chop and the mud from the storm as it reached the foothills far behind us. "I wouldn't have known anything, still less when I'd been a teenager fishing for striped bass right next to the logbooks, if you hadn't sent me Dad's article."

"Francis Pretty. I loved that name."

"You read it."

"That and other things. I was Sean Ballentine's property attorney until two weeks ago. I know an awful lot, Ethan. Too much. I know your Dad hid the papers and the older Willems died without telling anybody where. Both families thought he'd done it somewhere in the house."

"Did you ever see the real plate?"

"No. It was mainly depositions from everybody involved in finding the plate and storing it through the years. And building up the other historical sources in the Ballentine Museum into a credible case of ownership and authenticity. Did you get any time with the logbooks?"

"No. Not even a peek. Dad sealed them up in plastic vacuum bags. I was afraid something—oxidation, moisture, mold—would happen if I opened them."

"Bags like he stored the food in?" I nodded. She was silent for a moment, coiling the slack end of the bowstring-taut mainsheet and dropping it neatly over a cleat. "Is it over, do you think?"

"I don't know, Kay. There's a lot more going on than sixteenth-century seafaring paperwork. But after a while we'll just be bit players. Off the main stage."

"Bit players. I sort of like the sound of that. I truly want our old life back."

So did I. "You look soaking wet."

"I am. Did you throw all my clothes away again?"

"No."

She straightened and took a step towards the pilot house and companionway ladder, then turned. "You look younger without your beard, but promise me you'll grow it back."

While she was below, we passed under the Carquinez Bridge and into the Strait. There was a little ponderous traffic around the oil refinery, but otherwise we had the waterway to ourselves. Between the intermittent showers I could see how thickly green the hills had become, now that the grass had some longer days to grow. The human development on these slopes was modest for some reason, and had been there for a while: purposeful houses and muscular infrastructure. On this day and with this weather, it felt like a loch in Scotland instead of central California. Businesslike, thrifty, and very green. My father, who was originally from the East, always said winter green and summer brown were the exact opposite of what he'd grown up with, and it took him a lifetime to get used to it.

When Kay returned, I had her take the wheel while I took a turn below. I came back with coffee laced with Jim Beam; and then on the next trip Triscuits with cheese melted over them, thanks to the microwave. By that time we'd passed the second bridge and entered San Pablo Bay. I didn't like the look of the water or the sky. San Pablo Bay was shallow, like Suisun, but the deep water ship channel allowed long, high, oily swells to be pushed in from San Francisco Bay proper. A few minutes after we cleared the bridge, the wind slapped the trysail full with an enormous pop, and it heeled our tonnage over like a day sailer. *Drake* settled into a groove, though, and she was actually more stable than she'd been in the choppy seas earlier. I set the auto-pilot, which would hold under these conditions but not for long, took both Kay's hands, and nodded toward the shelter of the pilot house. She knew I didn't like to steer from there in this kind of weather, because the windows fogged and streaked with rain.

It was much quieter out of the wind. She pulled off her Gloucester hat. "Ask me anything you want," she said.

"You knew about my father, then."

"He was one of the first to think that there was another plate, and that the fake was a decoy. He apparently went out to Point Reyes to talk to the family that discovered it. Once he knew, it made sense for him to sign an affidavit that he had seen the logbooks. It was an independent verification for the recent generation of Ballentines that they still existed. No one actually told me, but I've suspected since last fall that he had a long and important involvement in the Willems collection."

"Why didn't you tell me?"

"I would have, eventually." I was watching out the windows as she talked, but she turned my head and searched my face to see if I believed her before going on. "But then I had this scheme of bringing you up to the institute, getting you involved. I thought you'd discover it on your own, and I wouldn't violate client confidentiality."

"But with Ballentine's blessing."

"Of course. They loved the idea. No one ever thought you were completely in the dark about Tom Storey's role. They even considered you might know where the logbooks were. Having you there convinced Sean that they'd finally come to light and all would be resolved, at last."

"He tried to get me to report to him directly, you know. Ballentine sent a message through Brian. The loss of the boat slip, my problems at the university, they were all ways of putting pressure on me. Did you know about that?"

She closed her eyes tightly. Of course she didn't know, or had denied it to herself. But if her world was in crisis and if her every deed was suspect and if she was terrified of being judged, and if this all was about to happen, the scene would not include Kay O'Toole breaking down. Not right now, not today. I found it reassuring somehow. Maybe we really were made for each other. "I should have," she said simply. The autopilot abruptly disengaged and we rounded into the wind, heading cross channel. I dashed back to the wheel and was instantly soaked again. She joined me a moment later. "What's the plan, skipper?"

"Paradise Cove. Take the wheel and keep The Brothers Lighthouse about thirty degrees off the port bow." We had about another ninety minutes before we would be anywhere near the anchorage, but conditions were deteriorating. "I'm going to get the anchors ready before it gets any worse."

I had two big anchors, one an enormous folding Herreshoff that I had never used. It took me ten minutes to find it, and another ten to wrestle it on to the deck, assemble it, and shackle it to the anchor rode. Several things had occurred to me while I got the ground tackle ready. The Ballentines had tried to bug the boat, had some sort of tracking device on my pickup, and probably had not let Kay out of their sight since she quit. In that regard, there needed to be a few things sorted out. There was pretty good cell phone reception right here, off Point Richmond. "Do you have your cell phone?" I asked, taking the wheel from her. She nodded. "How did you get to Suisun Bay?"

"Brian called last night and gave me your message. But he wanted to come separately."

"Call him and make sure he's OK."

"Why shouldn't he be?"

It struck me that, though Kay was back on my side, she still didn't realize what we were dealing with. "Listen to me. Sean Ballentine had Robert McNally murdered because they thought he knew something about the logbooks."

She shook her head. "That's not possible."

Another shower was on us and I had to shout over the cacophony of raindrops. "I'm not sure. But it's the only explanation for what's happened. Kay, all is forgiven. But you've got to believe me: what's going on is still dangerous to all of us—you, me, and Brian." I had reached another conclusion or two, but I needed her to swallow them one at a time. For the moment: could they listen in on her cell phone? Probably. "Call him, but don't let him say where he is. Keep it brief."

She disappeared into the pilothouse. She returned to say he was eating a Big Mac and driving fast to get over the mountains before the rain turned to snow. He was OK. I thought if they were going to go after Brian it would have happened immediately, so that part was good. If they were watching Kay, he was just the one who brought her out to the boat. Well and good. But it left me with the impression that they knew where Kay was, where we were, and that, there being no way to go but the way we were going, they knew where to find us.

The good news, I suppose, was that it didn't matter if we used the cell phone. But who was I going to call? The Coast Guard? Metaxis, probably still in Amsterdam? And who, really could do anything under these circumstances? Kay read my mind. "He knows where we are, doesn't he?"

"I think so."

"What will we do?"

"Check the tide charts, to start with."

She was back in a moment. She already knew what we were going to do. "A strong ebb tide that peaks at five knots, in two hours."

183

"Right, then. We'll go out the Gate."

"Anything I need to do? I want to move around. I'm freezing."

"Get life jackets for us. Run a line between the mainmast and foremast, as tight as you can." I thought for a moment. "And let the radar reflector loose."

She took me literally and before she did anything else, she untied the light halyard that kept the reflector aloft. Although it was metal, it had enough reflective surface that it sailed on the wind, dragging its halyard with it like the tail of a kite, before dropping into the bay thirty feet away. Hopefully, we were now off everybody's radar.

I WAS able to steer from the pilothouse for nearly an hour after that, the windows blown clear and visibility temporarily improved. I dried out a bit. But I knew these storms from long observation. The weather map showed them stacked up in long parallel fronts, one after the other all the way back to Japan. There would be plenty more rain. Kay had done a seamanlike job of rigging a safety lifeline down the middle of the boat, which we'd clip on to work on deck if the wind got any worse. She stood beside me now. "Do you know why the Willems never agreed to sell the logbooks?" she asked.

"Well, for the past twenty years, since Dad died, nobody knew where they were." I thought about it some more. "After the family came to the States, well through the 1950s, the elder Willems wanted no part of the transaction. They felt ill-used by the Ballentines, though I think their cold shoulder from Berkeley academia was mostly due to their connection with the German government. You must know the whole collection was impounded at one point."

"I think he actually was a Nazi collaborator. Sean and a couple of his staff thought so."

"But that leaves thirty years in the middle when nothing went on."

"Oh no," she said. "They were in regular contact all that time. There was correspondence going back and forth every few months. The Ballentine Library loaned materials to the Willems in Europe, and certain documents from the Willems Institute were always in circulation."

"What kind of materials came from the Ballentine Library?"

"You'd probably know more about that than I. I never saw any of it, but the attachment lists were all manuscripts and the like."

We had the bay to ourselves now, what I could see of it, with a single exception. Far to the south, upwind, was the deep blue hull and bright white topsides of a North Sea Cutter. An elegant pleasure craft but one rigged for serious seagoing, something over forty feet in length with a high prow and a long cockpit that allowed for her to be overflowing with gear. She was also bristling with antennas and had long booms on either side of a flying bridge for trawling. I'd seen the boat many times on Public Television when they followed the Ballentine oceanic research crew here and there around the Pacific Coast. Well, what were they going to do? Close with us and board? Fire a canon shot across our bow? I imagined Ballentine with his doctoral candidates in marine biology, his crew, explaining why he'd brought them out in these conditions to accost a wooden schooner. I put myself in Ballentine's position. He thinks we still have the logbooks, probably, so the more time he spent following us, the more time Brian had to spirit them away. He would negotiate, I supposed, before doing anything piratical. We could expect a call, either on the VHF or Kay's cell. Then what?

After Kay had watched them for a while through the binoculars, she said: "They don't seem to be getting any closer."

It was time for me to get to another piece of the puzzle. "Did you know that the fire at the institute was arson?"

"That's what they said in the newspaper. God, you don't think that was Sean, too? Why would he do that?"

I made my turn, now, from south to west. The light on Alcatraz passed under the bowsprit and I pointed it at the center of the Golden Gate. I felt the tide surge us forward. "I was hoping you could tell me."

"Ethan, I'm on your side now, no matter what. I made some terrible mistakes that hurt you badly. I'll sail with you into this storm. I know why you're doing it: we'll decoy them away from Brian so they don't just take the logbooks away from him . . ." She chose her words. "By force, if necessary. Sean thinks he owns them. He thinks he's already paid for them. He's single-minded and he's a bully. But I was the man's lawyer. I had dinner at his house. I played with his kids. He's not an arsonist and a murderer. McNally was killed by a crazy person. The institute burned down because it was an eyesore to some nutcase."

"He didn't want the logbooks found, if he couldn't have them."

"Why not?"

"I don't know." Whatever the case, the mission of the moment was to give Brian time to get to his destination. If he drove straight through, maybe two days or slightly longer. On cue, Kay's cell phone rang. She looked at the screen and nodded. "Don't answer it," I said. "Just turn it off. We'll chat with the Ballentines after Brian gets to Iowa."

"Iowa? Is that what you said to Brian?"

"To the university library there. It was Robert McNally's alma mater."

She looked at me. "My God, you're driving this thing now. The old go-along Ethan Storey is not on the bridge. You have a new plan."

"I suppose I do."

"And there are some things you're not telling me. I don't know if you're right about everything. I don't know if I want you to be. But I'm ready if you are."

Outside, I saw what happens when a luxury power yacht is asked to carry the equivalent of a research laboratory strapped to her topsides. Now about three hundred yards away, one of the trawl booms had broken loose and she pivoted around it, broadside to a following sea. She might not have caught us anyway before we cleared the Gate, where the swells over the San Francisco Bar would make any boarding impossible. The waves were not very big on this side, but the interval was short and they were moving fast, so the boat, which I now remembered was called *Goldrush*, swung broadside and rolled crazily until they had things under control. I opened the throttle and passed the wheel over to Kay, then went out into the wind and forward to raise the smaller of our two jibs, the staysail. The old schooner was sailing now, with the wind from the southwest, lee rail buried after I had the jib up, driving her tonnage to slice the waves like so many loaves of bread.

Then the bridge was high above us. The push of the tide astern meeting the southerly swell made a huge mess of winds and waves. The soundtrack was the booming bellow of the fog horns. When we were through, I looked astern. Kay was watching *Goldrush* and said: "I don't even see them, now." Which made me feel better, though it didn't mean they weren't in hot pursuit. It meant that it was hard to stay in sight when twelve foot swells appeared periodically in all directions. The seascape beyond the bridge was grey sky over a grey sea, with the crest of the swells breaking sometimes as the waves became their own beach. The *Drake's* motion was crazy corkscrews, climbs and drops without any logic to them. I had never been out in conditions like this. "Ethan," Kay asked. "Have you ever sailed in seas this rough?"

"No, but I know what to do." I paused for a moment. I knew that farther offshore the winds would be stronger and the swells higher, but they would be regular beyond the influence of the tides and the coast. I knew that the boat should run downwind under a kedge, which was something dragged behind to slow the boat and keep her straight. I knew that the one exception to this rule was when the wind would blow us into something, which the wind from the south would surely do. I knew that Plan B was

187

a classic heaving-to, bringing the bow as close to the wind as possible. We'd still drift slowly north, but only at a crawl. I knew all this because my father had taught me. A regular but random thumping came from below. For a gut-wrenching moment I thought one of the anchors had broken loose and was swinging on its line, banging against the hull.

"My God, what's that?" Kay's face was white.

I glanced below and saw what it was, as an immense contrary toss sent it partially airborne across the cabin, along with a book or two from the shelves. "It's the cooler, that big red box the documents were buried in. Go down and secure it, would you? Be careful." She took a bungee cord from the rack by the steering station and went below, almost hand over hand to keep her balance. I heard her swear and saw her lurch once or twice to grab it. Then all was silence from down there. I heard the bilge pump cycle, and started my stopwatch to time the intervals and see if we took on water at a uniform rate. After a moment, I shouted down to see if she was OK.

She didn't respond, but came up to the pilothouse with a very odd expression under her pallor. "There was a false bottom to the cooler, only an inch or so deep where the insulation along the bottom had been removed."

"What?"

"He did a really good job putting the bottom back in, but the knocking around cracked one of his glue seams."

"What's there?"

"More of your father's vacuum bags, one with a label that says 'Homemade Minestrone.' Do you know what it is?"

"It's not soup, Kay, that's for sure."

CHAPTER SIXTEEN

The coast of northern California is a stunning or appalling thing, depending on where you're standing. From your bed and breakfast in Mendocino it makes you believe in God, so wondrous are his works: the sea is throbbing, caressing, mightily sensuous, and the rocks like medieval castles with battlements sculpted out of bedrock, or oriental temples with graceful, heavenly arches. From the deck of a smallish ship, it inspires a sort of nauseating intimidation, and the only glory is the possibility of being somewhere else. Here's an interesting thought to consider in the twenty-first century. If Drake began to chart this coast in the 1570s, his work is not yet completed. With a single exception, the charting is poor north of San Francisco. If you sail inside the thirty-fathom contour, as someone who found the sight of the coast an unlikely source of comfort might do, there are outlying rocks and reefs up to a mile offshore. And it doesn't start out easy, either. The land north and south of the Golden Gate are like the jaws of a nutcracker through which the entire north Pacific struggles to make its presence felt. Battering through that, with a bit of staysail and the engine at maximum, only gets you in more trouble if you drift north as we were doing. The San Francisco Bar and Potatopatch Shoal were known for building huge swells even in fair weather, which this wasn't. Plus the tide that helped get us out the Gate now slid under these swells, giving them a boost and an unstable steepness before they even started to build.

"My God, those waves must be fifty feet high," said Kay. A certain but unnerving way to see how big the swells are over a bar like this is to watch your depth gauge when you're in the trough, then look again when you rise to the top. Twenty feet, was the reading.

"Not quite so bad."

"Are we in danger?"

"Not if the boat holds together." In the game of rain, we were now dry except for the blowing spray and we could steer from the pilothouse. Kay stood beside me. I could brace myself with the wheel and had a place to sit. She had only me and a sliver of teak grab rail. "Next time we crest, take the binoculars and look astern. See if *Goldrush* is out there anywhere." She lasted about a minute at the task, then dove below and was violently ill. She was not a novice, however; she recovered quickly and knew that staying below just made things worse.

"You're supposed to take your seasickness pills before you leave shore," she said. "Silly me."

"This will get better when we clear the shoals. And we should get enough westing by midnight so that I can heave to or run with bare poles."

She smiled weakly. "Run with bare poles. That sounds jolly."

"Either way it'll be better. The storm can't last forever."

"I didn't see anything. But it's getting dark."

"Can you turn on the radar?"

"I'd rather steer."

"All right. West, but steer directly into any wave that looks nasty." I stood with her for a few minutes till she got the hang of it. She was a natural at the helm, as indeed she'd been from our first day on the water together. But it was hard work just holding a course, let alone steering. She'd be able to do it just until dark, I thought. Maybe a half hour. Conditions would be very scary out here in the dark, but the almanac said the moon was full and I saw it rising on schedule as the daylight drained away. I heard the bilge pump whine and wrote the time in the log. About an hour since the last time. I went below, turned on the radar and lit all the kerosene lamps. Somehow these little points of flame in the tempest always made everything seem a little more controllable. I waited till the upstroke and looked, but all I saw on screen was the deadly incisor of Point Bonita, almost due north and abeam, which was good.

I sat at the chart table and continued to stare at the radar screen for a moment. I had a lot on my mind, but first the boat. She buried her bow about every third or fourth wave and looking forward with a flashlight I could see a little water coming in between the hull and deck when she swam like that. I checked the fuel reading: forty gallons, or about thirty-six hours of engine time. I stepped up to the pilothouse. "I'm going to kill the engine." I did so, and without its rumble we had nothing but what forty knots of wind had to say for itself, in the creaks and moans as it swept over us. I went below again and made a notation of the barometric pressure. I called Coast Guard San Francisco on the VHF and the cheerful bureaucrat took note of my general position and condition, in lieu of having left a float plan with anybody. The deck was next. Since it was getting cold, I fired up the propane heater below deck and in the pilothouse. I changed into foul weather gear and a safety harness, grabbed a spotlight and went out.

Nothing was amiss. As I clambered back, I looked at Kay through the pilothouse windows. In the reddish glow from the instruments, she looked as beautiful as I'd ever seen her, but about at the end of her endurance. It was warm in the pilothouse and I stripped the top of my gear off before taking the wheel. "You are relieved," I said.

"I'll be relieved when I have a chance to pee."

"It's almost cozy down here," she called up a few minutes later. "It's like an out-of-control elevator in a very fancy men's club. Do I dare try to make tea?"

"You must be feeling better."

"I think so."

"Just unlock the gimbals on the stove and only fill the pot half full." There was the noise of the water pump and a chorus of curse words and a dropped cup or two, but soon enough she was back at my side with a cup of tea and I drank it gratefully. She took the cup back, came up with one for herself, and asked me

191

if I'd looked at the contents of the box. She'd wedged it securely between the seat back and the salon table.

"No," I said. Outside there was a monster wave that we took badly, quartering before I had a chance to turn into it. She hadn't spilled a drop. "Jesus Christ, will there be many more like that?"

"Would you plot our position?" I asked. She needed something to do. If there was ever a mind that could get into trouble on its own, it was Kay's. She wrote down the GPS coordinates and scuttled down to the chart table where I heard her humming to herself as she worked the plotter. She came back with the chart folded where I could see her mark. "To answer your question, this'll be Four Fathom Bank. It's the worst part." I pointed with my finger. The waves were awful, but their tops were not breaking or streaming foam. The anemometer was reading forty knots. "Wind's down a bit, too." The moon was up and bright now. We sailed for a time with just the seas and each other.

At ten, Kay crawled into the pilot berth, the snug little cubby that ran aft beside the cockpit, and fell asleep. By midnight I needed a break and something to eat. Once clear of the shoals, I needed about thirty nautical miles before I could safely heave the boat to and sleep. We'd made perhaps half that, but the seas were a bit smaller and much more regular. The wind still southerly, which is how it would lie until we were officially out of the parade of storms. I could hold a course of south by west without feeling that the wheel would jump out of my hands, and I considered the autopilot, but only for a moment. Instead I'd try to heave the boat to for a few minutes. I started the engine, brought the bow into the wind, and tightened everything down with a furious cracking and flapping of sails. Then I put the engine in neutral to see how we would sit. The angle was critical. If it was parallel to the waves, we'd just tip crazily from side to side, risking a rollover. But she settled into an angle diagonal to the wave travel and to my astonishment (never having done this under these conditions), she just seemed to completely stop, going up and down with the waves but level, stable and quiet.

I found an overlooked twenty-eight-once can of Dennison's chili, opened it partially, then set it in the kettle to heat in the water. I poured Jim Beam into my cup, stopping at the halfway mark, and drank it in three gulps. Someday soon I'd have to try and get back to green vegetables. After a refill, I turned the radar back on and adjusted the proximity alarm to ring me at five miles. I sat down to wait for dinner at the salon table. Dad's 49ers cooler was on the seat beside me, and finally I looked inside. The white plastic bottom of the cooler, now torn free, lay askew over the contents. Under it were two familiar dark green, translucent bags, one with the minestrone label. Without the slightest hesitation but considerable care, I slit the top of one with my rigging knife and pulled out the contents. It was a three-ring binder covered in army drab with a cardboard label glued on the front cover that identified it as the joint property of the U.S. European Command/Allied Command Europe/ Headquarters Roquencourt, France, and the Seventh Army, G-2 Intelligence, and it was labeled TRANSACTION REGISTERS. Inside the cover were a series of cables from Seventh Army headquarters to Captain Thomas R. Storey, addressed through the U.S. Army's communications center on Mare Island. Mare Island, now part of the San Pablo Bay National Wildlife Refuge, handled all of the radio traffic during the Pacific war, which up until now I had thought of as Dad's war. Apparently, he'd stayed on in the Reserves.

The first page of the binder was a transfer from the Pacific Command to EUCOM (European Command); the second directed him to report directly to an office of the Pentagon. Stripped of their jargon and the alphabet jungle of military acronyms, my father, as an officer in military intelligence, was assigned to investigate the traffic in currency between a Belgian bank serving the University of Antwerp to U.S. account numbers held in the name of Curtis Ballentine. The rest of the binder comprised copies of these transfers, of which there were about thirty, seemingly randomly dated throughout the year, totaling over a million dollars. These were the wire transfers that Brian Haggerty had discovered in the FBI files, the ones reported in the book, now suppressed, that I had sampled the night of the fire at the institute. My father was too much a man of principle to store away government secrets as a legacy to his son. There was nothing else in the binder with a security classification, but at the end of the stack, there was an original receipt for one of the payments signed by Curtis Ballentine himself, with an address on the University of California campus that was still that of the Ballentine Nuclear Laboratory. Then, at the end of the binder, was the copy of a brief memorandum my father had written. It was to an address in Washington, D.C., no addressee, just a Mail Station number. Dated March 15, 1957. It read:

I've met on three occasions with William Hallowell in Point Reyes to discuss the finding of the original plate, the one now on display in the Ballentine Museum. The Ballentine family has apparently set him up or loaned him funds to start a business. Mr. Hallowell, of course, sticks with his original story. The quid pro quo is his continuing silence on what actually transpired, and the implication is that he has been given a script about his original discovery. But on my third visit he began describing the moment of discovery and gave some details as to color, patina, recognizable words, edge wear and so forth which were not consistent with the plate now on display in the University Museum and soon to be exposed as a fake. In my opinion, at first, I thought that there might be two different plates, one on display and one in hiding. Now, frankly, I'm not sure what to think. Curtis Ballentine is an extremely complex and devious man and hiding the original behind a fake is very much in character with someone who loves secrets and intrigues. However, the close contacts and funds transferred between the Willems Institute and Curtis Ballentine involve something else. There is very little public contact between the families; they are publicly at odds over perceived insults after the collection was moved to Berkeley just before the war. I am currently affiliated with a different school and it may be possible to offer my services as a nautical historian to the Willems Institute. Please advise.

I repacked everything in the cooler and put the top back on. The ocean doesn't deal kindly with inattentive skippers, radar or no radar. Fifteen minutes of unattended helm is about as much as you dare. All looked OK in the world through the pilothouse windows, and the rest of the box, and God only knew what it was, could wait. The boat gave a lurch and a wallow and the bilge pump cycled. I turned the long range radio to eight megahertz and put on the earphones, and through the headset the National Weather Service gave me a forecast of continued southerly winds and very high swells. Within twenty-four hours, though, winds would start backing to the northwest, which was the good news, accompanied by unseasonable cold and heavy fog. Where was Brian Haggerty by now? He was not one to drive all night, much too fond of his comforts. Let's give him the rest of tonight and tomorrow night, assume he'd be in Iowa the following morning. Meanwhile, we'd be as unfindable as if we were on a different planet.

The alarm on my wrist told me fifteen minutes had passed. I looked around again, then cautiously approached the stove. As if I did this kind of thing every day, I placed the chili in one of Kay's china bowls, refilled my mug with JB, and back in the pilothouse seated myself at the smaller chart surface next to the wheel, where I could eat and watch the sea at the same time. We were doing very well, and in the warmth of the pilothouse, having my dinner and my third ounce of hard liquor, it was like watching the waves on a particularly good TV documentary. The relative quiet seemed odd, and I think that was what woke Kay, because when she appeared up the companionway she said, "Are we there yet?"

195

"We're between storms at least. Get some chili; it's on the stove."

"I never liked chili and you always thought I did."

"Did you ever tell me?"

"Not more than a hundred times." She picked up my cup and sniffed. "We have to talk about your drinking, too." Then she smiled and kissed my forehead. "I feel like an old married woman, kicking around stuff like this." She came back with a bowl and a lukewarm can of iced tea. "I draw the line at starting bourbon at two in the morning." She paused. "You looked in the cooler," she said.

"Just the first package."

"Well?"

"My father went to work for the Willems, at the direction of Military Intelligence, around 1957. He was still in the Reserves at that point. He was asked to investigate payments made by Willems to Curtis Ballentine just before the war. The first package had that traffic, plus the paperwork on the transactions, including proof that they took place."

"Wait. If all this was about Ballentine's wanting to acquire the Drake logbooks, why would the Willems be paying him? And what proof, by the way?"

"Curtis Ballentine's signature on a receipt for one of them. I guess it's obvious now, because all of this stuff eventually was taken over by FBI counterintelligence, but Curtis was sending technical information about nuclear research from the Ballentine labs, and Manfred Willems was passing it along to Germany."

"The Ballentines were *spies*?"

"I don't think it started that way. The early years of technology were just about the science, and it wasn't classified until later in the war. Nor did Curtis Ballentine necessarily know he was dealing with anyone but an academic wandering around from Luxembourg to Belgium being persecuted by the Nazis."

"Who happened to have an interest in nuclear science?"

"I can only imagine how it went down. Maybe he just needed the money."

Kay ate for a few moments and then said, "The family lost nearly everything in the 1929 stock market crash."

"How do you know?"

"Sean told me. It was why they wanted the logbooks so much, why all this was so important to them for so many years. Now, they seem to have all the money in the world. . . . What's that sound?"

"The radar alarm." I ducked below to look at the screen. Visible only on the wave crests, the blob was the size of a thumbtack. "Ten miles, due east."

"Is it them?"

"No way to know, but it's not a container ship, I can tell you that."

"Can they see us? I mean after I let the reflector go?"

"No, not very easily. They could if they were close enough." What was close enough? I had no idea. We could stay where we were, I supposed. But Sean Ballentine was a sailor, and I had done exactly what any sailor might do in these conditions: get over the bars, get enough westerly to clear Point Reyes, heave to and drift slowly north until the wind and seas abated. The wind was down to thirty-five knots, the seas now less than twenty feet. I started having some doubts. "Maybe I shouldn't have played it this way."

"What do you mean?"

"Maybe I should have put into Pittsburg Marina yesterday and called the police, or . . . something." For a moment, I couldn't track my own decision-making process.

"Maybe you just had your boat and your woman back, and you went for it. What're your orders, skipper?"

Fuck it. If they were going to find us, it wouldn't be when we were conveniently sitting still for them. "Let's get some sails up."

CHAPTER SEVENTEEN

M y father had built *Drake*, whose name my father said came
from the term for male mallard, in the 1950s of Port
Orford cedar over California live oak. Her design followed that of
L. Francis Herreshoff's *Joann*, lines laid out by the master sometime in the late 1940s and of which he said: "the *Joann* smacks
of tradition and wholesome good looks; she could be counted on
to behave herself at sea." Dad had started work on her during the
long winter after my mother died, and it took most of a decade
of his spare time. By thirteen, I was old enough to help him
sometimes, during the final fitting out, working almost always
in silence while his radio played Bach or Handel. I bought him a
present the day she was launched, a small St. Christopher medal
done in nautical bronze. He was wearing it the day he died, as he
did every day.

Here was the problem: turning the boat around to face
down wind and down wave, without getting rolled over in the
trough. Then, having the right sails up to move us forward
without driving her bow down into the wave ahead of us while
she was riding up the one behind. So, the little staysail and the
storm trysail would stay where they were. I had no choice but
to work with the mainsail to propel us along, all 614 square feet
of it. But to set the whole monster was asking for trouble with
only the two of us. Also, she'd be overpowered and hard to hold
on course. So . . . raise the sail a third of the way, reef it down to
a third of its size while we were still hove to, then when all was
ready, gun the engine, pivot 180 degrees, sheet everything down
and pray.

I described this to Kay, and as I did so I had a strange recol-
lection. The dream I'd had in Amsterdam, of sailing in a storm

198

with both Kay and my father. I told her. "What happened in the dream?" she asked.

"We had wonderful time," I said.

"Liar."

It was by now around two in the morning, a good five hours until we could see anything. I scrambled down into our tiny engine room so I could read the gauges mounted to the panel, which I always thought were more accurate than the set on deck, and shine a light around. The bilges below the diesel held a good deal of angry dark water, but it was nothing the pumps wouldn't handle, and indeed they came on just as I shined the light into the darkest, dampest corner. I called to Kay to start the engine up. I gave it a few minutes to warm—it was starting to get very cold as the barometer rose—and called again, this time for Forward and 2500 rpms. I watched the propeller shaft turn in its mounting. No water coming in that way. With the engine running I could now turn all the radios on, and switch the speakers on in the pilothouse. The blip was still on the radar, a little closer. Then without further ado, I turned the spreader lights on and went out onto the deck.

The cold made it all seem much worse, that and the darkness. My fingers were stiff by the time I had the sail untied and they began to go numb. Unfurled, the sail wallowed and billowed and slapped me in the face from time to time. My knees were already bothering me, and I could feel an attack of bursitis coming on. I went down the lifeline to where Kay was standing by the winch. Her back was to the wind and spray, and as I approached, the top of a wave broke off and slapped a bucketful of Pacific Ocean onto the back of her neck. She barely flinched, but she was shaking and could only control it with great effort. We both put our hands on the handle and cranked. We managed the operation in about ten awful minutes. We were then sailing awkwardly, into the wind and waves, but not making any serious forward progress. I nodded, and we edged our way back to the pilothouse.

Kay's teeth were chattering and her skin was the color of the foam that blew by the portholes. She stripped off her gloves and held her hands in front of the propane heater, wincing as circulation returned. Our companion was less than a mile out, now. The wheel was still tied down, and we could afford to take a few minutes before we turned downwind. I went below, where the motion was actually less than it had been before our sail change, and pulled open the door to the head. There was a tiny vertical locker there, a hanging locker as we say, where Dad kept his gun. It was a conventional twelve-gauge Winchester pump shotgun which he used to hunt quail in San Luis Obispo, in what was now a very long time ago. But like everything else he left behind, it was tightly wrapped, protectively oiled and ready for use. I loaded it with the heaviest stuff he had, put it back in its bag and handed it up to Kay, who was now looking much better. As I watched her slight smile, the light around her head changed, just for a split second. She noticed it too. "What was that, lightning?"

"No. Somebody just picked us up with a spotlight."

I hit the electrical master switch that cut power to everything but the fuel and bilge pumps. It was an unsettling, deep black world that closed around us, and with the main up and doing something, the ship seemed more alive now: noisier with the sail, a change in the note of the wind as it blew around the tightened shrouds, a creak from a mast under load. The kerosene lamps were still lit below and I could see her face clearly. She had never looked as beautiful to me as she did at that moment. "I always thought that was a fishing rod," she said. "Will you shoot at them?" Kay asked.

"They want the logbooks; they think we've got them. Two people are dead already. You're fucking right I'll shoot at them."

"I never heard you say 'fuck' before."

I opened the throttle slowly and took the lashing off the wheel. "Kiss me for luck," I said. She did so. "Now hang on to something." I waited until we were entirely within a trough between the swells, then as we rose, pushed the throttle all way open, rpms at red line. We began to climb rapidly, coming at the wave as it came at us. A third of the way up, I spun the wheel hard to starboard and pinned it there. For a long second nothing seemed to happen. I was listening for the sound of steering cables breaking. But no, we were OK; here we came, pointing across the wave. We were at the same angle as a surfboarder, but we weren't surfing. The wave was starting to roll us. Some part of my mind told me to rush out and ease the sheets, but I was terrified and nothing could have pried me loose. I would ride the steering wheel all the way to the bottom, after we turned over, filled with water and sank. I felt the starboard rail go under and we had every reason to believe we were capsizing, since it felt like we were already on our side. I glanced to my right. Out the pilothouse glass I saw the water come rapidly up almost halfway, so that I was looking at something in an aquarium, though what I saw were pieces of webbing floating by, the orange harness that held the inflatable dinghy in place. Why didn't the glass break? Then it slowly began to recede.

"Oh my God," said Kay.

"Get ready, here comes the hard part."

"I HATE YOU, ETHAN STOREY," she called after a second.

We shed the water (and presumably the dinghy) and were stern to the waves. The trick now was to keep from being washed the rest of the way around and going through it all over again on the other side. For that we needed speed. "Keep pointed just a little west of north," I said, and gave her the helm. On deck the wind felt much easier as we moved in the same direction, but seeing the sea coming from behind was unsettling until I'd watched a couple of waves lift *Drake*'s butt and pass under us. I adjusted the small jib, trysail and reefed main, and with them all pulling as sails are supposed to, we were suddenly calling the shots, charging along with the storm. It was maybe twelve knots, but it felt like an amusement park ride.

I took the wheel from Kay. We were a dark wooden boat, with a poor radar image, racing away from them at speed in the storm. Moonset was upon us, 0235 hours of a new day. We would call Brian in the late afternoon of this day which had just begun.

If his errand was accomplished, we wouldn't really matter anymore. If they were somehow able to listen in on Kay's cell phone, so much the better, because they'd know that the logbooks were out of their reach once and for all, before anything got out of control between myself and Sean Ballentine.

WITH THE moon down, and looking ahead, I steered by feel, as I was unable to check the direction of the waves coming up from behind, or their height or speed. I wanted to keep wind, wave, and *Drake* all headed in the same direction, but the sea is never like that. The backs of the waves as they hissed away were marbled with white that flexed like netting, trying unsuccessfully to hold the ocean in place. This storm was nearly over, the barometer back up to 1013 millibars; but something else was brewing far up in the Gulf of Alaska and it was sending a counter swell that would either homogenize with the southerly we were riding, making every third or fourth one a large maverick heading northwest, or it would keep its identity and slap us sideways. It meant an almost constant vigilance. After the initial exhilaration of moving greater than hull speed, which might have lasted five minutes, I was worried about getting knocked down again if I couldn't steer straight by making constant adjustments to the helm. The motion of the boat was steady and level when she surfed down these waves perfectly, but a brutal corkscrew when she wasn't. No autopilot would handle these conditions. There was really nothing for it but to steer from the spray-tormented, freezing cold cockpit. The effort was like lifting a cinderblock, or keeping one from falling out of your hands, and that kept me warm, but I didn't know how long I could keep this up. I wanted to last until dawn, when Kay could manage. She stood watching me as I got settled, with every intention of staying with me. "Please make me a cup of coffee," I asked, to give her something to do.

It took an extraordinary amount of time, it seemed, and when she brought it in my San Francisco State commuter mug she said: "I fell asleep while standing at the stove. I'm sorry."

"That's all right, Kay. Listen, one of us is going to have to get some sleep. These conditions aren't going to go away for another twelve hours or so. When it gets light, I can rig a drogue, and you'll be able to stand watch. Until then, it makes sense for you to sleep. If you're in the pilothouse, I can always wake you if I have to."

"What's a drogue?"

"A fancy name for something heavy that has a lot of water resistance. We stream it astern; it slows us substantially but keeps us exactly in the direction of the wind."

"Why don't we set it up now?"

"I can't do it in the dark," I lied. My real reason was that I wanted to move as fast as possible for as long as possible.

"Do you need anything here?" Our voices were getting hoarse from having to shout so much.

"The rest of the crackers with peanut butter, the spotlight, the handheld VHF radio, and the shotgun." I added as an afterthought: "And four of my bursitis tablets."

She made little cracker sandwiches, and tied everything off to cockpit cleats within reach so they wouldn't blow away. Then, without a word, she went into the pilothouse, pulled out the leecloth that would keep her from rolling off the bunk, and lay down. "Just you and me, old girl," I said aloud after I'd wolfed the crackers, loaded the shotgun, finished the coffee, and dealt with my bursitis.

I was exhausted a half hour later, but could keep going because I learned rapidly how to correct for the swells just before they made me their slave; and I began to think I might last four hours under these conditions. I knew my limitations in other ways, though, and they were apparent within the first hour. I was so tired I began to hallucinate, seeing waves where there were none, spectral beings made of foam swimming against the wind, and my father smoking his pipe in the pilothouse. Judgment thus impaired I steered on instinct, brought up into alertness when a muscle cramped, and it was during the first of these (a calf muscle) I checked my watch to see I'd done a respectable two hours—half way through—and during the second (in my foot) I saw *Goldrush*, working her way up to us from down wind.

They were about a hundred and fifty yards away, and brightly lit with working lights on their radar mast and in the cockpit. It couldn't have been any other vessel, unless there were several other boats which had lost trawl booms in this storm, had dark hulls and white topsides, and were out looking for me. Their approach was slow; they didn't use the searchlight, and they had their own problems working up through the swell. It gave me time to think things through. What would they do? They couldn't board me or take me in tow without risking severe damage to both vessels, and wood or not, *Drake* was much heavier and likely to suffer less in a collision. They could simply follow me until conditions improved, but they may have fuel limitations. We'd both been out about twelve hours at least, but we'd burned an hour's worth and they'd been running full time. On the whole and for the moment we were at a stalemate, I thought.

And behind this was the sense of unreality that had kept me from understanding any of this until it was thrown in my face. My father had been an FBI informant for many years, getting the goods on Sean Ballentine's grandfather. He'd hidden the Drake logbooks twice, first when the building was renovated in the 1950s, and he moved them again, to where I'd found them, sometime after 1969. I couldn't imagine why, unless the Willems were afraid the Ballentines would show up one day and just tear the institute apart. Manfred's son Kurt must have known about the new hiding place, but . . . he was killed in 1990. Before he could pass along the information to his son Lucius, the man I'd met in Amsterdam? I lost my train of thought. My eyes went blurry; now what was I thinking?

I was thinking that my father had died the same year as Kurt Willems.

I blinked hard and cleared my eyes of the salty tears and spray. They were fifty yards to starboard now, alternating between a shining city on a hill of waves and a blue-white glow when on the other side of a wave. I could see the bridge, though, and a man in a red survival suit. I leaned down and pulled the VHF handheld radio out of its bag. When I turned it on, it was clear they'd been hailing me for some time. *Schooner running without lights upwind of us, please respond.*

I thumbed the switch. *This is the Drake, go ahead.*

Do you need anything?

Sure. How about giving me some sea room? Wouldn't want to ruin your nice plastic boat.

There was a silence on the radio. They had no plan, I realized. In their place I guessed I would just keep me in sight until conditions improved, then just come up and board us like pirates. This no longer seemed unlikely. This was not the world that I knew, but it was real and I had to play by its rules.

Drake, stand by; we're gunning you a line.

No, you aren't. Stand clear.

Fifty yards. No one on deck, yet. I didn't think I would kill anybody, and I raised the gun and fired, pumped it and fired again. The glass in the wheelhouse exploded but the helmsman was not hit. He turned away, in a large, careful circle. The *Drake* yawed badly, the helm lashings having slipped, but as I grabbed the wheel Kay's hands were already there. It was a two-person job now, getting her back under control. She had come out at the sound of the gun, but for the past minutes I'd only had eyes for Ballentine's vessel. "You tend to that business, there," she said, and nothing else.

When *Goldrush* completed her circle, safely out of range, Survival Suit was positioning a piece of plywood over the shattered glass. Serious work boats sometimes carry these, precut for this kind of thing—a wave taking out the window, say—and the frame of the window is equipped with fittings and the plywood with matching holes. They were now headed straight towards us, still brightly lit. Sean Ballentine was at the wheel, his Norse God bronze hair making him unmistakable for the rest of us mortals. When the radio broke squelch again, it was him. "Good morning, Dr. Storey," he said. "Can't blame you for feeling vindictive. I fucked your wife, after all."

205

I picked up the radio and thumbed the switch, but no words came. Then finally: "Was my father killed?"

There was a long silence. He was holding position, coming closer now, but staying where he could see us and we him. "Just an untimely death. His buddy Kurt Willems, though; he was a problem that had to be dealt with. We're very serious people, we Ballentines." We went on like that for a time; then I thought, *that's about enough from you, asshole.* They were positioned off our starboard bow, at maybe the two o'clock position. I took the wheel from Kay and pointed straight at them. We now had all the wind behind us, and *Drake* took the hint. Ballentine looked at the full six feet of bowsprit, eight inches at the base, coming his way. We could skewer them like a kebob; they'd roll over and sink in minutes unless both boats stayed pinned to each other. I didn't think it would happen that way. I thought it would take only a foot or two of the sprit to stop us and I could lever us free, using our momentum and doing more damage as I pulled out. Either way, they would all die.

There were at least a couple of people standing behind him now, but all of them frozen. *Is that guy for real?* There was no doubt in my mind, and within a minute I couldn't have avoided a collision even if I wanted to, unless they moved. With our tonnage and everything pushing us forward, we'd be in a straight line for the foreseeable future. I was suddenly warm; hands strong, back and shoulders limber. The world was in absolutely clear and sharp focus. The black of the water was distinguishable from the dark blue of the hull; the soapy white of the spume from the blue-white of her topsides; the sound and smell of her diesels idling; the hiss of the uncaring waves passing under us both. "I don't care, Ethan," Kay said, beside me. "Do what you have to do."

At fifty feet, there was a scuffle on the bridge of *Goldrush*, which flashed across in a burst of time-lapse images that began with Ballentine shrugging and shouting, and ended with Survival Suit at the wheel. Then she fairly bloomed with a scream of engines and a vast cloud of milky smoke. The bow came sharply around and for a moment she wallowed seriously in a trough, and I thought we'd take her broadside, my mind reflecting in an unreal, detached way that dead-on was best for *Drake*, taking the blow on her stoutest members: stem piece, forefoot and iron-ballasted keel. But now *Goldrush* leapt forward, digging her in like a runner collecting his legs and we passed her stern, the wake a caldron of intensely churning water. I didn't even turn to watch, and the radio was silent as the distance grew.

Neither of us said anything for many minutes. Eventually Kay said, "I don't see them anywhere." And then: "I think the wind is less."

I killed the engine. "Take the wheel, Kay." She did so. I checked our position and decided we could drop the drogue and the mainsail, and drift with the rest of the storm. Three hours at this rate would put us off Point Reyes by full light, but not close enough to worry. The act of setting the canvas cone properly, attaching its line and lifting it over the stern seemed impenetrably complex and requiring superhuman strength, and I only accomplished it as a series of very small, orderly steps. My father once said, in what had seemed an odd comment at the time: *save your passion for the bedroom, Ethan. Think everything else all the way through.* The line played out without snagging anything or tangling, and when it pulled taut at 200 feet we straightened out and slowed, but only slightly until I took in the sail. With the jib still pulling we were now dead down wind, just flotsam and not fighting the Pacific anymore. I could barely stand. There was nothing on the radar screen that was not attached to the coast of California. "Kay, I don't want to know. I don't have to know," I said. She bit her lip, looking very small in the bulky parka hood, and nodded. I lashed the wheel just to keep the steering gear from wearing out. "Listen for the radar proximity alarm, sweep the horizon every ten minutes whether you think you can see anything or not. Wake me if anything feels wrong or the water gets less than a hundred feet, or in a couple of hours."

"Okay."

"And if he sends a helicopter, shoot it down with one of Dad's rocket-propelled grenades."

I paused at the step into the pilothouse and I heard her say behind me: "You're my hero." She said it quietly, and I wouldn't have heard her at all, but for the wind at her back.

CHAPTER EIGHTEEN

I stood stupidly in the pilothouse for a full minute, too tired to remember what I was supposed to be doing. Then I pulled off the top two layers, foul weather slicker and pants, fisherman's sweater. No fancy survival suits for the crew of the *Drake*. I had never really intended to encounter these sea conditions, let alone the rest of it. I sailed in the classic boat parades and made one overnight cruise every summer. The long ocean passages, the testing of oneself against the sea, even the romance of it never really got to me. I took my students out sometimes, so they could see the coast the way the Spanish saw it. Once every few years I'd make it to Baja.

Kay had spread out a sleeping bag on the bunk and I could feel her warmth still in it. It smelled of her too, and somewhere in the ten seconds before I slept I was very aroused. When I woke five, not two, hours later, the motion of the boat was much reduced, along with her speed. I felt as though I'd been beaten up, pummeled by the events of the night. When I tried to rise, my lower back protested; when I rolled on my side I found a bruise. I was getting too old for this kind of shit, as they say. In the little repeater compass over the bunk I read us as slightly west of north. The external thermometer was in the mid-fifties and the day was full on; and though the cloud cover was low there was no fog around us. I sat up, a movement of three distinct stages of pain and soreness, and saw Kay's cell phone hanging on the charger. Could we call Brian? Incredibly, he'd only been traveling for less than a day. It would be mid-afternoon at best before he got to Iowa. We had some more sailing to do.

I stepped down to the main cabin from the pilothouse, loaded the twelve-volt percolator and got coffee going. While it bubbled and made the galley smell like heaven, I listened to the nautical weather, which said we were in a lull between storms, with the next one bringing much more rain; lots of snow in the mountains, chains likely required at Donner Pass within the next seventy-two hours. I found a pouch of Dad's lamb stew and dropped it into a pan to heat. When all was ready, I thought about having her come below to the salon table—conditions would almost allow it—but that seemed irresponsible given the fact that Point Reyes was somewhere under our lee and that I'd declared war on the most powerful family in northern California. In the end I compromised and brought a bowl up to the smaller flat surface in the pilothouse. It was impractical as a chart table, but one person standing could make it work and it was much better than trying to manage it on deck. I took Kay a cup of coffee in the cockpit first. She was so intent on the boat and watching the horizon that she gave a start when I said good morning. "Coffee?"

She took a sip. "Oh my God. You make the best coffee in the world. How about a muffin and the Sunday paper?" It was actually Sunday, I realized, and I had a disconcerting moment thinking how Brian would handle waking up the history department in a snowy Midwestern city on a Sunday morning. I put the thought aside. If anybody could make it happen, it was Brian Haggerty.

"How's she sailing?"

She blew on her coffee. "I haven't had to touch the wheel since dawn."

"OK. Let's steer from inside."

There was no real steering to be done. She still ran softly, slowly over the swell that pushed her north. We ate ravenously, Kay at the table and me with my plate in my lap. Neither of us spoke. When we were done I took the bowls below, wiped them out and left them in the sink. I found my father's meerschaum and lit it and joined her. She sat like a little girl on the starboard settee where the heat from the propane heater could reach her directly, one leg under her and the other swinging. She watched me for a minute, then asked if that was my father's pipe. "Yes."

"You've spoken of him so little."

"We had sort of a strange relationship. Maybe he was different before my mother died, but I don't remember that."

"Did you love each other?"

"I think so."

"You just had no idea what he was up to, this whole business?"

"I guess I knew he had some other interests besides the boat and teaching. He called them research, and of course that's what they were." I paused in thought. "You know, it's strange that as a professional historian I never really knew about the Willems collection until last fall, when Brian gave me the backstory. I put it down to my academic laziness, but there's no doubt now that he kept me in the dark on purpose."

"Why?"

"To protect me, I think."

She nodded, finished her coffee and yawned. Coffee under these circumstances was like a sleeping draught. "Didn't it make you feel lonely, not having him in your life more, not more involved?"

"He was the only family I knew."

A tear rolled down her cheek and she dabbed at it with her cuff. "It's so sad."

"Well, no Kay, it wasn't. I don't know how to describe it, but each of us knew we'd be there for each other somehow. I became a historian, just like him. He made the boat that kept us safe last night, and he made us the dinner you just ate."

"Well, you can see how everybody thought you must know something about the logbooks." She paused. "I saw there was something else in your Dad's treasure chest when I came down to pee last night. Another package. Do you know what it is?"

"More dirty laundry on the Ballentines, I suppose."

"I think it's maybe a letter to you."

"I doubt it."

"Are you going to open it?"

"Not right now."

She smiled. "Between the two of you, there's not a woman in the world who wouldn't be driven crazy."

"Why don't you get some sleep? I'll go on deck and finish my pipe."

"Where are we going?"

"I'll reach out towards the Farallons, then gybe around and head in to Drake's Bay in the afternoon. It'll be pretty exposed to the southerly swell, but with both anchors down we should be OK."

From the cockpit, I walked forward. The inflatable was gone, and one of the dorade vents that funnel fresh air below while keeping out the sea and the rain. The starboard berth would be soaking wet. I covered the hole with duct tape. But that was about it. The bilge pump ran only once in the hour I spent on deck before changing course. The boat had been worked very hard and if she wanted to leak a little that was fine with me. When I was satisfied we were OK, I altered course and sail to take us offshore till noon. I thought I could make it as far as Bodega Bay before the next storm hit—all of this high seas adventure was within a day's drive of San Francisco, after all. But I knew there wouldn't be anybody at Drake's Bay. Given its southern exposure any sensible mariner would run to Bodega, because although its entrance was tricky it faced northwest, or else they'd go back into San Francisco Bay.

I smoked my pipe and thought about things. My Dad, the counterspy. Things heating up to the point of Willems asking Dad to hide the documents a second time. Let's see . . . Manfred Willems was the one who came to the U.S. in 1939. His son Kurt was my father's employer; Kurt had died at the hands of the Ballentines just the way Robert McNally had, because by that point in time, 1990, they only wanted evidence of their wartime spying erased. McNally didn't know where the logbooks were; if Kurt knew, he didn't say. At the end, only Dad knew. Karen had died because they burned the house down. All to get the logbooks of Francis Drake; and if they couldn't get them, destroy them. Months ago, Kay suggested using her boyfriend, son of the mysterious Tom Storey, as an inside source without telling him. She was manifestly stupid there, granted, but Kay could talk herself into anything. Of course, I reminded myself, she didn't know about Dad. Ballentine had recruited her as his attorney because *he* knew she was my lover and he knew who I was. But what had started it all, last fall, was Lucius Willems simply deciding to sell the collection, and in all likelihood he was not going to sell it to Sean Ballentine.

Here was a thought, flashing brightly through my mind: she hadn't slept with Ballentine. I was sure of it. He just knew about her history with Peter Peckerhead. Sean had played a head game with me and all it got him was a berserker history professor.

But suddenly the "if he couldn't have them, he wanted to destroy them" was a non-starter with me, though that was the only explanation for what had happened. It made no sense, with my pipe, a belly full of stew and a fine view of the Farallons off the port bow. Even now, his worst-case scenario was the documents surfacing in Iowa, not in his possession but showing all the world that their plate was the real thing. Surely that was most of what he wanted? In history, you sometimes never found the central principle that explained a war, or a generation, or a tide in human affairs, or a mass migration, or the fall of an empire. But you searched for it, that was what historians did, and once or twice in a career you had it: the reason why.

There had to be one final rock to be overturned.

I<small>T WAS</small> not what you'd call a fine sailing day, but given what came before and what was coming again, and the fact that we were still running under shortened sail, it felt pretty good, a long, slow passage over the swell, deck steady, wheel easy. When I got cold, I could go into the pilothouse and let the autopilot handle things. On one of these trips, around mid-morning, I got on the long-range radio and called John Davenport, my old harbormaster, to see if he had seen *Goldrush*. They had my old slip, after all, and if they weren't around here that's where they'd be. I tried to think of a roundabout, camouflaged way of putting the question to him, but John was a straightforward man and if he wanted to know why I was asking he'd wonder aloud, and I simply wouldn't say why. And then he'd answer the question. Shorn of the radio jargon and call signs, this is what was said:

"Hello, Ethan," came his voice, with the usual nasal twang that flavors all single sideband transmissions. "Did you miss this storm?"

"No, but we're in good shape. Kay's with me, you know."

"I'm glad to hear it. For a while there I thought you were running away again, the way you did a few years back when you went to Port San Luis without her."

"No secrets from you, John."

He replied, "The harbormaster is the master of the harbor, you know."

"Tell me. Is *Goldrush* in port?"

"They came in about an hour ago. They were low on fuel. They'd gone right out into the teeth of the storm and lost a trawl boom before they even cleared the Gate. Then they had a rogue wave blow out the wheelhouse window. Most of the crew just left, pissed off. The boat's still here."

"Thanks, John."

He didn't ask why I wanted to know. "Don't forget that post-card from Baja," was all he said, and signed off.

On the strength of that information I set course for Drake's Bay, now due east of us, with the wind now southwesterly and our friend, at least for a while. Kay woke up around eleven and we sat quietly together as we made our way back to the coast. We passed a pod of migrating grey whales on our way in, and a couple of humpbacks who showed us their tails as we rounded Point Reyes, four hours after making my decision and twenty-six hours after parting with Brian in Suisun Bay. The swells were there, still from the south and making the spot, theoretically, a bad place to anchor. But they were large and low, more of a nuisance than a threat. There was no one else here. The shore inside the point was the steep, rocky escarpment and pocket beach common to this coast and had only a few manmade features: two piers and a fish buyer's warehouse. With its boxy shape and white clapboards with neat rows of small windows, the warehouse might have been a roadside inn in Maine, pricey but authentic. I was choosing my spot to anchor when Kay said: "There's no cell phone signal." Damn. I realized we would never get a cell phone to work at water level, though I knew from a previous trip that there now was a repeater at the lighthouse itself. That meant getting ashore without a dinghy. "What are you thinking?" Kay asked.

"I'm going to have to drop you at the fish pier." Although it may seem odd to non-sailors, I was much more afraid of this maneuver than anything we saw last night, apart from the near-knockdown. Boats are made for the sea, not for unforgiving steel structures bolted to the bottom. I would have to drop Kay at the end of the pier, where there was a platform at water level, directly in the paths of the swells. Watching the platform through binoculars I saw it rise abruptly five or six feet, then drop quickly back down. It would require a very agile leap given that the period between swells, the effective window for jumping, was narrow. In fact, I thought, I might as well just plan on hitting it and minimizing the damage. But I knew the limit of my skills. I turned in a wide circle while I thought some more, and ultimately came up with the unworthy notion that technical difficulties aside, I didn't want Kay to make the call to Brian.

"Are you afraid I'll get hurt?" She asked. "Don't worry, I can make it."

"I have another idea. The top of the mainmast should give us enough height." Failing that, I could probably get Davenport to patch us through his radio, but broadcasting completely in the clear, for all the world to hear us, was out of the question. I poked around for a while, with Kay, out on the bowsprit, warning me off the kelp beds that would foul our anchor. When we found a clean spot, I took a GPS reading and switched places with her. The anchors had stayed tucked down throughout the wild night, but only at the cost of thick wet lines that had tightened up as they dried. I had to cut the starboard lash line away, and it was like sawing through solid wood with a paring knife. I waved back to Kay and she puttered us slowly back toward the waypoint. When the GPS beeped she called On Mark and dropped the engine into reverse, and I let the anchor go. When it set, with a jerk, I let out 150 feet of anchor chain, then motored up at an angle to the first and dropped the other one.

With what seemed like an exhausted sigh, *Drake* gave herself over to the security of the double anchors, ran her pumps one more time and all was suddenly quiet. There was no wind, only the gentle if substantial swell. I lowered and furled the sails. We had a cup of tea while I sorted out the bosun's chair and its blocks and tackles, then it only made sense to go ahead and do it. We ran the tackle up to the top of the mast and the lead line down to the winch. "I'm lighter," Kay said.

"It is the captain's pleasure," I replied, "to do this himself."

"I'm afraid I'll drop you." She had always hated this routine.

"You can't. There's a jam cleat and the winch only turns one way."

I sat in the canvas sling, feet barely touching the deck, while she got her phone. As she handed it to me, I asked for Sean Ballentine's cell number. "Why?" Her voice had a painful, defensive edge, as if I'd accused her of something.

"I want to be able to call him and tell him the game is over."

"It's on the electronic book in the phone."

She gave me the handheld VHF so that we could communicate without shouting, and up I was trundled, fifty feet up to

216

the spreaders, where I could sit and dangle my feet. This high up the motion of the boat was magnified many times and I was in for a wild ride with each wave; it felt like a ten or fifteen foot arc back and forward. But it was much better than side to side, and tying myself to the mast at the crosstrees, leg over the spreader on both sides of the mast, it was a piece of cake compared to last night. Everything was a piece of cake compared with last night. I took a breath and dialed Brian. It was just about to roll over to voice mail when he answered. "Ethan," he said. "I have news." The reception was perfectly clear: there was a voice in the background I could almost recognize.

"Who's with you?"

"Helen McNally. She knew who to talk to at the university. I'm having a late lunch at her house. Twenty hours of driving has left me quite famished." He paused. "Helen says to say hello and that Sally the cat misses you." This was such a normal conversational turn I didn't know whether to laugh or cry. "I won't keep you in suspense. The chairman of the history department knew a little of Bob McNally's history with the Willems collection; he was able to loan them some stuff when he was the archivist. However, he's a medievalist and was pretty slow in figuring out what I had. But he met me at their documents lab—pretty good even by Cal standards—and I opened the package under their hood not an hour ago, surrounded by Midwestern scholars with their mouths open. Parchment, sixteenth-century binding."

"Is it Drake's?"

"Ethan, his signature is at the bottom of every page; the usual barely decipherable scrawl." Drake's execrable penmanship had followed his legacy down through the centuries. "There was an accounting of all of the loot he'd captured from the Spanish on the last page, which was . . . are you sitting down?"

"In a manner of speaking."

". . . countersigned by Queen Elizabeth, with the royal seal."

Now I felt some vertigo. "What happens from here on?"

217

"Typical academic stuff. Call the British Museum, the Willems family, the lawyers. They'll keep the lid on it till tomorrow, then have a press conference. But it's not going back on the shelf or in the vault. They're scanning it and doing some ink and paper tests, and some Drake expert is flying in from England. We should have a readable text by late tonight or tomorrow. Congratulations." He stopped talking, out of breath. "Where was it, can you tell me?"

"It was with my father's papers."

"What?"

"I'll tell you the whole thing, Brian, soon. You've earned it. Have your lunch. I'll be in and out of cell phone range for a time. You can still e-mail me, though." My e-mail was on satellite.

"What are you up to?"

"It's time to let Sean Ballentine know. I'm beyond harassment now."

"God, I'd love to listen in. Be careful, Ethan, the man is a snake. But you already know that."

I found Ballentine's name on Kay's phone and punched the button. He answered immediately: "Kay, is that you?"

"No, Sean, sorry; she bats for the other team now."

I paused for him to make a move, then he said: "You have Drake's papers, don't you?"

"Indeed I do. It'll be in the news tomorrow."

"Are they in your possession?"

"That's why I'm calling. The game is over. There is nothing more you need from me that I can provide. Pull the plug, Sean. We're done. The papers have been donated to the University of Iowa in memory of Robert McNally. Do you remember who he was? Died in New York some months ago?"

"He tried to extort money from me. The man was an incompetent charlatan and he got what he deserved. Look . . ." he was putting himself back in his box. I could feel it. "All right, you win. But let's talk like gentlemen. Maybe we can help each other get things back on track. I have resources . . . I can help your career, and Kay's."

218

"We have nothing more to talk about," I said, and dropped the connection.

I was feeling queasy, and not from my soaring arcs forty feet above Drake's Bay. I was feeling queasy because I'd just taunted a man who was clearly a sociopath, or worse. I had no idea what he would do.

CHAPTER NINETEEN

I lowered myself back down because Kay was nowhere to be seen. With my feet on the deck, the feeling of not knowing what I was going to do now was accompanied by a certain lethargy. I'd had enough, for the moment, of being purposeful. My mission was accomplished, after all. I unshackled myself and coiled all the lines. The wind was almost gone and the air was full of the smell of kelp and a wisp of smoke from the pellet stove, which Kay had evidently fired up below. One more turn around the deck and I went through the pilothouse and down into the salon. There were candles burning on the table, an old sign between her and me, a way of making sure I knew what rung on the ladder of love she was on, and it made me gasp slightly. I took off all my layers save thermal underwear, and examined myself in the small mirror in the companionway. Was I still pretty? I heard Kay in my mind, as I frequently did even when we were out of love. *No, but you're still an idiot.*

She was lying on the forward double berth, wearing the pink BERKELEY LAW sweatshirt from the first time she'd sailed with me, her breasts loose inside it, and nothing else. When she saw me, she slid her legs under the blankets. "The legs are all for you, skipper," she said, "but I'm cold." She was drinking from my mug and handed it to me, nearly full of Jim Beam. I drank only a swallow and set it on the locker. She opened the blankets for me. "Take off that silly underwear," she said, but her tone said she loved my long johns and everything else about me. When she'd first told me she loved me, she'd said, "I even love your shoes." Her skin was very warm. She raised the shirt above her nipples and held her breast for me. I kissed it for so long it seemed I didn't want anything else, but she took my hand and placed it between her legs. They remained tightly shut: an old part of the ceremony. After kisses and caresses she opened herself bit by bit to my hand, and when I found her passionate core we were both beyond ready. We moved together and as we joined I felt I was finally and fully restored. I didn't need sleep. I only needed her.

We lay joined for many minutes, and then she said softly, "You've lost weight." I shifted off her and blew my nose, something which always added a hint of the ridiculous to our lovemaking. "I've never loved anybody else," she said. "You know that?"

"Yes."

"Tell me what transpired up there."

"The documents were Drake's sailing records, along with a long list of his booty. If the seal hadn't been already broken, the whole package would have been under Elizabeth's wax."

"He was sort of the Queen's personal pirate, wasn't he?"

"Very much so. A bit of a scoundrel, but he knew which side his bread was buttered on." I paused when she said nothing. I could do better than that. "Power, gender, money, adventure, discovery. Codependence, lifelong loyalty. A relationship not unlike ours, come to think of it."

She poked me gently under the covers. "Did it mention the plate?"

"I don't know. They'll be transcribing it all night and into tomorrow. Press conference sometime tomorrow afternoon. But I expect it will. We know he was in San Francisco Bay. Dad's paper proved that."

"What about Sean?"

"He said we should sit down and discuss our future together."

"What?"

"That was my reaction. He's more dangerous than ever, especially if we release the records of his family history of espionage."

"What will we do?"

"I'll think of something. Sail to Tahiti?"

"Right now?" She reached for me under the covers. I felt sleepy and passionate at the same time, a wonderful mixture. I gritted my teeth and slid out of the bunk, to do my captain's duty. It was 1700 hours of a stormy late February Sunday. I checked what needed to be checked, set the radar proximity alarm to a quarter mile, blew out all the candles but the one beside the bed and climbed back in. The color of the sky through the hatch was a marbled white, and against it I could see gulls, grebes, surf scoters, and buffleheads, inspecting us and coming in for landings. The storms past and future had brought them here, as they had us. Kay swung herself on top of me. After this time we both slept, curled up in each other.

WHEN I woke the sky was almost the same color, though somewhat dimmer, a dawn light that meant we'd slept twelve hours or more. The seabirds were silent. I could tell that we were lying slightly differently to our anchors, which meant a wind shift. I bundled myself in the spare blanket and went back to the main cabin looking not unlike a toddler, with my sleepy eyes and unsteady gait. Barometer was back down to 1009 millibars. Not as bad as I thought it might be, but all depended on the direction it would take. I poked my head out of the pilothouse and looked around at the slowly heaving anchorage, the misty shore and the sky. A high-prowed crab boat had come in during the night. She sat about fifty yards to port, looking businesslike but not busy. There was a soft yellow anchor light at the top of her stubby radio mast, but no antenna, and streaks of rust from her deck fittings that ran like tears from her bow to the waterline. Through the glasses I saw her name and port of call—*Patty Lee*, Monterey. The boat seemed empty and harmless. I reached this conclusion by virtue of the fact that the proximity alarm must have gone off, that we had slept through it, and that the crew of the *Patty Lee* had not boarded us and taken us prisoner while we slept. The main batteries were almost dead, from half a day of continuous radar surveillance. I switched the battery bank over to the ones which had been in reserve, started the engine, the heaters and the teapot. When Kay joined me she kissed me in a perfunctory, wifely sort of way and took over breakfast.

There were only three packages left of Tom Storey's delights, and they all showed signs of having lost their vacuums and acquired traveling companions. We were down to canned goods. "Tomato soup?"

"Breakfast of champions." While she heated it, I dressed in dry, clean clothes and turned on the computer. There was no satellite e-mail from Brian, but there was one from George Metaxis with a *us.gov* extension, dated last night around midnight. It just started in the middle of things and was cryptic in the usual Metaxian way I'd grown used to over the course of this thing.

> *Your cell phone was found on the seat of a taxi in the red light district. Honest folk, the Dutch, if a bit given to bad habits. I presume you're all right. The first trace of you since Amsterdam was the position report you radioed to the Coast Guard night before this one. I assume this was not a pleasure cruise. Lucius Willems received a call at his home six hours ago and a very excited man who identified himself as a Dr. Kent Sturgess left an urgent message to call back, to an area code in Iowa. You can probably further assist us in our inquiries, as they say at Scotland Yard, and we may be of some service to you as well. My contact numbers below, in case you've mislaid them. Congratulations. George M.*
>
> *P.S. SF Office is attempting to locate SB without success.*

I left the computer on, just in case.

"Oh, good." Kay said. "I found some Bisquick and powdered milk. I believe we may have some scones, of a sort." While she was at it, I turned on the radios and heard a general bulletin from Coast Guard San Francisco about an SOS transmission they'd received just at dawn, which had ended before a position or a vessel name or condition was broadcast. Any station which had received it was asked to call in. Then, the weather. The meteorologists had got it wrong, but then so had the seabirds which had flown in last night. The second storm was being pushed north and we could expect a typically northwesterly flow (this is what had turned us around on our anchor), with light winds but heavy fog. I supposed that was good news.

Kay handed me a cup of tea and looked over at the computer screen. "George Metaxis? Isn't that one of the policemen we talked to last fall?"

"Yes. We've been . . . corresponding."

"Is SB Sean Ballentine?"

"Yes."

She didn't reply, and I went back to the computer. It was two hours later in Des Moines. Typing in "Drake's Logbooks" as a search term, I had a hit on the *Des Moines Register.*

Dr. Brian Haggerty of the University of California at Berkeley and Dr. Kent Sturgess of the University of Iowa announced last night that the original nautical logbooks of Sir Francis Drake, famed sixteenth-century explorer and hero of the battle against the Spanish Armada, had been rediscovered in a private collection and donated to the University of Iowa. "These priceless artifacts, placed under seal by Queen Elizabeth I and lost for more than four centuries, will have quite a story to tell," said Dr. Haggerty. A press conference is scheduled for this afternoon.

"Cat's out of the bag, now, isn't it?" Kay said.

The cooler and its last package of documents were neatly lashed to hooks behind the port side settee. We both glanced at it. "It'll keep until after breakfast," I said. She set the table with cloth napkins and a checkered tablecloth.

We ate the biscuits and soup in silence at first, then Kay said, "Is there anything you want to ask me?"

"Is there anything I need to know?"

She thought about it. "Sean was working directly with another man at the institute. Adrian Burke. He's English and doesn't seem to mind working for both families. He's kind of creepy. Sean has his own security team. I always thought they had something to do with security at the Ballentine Labs, but they were always around. One is named Mike something. He's a big Samoan. I haven't seen him in months."

"He was at the institute, too. Messed around with the boat, while I was at Richmond. How many others?"

"Two or three." I couldn't think of anything else to ask. We finished eating and cleaned up. The diesel rumbled. The bilge pump did its duty. The computer beeped to signal new mail had arrived, and it was Brian at last. His message was simply:

There is no real Plate. There is only the fake Plate and that's all there ever was. Call me ASAP.

I tapped a reply that we had no phone contact and sent it. Then we stared uncomprehendingly at the screen. "Does this mean anything to you?" I asked.

"Of course there's a real plate. That's what all this has been about."

We had no phone, but we had radios galore, and now one of them said: *All vessels, this is the United States Coast Guard San Francisco. We have an Emergency Position Locator Beacon activated at the following coordinates.* He repeated them twice, and out of habit I took them down. *Position is approximately five miles west of Point Reyes. Area is in heavy fog and helicopter searches are not successful. All vessels in the vicinity are requested to give assistance and respond Channel 22A.*

I stood, dialed 22A and plucked the microphone from its bracket, then paused. I would rather not have to deal with this just now. But as the dead air extended to thirty seconds, I could feel my father's mildly disapproving stare.

Coast Guard San Francisco, this is sailing vessel Drake. *We're at Drake's Bay. ETA to those coordinates forty five, four-five minutes. Do you have any other information on the ship?*

Drake, SF. Thank you, skipper. It's been busy out there. Information on the EPIRB will be in shortly. Stand by this channel. San Francisco out.

"What does that mean?" Kay asked.

"The EPIRB beacons turn on automatically when the boat they're registered to goes down, with a message about location and the boat's registry." I thought for a moment. "Get all the fenders together. We'll just tie them to the anchor lines. It'll save time."

"Do we have to do this?"

"I'm afraid so."

We went on deck, where the headland was now hidden in fog, though there was enough visibility to safely get under way. Kay tied off the anchor lines to a couple of fenders each. I put the engine in gear.

"It may be Sean, somehow," Kay said, coming back from the bow.

"Kay, now you're more paranoid than I am. It's too far-fetched. Besides, we're not going alone." I nodded towards the *Patty Lee*, which Kay had not noticed, but which was now sending some fine black diesel exhaust into the air. Kay went below to enter the EPIRB coordinates into our handheld GPS. As we headed southeast to clear the Point, *Patty* came close enough to hail me. "Are you headed out to the beacon?"

I nodded. The sea was dead flat and he came quite close. I could see his face: an aging hippy, the kind of baby boomer who chose to work in dying professions out of sheer spite for their generation. "What speed can you make?" he asked.

"Six knots."

He pointed toward the radio he was holding in his hand. Ours was still in its bag in the cockpit. "Hello, *Drake*. OK, we're not much better. We're having engine problems and we lost our main radio antenna off Point Arena three days ago. You may have to tow us to the rescue."

He didn't really mean that, but it meant he would keep us in sight. "Roger that. *Drake* clear." I moved the throttle forward and made my turn to the west. Beyond the point, the sea was as waveless as the bay; but where the kelp beds floated you could judge there to be a strong, slow swell running, residue from the storm. But I could only see about fifty feet of it ahead of me. Beyond that was fog so thick I thought it would stop us when we went into it, and as soon as we did so the temperature dropped ten degrees. I looked astern to see *Patty* take up position off our starboard quarter. My fifty foot estimate was about right. If she drifted back any more than that, she immediately disappeared like she'd been dropped in a bowl of milk. I set the autopilot to match the course to the beacon from the GPS, put on a sweater and turned the volume up on the radio in the pilothouse so I could hear it on deck. Over any distance other than boat-to-boat the handheld was unreliable, though it got some of it; and when either radio scanned back to channel 16 it was quite busy with transmissions, much of it dealing with other casualties from the storm, both to the north and west of us. Twice we heard the deep pulse of the Coast Guard Dolphin helicopters overhead. Farther from the coast, I surmised, there was less fog as the temperature of sea and air became more equalized.

The main threat to life under these conditions was hypothermia if anyone from the wreck was in the water. Just a few minutes to unconsciousness, in the worst-case scenario. Kay was bundling blankets and towels up into the cockpit. I suppose we had talked about this kind of thing when we started sailing together, because she set out the boarding ladder, our life-ring, and a floating strobe light attached to a life vest. What a gal; I was proud of her. The GPS would take us to the beacon, but that was not necessarily where the survivors would be; so when we were a mile or so out from it I stopped to listen. But *Patty* came out of the mist and having us both shut down completely, which

227

we'd have to do to hear anything, seemed like a waste of time. I changed my mind and throttled up again, this time to maximum, so close to hull speed the boat vibrated slightly from the strain.

0.25 nautical miles. *Patty* was still gamely keeping up, though her exhaust was distinctly darker than it had been. 0.1 nm, then it started reading in feet. When it dropped to 500, I slowed to idle. "Kay, go forward, right up on the bowsprit, so you can see dead ahead." I gave her the handheld VHF. It was tempting to go to the pilothouse and to steer from there to be close to the main radios, but I was afraid I'd miss something in the water, which was a confused mess of torn-up kelp. I compromised by pulling the microphone off its hook and hanging it out the porthole, where it was three steps from the wheel in the cockpit. We were as ready as could be. At 250 feet, she said, "Slow, Ethan. I see something." Then: "Stop, stop!" I threw the engine into reverse, hoping they'd heard Kay over on *Patty Lee*.

Sailing vessel Drake, *this is Coast Guard San Francisco Channel 22A.* I jumped to the microphone.

San Francisco, this is Drake, *go ahead.*

Kay stood on the bow pulpit, frantically gesturing for me to turn right. Our way was almost gone now. I jumped back to the helm and spun the wheel. She leaned over and plucked the EPIRB from the sea by its little mast and flag. Just as she pulled it aboard, she glanced at its identification tag and immediately threw it back over the side. She arrived at the cockpit, running, just in time to hear the Coast Guard announce *EPIRB is registered to a 40-foot North Sea, a research vessel, name* Goldrush. *Repeat* Goldrush. Washed over the side during our little game, I thought with a flash of satisfaction. How appropriate. Then there was a soft crunch as the *Patty Lee* came alongside, and the two of them had me down long before I got to the pilothouse to reply.

CHAPTER TWENTY

The other one had Kay's arms pinned in a bear hug, and when she struggled he simply handcuffed her hands in front of her and threw her down on the deck. From my perspective, all I saw of this was through a spotty haze of vision while the choke hold drained my brain of oxygen. The one who'd thrown Kay down walked calmly to the microphone and said *Coast Guard this is* Drake. *We have the EPIRB and will continue the search in rectangular grids and report back within the hour.* Drake *clear.* CG San Francisco acknowledged. They stood still then for quite some time, a few minutes anyway, as if expecting something to happen. During this time I was allowed to breathe, but any motion tightened the grip on my throat. This was probably my aging Hippy Boatman. The other was Samoan Mike. Hippy Boatman was light against my backbone where he placed his knee, but his arms were hard as redwood rounds.

"Don't move, you two," I heard Adrian Burke call from the deck of the *Patty*. The two ships were now securely rafted together, and the large platform they comprised was steady as a landform under these conditions. "We'll be with you shortly." Mike sat down and lit a cigarette, keeping an eye on Kay. The silence stretched away. What were they waiting for? When it came it was obvious:

Drake, *Coastguard San Francisco.*

Drake, Mike replied.

Yeah, EPIRB was a wash-over. Vessel is safely in an East Bay marina. Thank you skipper.

You're welcome, Mike replied. Drake *clear.*

Burke came aboard and said, "Excuse me," as he stepped, with some delicacy, over Kay and went below. He was there

229

quite some time, but he eventually emerged with the last vacuum bag, which had been opened. In his other hand was an eight-and-a-half-by-eleven photograph. "Let them sit up," he said.

Kay and I did so, to positions sitting side by side on the cockpit sole. Samoan Mike pulled an automatic pistol from his belt and lit a second cigarette. Mike asked, "Where's your scatter gun?"

"Shelf in the pilothouse, starboard side." He came back with it and threw it over the side.

Adrian watched this little tableau as if grateful to have more time to think. "Where are the logbooks?" he asked, sitting down. He looked very tired; thinner, if possible, than when I'd last seen him the day the Willems Institute burned down and Karen Molina died. He also looked very confused.

"Are you all right?" I asked Kay, who nodded. "They burned up the night you set the institute on fire, Adrian," I said to Burke.

"Oh my God, that *wasn't me*. It was a tragic *accident*. It's only about the logbooks. That's all I've ever wanted. Please tell me you're lying."

I thought for a moment. What would the truth get me? "Go below and type 'Drake's Logbooks' into the internet search window," I said.

"Internet afloat, what a concept." But he did so. There was more silence. Boat Hippy and Samoan Mike were the sort of thugs that historians sometimes called centurions, and they were always around powerful people to do whatever they were bidden. The gene pool bred them as instruments of history, from Nebuchadnezzar's palace guard to the Watergate burglars. They transcended evil. They were just there to serve, but they would do anything, including evil. Adrian was different, his own man, but a very disturbed and conflicted one. When he returned he looked more perplexed than ever. "The University of Iowa? Didn't you find them? Didn't your father hide them somewhere?"

"You've been a bit out of the loop, Adrian. My father hid them and I found them a few days ago. They went to Iowa in memory of Bob McNally."

"McNally. Robert McNally who worked at the institute?"

"Yes, the same. He was killed in New York when this whole business started. A decent man. Not a great scholar, but married to a woman who grieves for him now."

"But . . . what's this?"

He held out the picture. It was of a younger Sean Ballentine meeting a dark-haired, jowly man in what looked to be People's Park in Berkeley. Telephoto lens, but they were both in nearly full face focus. It was dated in indelible ink 7/7/87 and annotated in my father's hand "SB and 242 at meeting. See tape of same day, 1000 hrs."

"Are there tape cassettes in the package?" I asked.

"Yes, and more pictures and some documents that appear to be technical. Nothing of any antiquarian interest whatsoever."

"Depends on how you define history," I said. "These are contemporary but—" I was sure of it now—"it all links up, every evil and every blessed thing anyone has ever done." My father's words.

"What the bloody hell are you talking about?"

"There never was a real plate, only the fake one. The plate was a legend concocted after Drake returned—by him, his mate Pretty, Elizabeth and her advisors to make the Spanish think there was an English claim to this part of the world. The log-books don't make any mention of it."

Burke still looked mystified. He stood by the pilothouse door holding the photo in one hand and the plastic bag in the other. Then his gaze lifted to the right of Kay and me. I turned, and emerging from the mist was *Goldrush*, virtually silent with everybody's diesels idling. Sean Ballentine was handling her alone, which I could see through the window to the steering station, the one without the plywood cover. Hippy Boatman moved to take his lines, nodding first at Mike, who waved his weapon nonchalantly at us. He had us both covered. My neck hurt from turning to look and it didn't matter anyway, with our three boat party motoring slowly westward toward the twelve-mile limit of state and federal jurisdiction. When Ballentine arrived, his first words were not to Kay or me but to Burke: "Bad boy, Burke. You shouldn't have opened that."

Burke was more petulant than anything else. He was a long way from understanding. "I had to look, didn't I? No good not making sure we had the right property." A little Cockney was creeping into his voice.

"Point taken. No harm done. Was that it?"

"Some other papers from the 1930s. Bank statements or something."

"Why don't you bring them all up here and we'll set fire to them. Get started on torching this once proud schooner and burning her to the waterline."

He brought out Dad's cooler and he prodded the contents without great interest. Burke said: "Storey says there is no real plate. I'm a bit in the dark, here."

"Well, he's right. Old Curtis was a pompous gasbag. Bought a hoax by a couple of students out to embarrass him, and by the time he realized it, he'd already made a complete fool of himself. So he got an old boy to say he'd found another plate, when no such thing happened. Then he could declare one plate a fraud; but he led everyone to believe he had two plates and he was the only person who could validate one as genuine—all he needed was Drake's Logbooks." He paused. "It's all a bit complicated. The more so because after he started dealing with the Willems he decided the real money wasn't in Elizabethan artifacts, but in passing the particle accelerator test data to the Germans. From that point on it didn't matter because it was all just a cover story, all the interfamily hostility, all the mysterious feuds, the conundrum of the logbooks, all so much cover for a lucrative enterprise in espionage which in due course I inherited. Hello, Kay. Are my people taking good care of you? Handcuffs comfortable?" She didn't reply. "And the good doctor?"

"I've had better days," I said.

"Just so we're all clear, I largely reformed after the Soviet Union decomposed and my family and I are now productive citizens. Just a little dabbling in the old business from time to time. My wife and I had dinner with the governor twice in the past month. But I have been haunted by a communication from your father shortly before his death, rather cryptic, but definitely threatening. Knows where the logbooks are, no plate mentioned therein, proof of malfeasance on the part of both my father and I; etc., etc. One move against him or his son it all goes to the FBI, blah blah. Then Storey Sr. dies of a fucking stroke and I live on tenterhooks for fifteen years waiting for the other shoe to drop. Then, the collection goes up for auction and, well, it was time for me to worry about *my* family." Mike put his gun down to light another cigarette and Kay was no longer at my side; she was diving for it and then had a hand on it. I had time to actually form the mental words *this woman is something else* before I stood and threw myself at the Samoan, who simply stepped out of the way. I bounced off the lifelines like a punch-drunk boxer. When I turned, she was pointing the gun at Ballentine, at all of them, and before any of the professional criminals figured out what to do, she just started blazing away. Eight rounds, as fast as she could squeeze them off. I felt the muzzle flash and the zipping sensation of a bullet close by my head. The only one she hit was the Boatman and that just by chance, as he was still in the well of the *Patty*. He collapsed and started yelling, "FUCKING SHIT" over and over. When the clip was empty, Mike kicked me in the stomach, and Adrian Burke stepped forward and plucked the gun from her fingers. "I hope you rot in hell," Kay said without inflection, but her voice was loud and clear and she was talking to Ballentine.

"I gather you're no longer my attorney," said Ballentine, an adrenaline quaver in his voice. Then, "Mike, you're quitting smoking right now."

"Yes boss," said Mike, who was in fact reaching for a cigarette.

"Adrian, give me the gun." Adrian stepped around behind Mike, to keep him between himself and Kay, and turned the weapon over meekly to Ballentine. Ballentine took another weapon out of an ankle holster and handed it to Adrian. "Time to decide whose side you're on."

"What do you mean?"

"I mean shoot them. We just have too much to lose, you and I, and I've been putting money in Mexican banks for fifteen years. The doctor and his lady have nothing but this old boat, which will be in flames shortly."

Burke stepped back and leaned against the pilothouse, facing us. He gestured for me to come back to the cockpit. I stood beside Kay. I heard a distant gull and realized Kay was wearing perfume. I thought of my father and his blessings. I smelled kelp and bilgewater, dry rot and diesel exhaust, and I took Kay's hand and squeezed it hard. After a few long instants of my life, Burke turned and shot Sean Ballentine through the chest. The force of it tipped him over backwards and he fell into the sea between the two boats. Burke looked at Mike. "Can you work the boat?"

"Sure," Mike said. "Can we get Paul to the hospital?"

"Paul will be fine," Burke said, but how he knew that I couldn't tell. He turned to us with only mild interest. "That was for Karen," he said. "She was very dear to me. I told them you were almost to the documents, behind the wall in the small library. They set the institute on fire, I know now. Ballentine denied it, but now it makes sense. She died for nothing."

He and Mike climbed onto *Patty* and cast off her lines, first from us and then from *Goldrush*, and we all drifted apart, lost in the fog within minutes.

THE COASTGUARD cutter *Mendocino* found us shortly after we made our distress call—"PAN" not "Mayday" because we were in no real danger. She had been brought in for the multiple rescue operations, but I was not surprised to see George Metaxis aboard, looking sea-sickly in an undersized Kevlar vest, as he waved at us from her deck. There would be much in the day of debriefing that followed. Tom Storey as FBI Confidential Informant from the end of World War II until he died; the old case against the eldest Willems lost in the post-war confusion; Ballentine's use of lab secrets for personal gain never quite a provable thing, languishing until he started looking for new clients in the post-cold war world. I was not quite convinced; I also knew it was all they'd tell me.

But that moment, looking up at the big red cutter's side, was what I'd remember the most clearly. In spite of having been equipped by my father for every possible contingency, I'd been unable to find a bolt cutter or a hacksaw to get Kate out of the handcuffs. When she hugged me, she had to do it by dropping her arms over my head. Before they came alongside, Kay said: "I've got you. There's no escaping me."

"Where did you ever learn to shoot?" I asked.

"Never. That's why I had to close my eyes."

A Coastie paused with his lines, waiting I suppose for a signal from me.

"I think we should get married now," I said.

Kay waited for a moment and said: "I thought you'd never ask."

WE TOOK *Drake* to Baja three weeks later. I was on paid sabbatical, as the university tried to cope with what came out in the press. It wasn't the whole story, but there was an ongoing investigation of security problems at the Ballentine Laboratory that had already made the papers, and Ballentine's disappearance, as it was first reported, was suspicious. That was just enough for SF State to rapidly offer me my job back, and the gift of the semester to put myself back together. The FBI didn't want to go much farther until they'd completed their investigation and were able to bring somebody to trial. At first it was thought that there were just a few scientists at the lab who were careless with their laptops, but the press knew this was just the beginning and the story was a long way from its apogee. Metaxis sent a brief e-mail and said that since we'd already filed our

235

sworn testimony we wouldn't be called. And just to make sure there was no more fuss in our lives, maybe we should go somewhere for a few months. He ended it with one of his cryptic remarks: *Meet you in Ensenada on your father's century?* May 18th would have been his 100th birthday.

So we headed south, just as all the boats that had wintered in Mexico were headed north. It was a long, slow trip, but with the wind always fair and just a few late-spring squalls. We married at our first stop, only thirty miles south of San Francisco at Santa Cruz. They'd had a cancellation at the Mission church there, were not particular about me not being Catholic (this was Santa Cruz after all, pagan ground where all conventional people have to stick together), and had a retired priest who'd become a Buddhist. We had only Brian and his wife and a few others I did not recognize from the Haggerty/O'Toole clan in the Central Valley; most brought some form of honey as presents. Also one of my Ph.D. candidates, who deserved better from her committee chairman than to be abandoned in the middle of her dissertation. Brian was oddly reticent and did little but beam at us. When he hugged Kay there were tears in his eyes. He never asked a single question about the night of the storm. I never thought to invite Metaxis.

Then, the broad, sweetly calm San Simeon Bay, with the Hearst Castle on the hills above; a tie-up overnight in Santa Barbara for a shower and an obscenely expensive dinner. I was able to make the arrangements for entering Mexico from there and our next stop was Ensenada, exactly a month early for meeting Metaxis. We dawdled south down the Pacific Coast, buying fish from passing boats, swimming in water as warm as our skin, sleeping on deck and venturing ashore to explore the desert and avoid history, for a time. All the days seemed the same; all bright and drowsy and eventful only in our relationship with the schooner and the sea. "We're a happily married couple, aren't we?" Kay said on our last stop before we trained north again. In the light of the kerosene lamp, she looked younger than the day we'd met.

"I'm not afraid to be happy with you anymore," I said without thinking about it.

The anchorage at Ensenada was not especially nice, crowded and not quite clean, and we could find no slip space. It was OK. We were headed back to life. There was no e-mail from Metaxis and the boat was anchored a long way from shore. But I had no doubt he'd find us and he arrived at dinnertime, coming out of the long orange rays of the Mexican sunset in a fishing skiff, sunburnt and in preposterous Bermuda shorts and a straw hat. He carried a tacky leather satchel from the market ashore. It had a long strap to pass over his shoulders and was engraved with sea creatures. He negotiated the boarding ladder with surprising agility and came aboard. He said, "Hello, Mrs. Storey. Found you, Ethan."

"Well done."

"We've had your boat locator-bugged since, oh, January? I always knew where you were within a hundred feet or so. I'm here to take it off, among other things." The FBI bug had been attached in ridiculously plain sight on the very end of the bowsprit, and while he retrieved it, we set up the table in the cockpit and laid out dinner, pasta with shrimp and a Baja chardonnay. He proposed a toast to Thomas Storey, then ate attentively till we'd reached the coffee. "So," he said, "it's all come out, as it always does. I'm sure you've been following the news."

"We're on our honeymoon, George," Kay said. "We never even turned the radios on, except for the weather."

"Good for you," he said, although he looked at us as if she'd said something very strange. "So, what's not in the public domain is anything about you or your father. It stuck to the current case of secrets, mostly computer models the lab used to test nuclear warheads, passed by Sean Ballentine to China in recent years. An accomplice testified, will plead out to twenty-five years or so. Ballentine's body washed up on the beach at Bolinas Bay and it was ruled a suicide. The *Goldrush* has never been found. Drake's Logbooks are now on loan to the museum at Cal."

"Was my father killed?"

"We don't think so. You know he started working for the Bureau shortly after the war?" I nodded. "OK, well, that information wasn't passed back to us until the mid-1960s. We never moved on it, never arrested old man Ballentine because, thanks to your dad, we knew the content; and from the lab end, we were able to inject enough disinformation into the stream so that it didn't add up to much for the Germans, or later, for the East Germans."

Kay said: "You mean Ethan's father told you what was going on and you didn't do anything?"

"Well yes, but, you know, if you stop one spy, another just comes along. The whole Ballentine thing—and your father was fully willing to do this—was deliberately maintained by us and the Ballentines, for almost thirty-five years. Because he gave us all the information on how the stuff was transmitted and where it came from, our people at the lab made sure that what Ballentine got was about half garbage. None of the Ballentines ever had any training in physics or engineering, so they hadn't a clue. Neither did the Willems, who were never more than a conduit for the money."

"But he was worried about Ethan," Kay said, "and that's why he moved all the documents—"

"—not all, just plenty of them—"

"To the place in the Delta. He didn't trust you to protect him?"

"That wasn't what the game is about, Kay. Ethan's father was trained early, but trained well, in counterespionage. There was only so much we could do for him. He made his own arrangements."

I hadn't said much because I'd guessed most of it. "Like you, George," I ventured.

"I'm just a humble document specialist, but yes, I work off the clock quite a bit."

"Like now?"

"Yep, as a matter of fact. I'm here to consult you on another matter." The last of the light faded but the air was still warm.

Kay looked at me questioningly, and I knew she wanted to say something like, *You can't be serious.* But I shook my head. She cleared the table and turned on the spreader lights while Metaxis removed something from the satchel. "Take a look at this and tell me what you think."

I stared at the little pile of documents, and drank the rest of my wine, while the two of them watched me. In truth, though, I wanted to see what he'd brought. Eventually I reached for them with what they must have seen as a rueful smile.

I was my father's son.